The Day
of the
Triffids

JOHN WYNDHAM

★

*The Day
of the
Triffids*

London
MICHAEL JOSEPH

First published by
MICHAEL JOSEPH LTD.
26 Bloomsbury Street
London, W.C.1
1951

Set and printed in Great Britain by Tonbridge Printers
Ltd., Peach Hall Works, Tonbridge, in Times ten on
twelve point, on paper made by John Dickinson at
Croxley, and bound by James Burn at Esher.

CONTENTS

CONTENTS

1. The End Begins

WHEN a day that you happen to know is Wednesday starts off by sounding like Sunday, there is something seriously wrong somewhere.

I felt that from the moment I woke. And yet, when I started functioning a little more sharply, I misgave. After all, the odds were that it was I who was wrong, and not everyone else—though I did not see how that could be. I went on waiting, tinged with doubt. But presently I had my first bit of objective evidence—a distant clock struck what sounded to me just like eight. I listened hard and suspiciously. Soon another clock began, on a loud, decisive note. In a leisurely fashion it gave an indisputable eight. Then I *knew* things were awry.

The way I came to miss the end of the world—well, the end of the world I had known for close on thirty years—was sheer accident: like a lot of survival, when you come to think of it. In the nature of things a good many somebodies are always in hospital, and the law of averages had picked on me to be one of them a week or so before. It might just as easily have been the week before that—in which case I'd not be writing now: I'd not be here at all. But chance played it not only that I should be in hospital at that particular time, but that my eyes, and indeed my whole head, should be wreathed in bandages—and that's why I have to be grateful to whoever orders these averages. At the time, however, I was only peevish, wondering what in thunder went on, for I had been in the place long enough to know that, next to the matron, the clock is the most sacred thing in a hospital.

Without a clock the place simply couldn't latch. Each second there's someone consulting it on births, deaths, doses, meals, lights, talking, working, sleeping, resting, visiting, dressing, washing—and hitherto it had decreed that someone should begin to wash and tidy me up at exactly three minutes after 7 a.m. That was one of the best reasons I had for appreciating a private room. In a public ward the messy proceeding would have taken place a whole unnecessary hour earlier. But here, to-day, clocks of varying reliability were continuing to strike eight in all directions—and still nobody had shown up.

Much as I disliked the sponging process, and useless as it had been to suggest that the help of a guiding hand as far as the bathroom could eliminate it, its failure to occur was highly disconcerting. Besides, it was normally a close forerunner of breakfast, and I was feeling hungry.

Probably I would have been aggrieved about it any morning, but to-day, this Wednesday, May 8th, was an occasion of particular personal importance. I was doubly anxious to get all the fuss and routine over because that was the day they were going to take off my bandages.

I groped around a bit to find the bell-push, and let them have a full five seconds clatter, just to show what I was thinking of them.

While I was waiting for the pretty short-tempered response that such a peal ought to bring, I went on listening.

The day outside, I realized now, was sounding even more wrong than I had thought. The noises it made, or failed to make, were more like Sunday than Sunday itself—and I'd come round again to being absolutely assured that it *was* Wednesday, whatever else had happened to it.

Why the founders of St. Merryn's Hospital chose to erect their institution at a main road crossing upon a valuable office-site and thus expose their patients' nerves to constant laceration, is a foible that I never properly understood. But for those fortunate enough to be suffering from complaints unaffected by the wear and tear of continuous traffic, it did have the advantage that one could lie abed and still not be out of touch, so to speak, with the flow of life. Customarily the westbound buses thundered along trying to beat the lights at the corner; as often as not a pig-squeal of brakes and a salvo of shots from the silencer would tell that they hadn't. Then the released cross-traffic would rev. and roar as it started up the incline. And every now and then there would be an interlude: a good grinding bump, followed by a general stoppage—exceedingly tantalizing to one in my condition where the extent of the contretemps had to be judged entirely by the degree of profanity resulting. Certainly, neither by day nor during most of the night, was there any chance of a St. Merryn patient being under the impression that the common round had stopped just because he, personally, was on the shelf for the moment.

But this morning was different. Disturbingly because mysteriously different. No wheels rumbled, no buses roared, no sound of a car of any kind, in fact, was to be heard. No brakes, no horns, not even the clopping of the few rare horses that still occasionally passed. Nor, as there should be at such an hour, the composite tramp of work-bound feet.

The more I listened, the queerer it seemed—and the less I cared for it. In what I reckoned to be ten minutes of careful listening I heard five sets of shuffling, hesitating footsteps, three voices bawling unintelligibly in the distance, and the hysterical sobs of a woman. There was not the cooing of a pigeon, not the chirp of a sparrow. Nothing but the humming of wires in the wind. . . .

A nasty, empty feeling began to crawl up inside me. It was the same sensation I used to have sometimes as a child when I got to fancying that horrors were lurking in the shadowy corners of the bedroom; when I daren't put a foot out for fear that something should reach from under the bed and grab my ankle; daren't even reach for the switch lest the movement should cause something to leap at me. I had to fight down the feeling, just as I had had to when I was a kid in the dark. And it was no easier. It's surprising how much you don't grow out of when it comes to the test. The elemental fears were still marching along with me, waiting their chance, and pretty nearly getting it—just because my eyes were bandaged, and the traffic had stopped. . . .

When I had pulled myself together a bit, I tried the reasonable approach. Why *does* traffic stop? Well, usually because the road is closed for repairs. Perfectly simple. Any time now they'd be along with pneumatic drills as another touch of aural variety for the long-suffering patients. But the trouble with the reasonable line was that it went further. It pointed out that there was not even the distant hum of traffic, not the whistle of a train, not the hoot of a tugboat. Just nothing—until the clocks began chiming a quarter past eight.

The temptation to take a peep—not more than a peep, of course; just enough to get some idea of what on earth could be happening, was immense. But I restrained it. For one thing, a peep was a far less simple matter than it sounded. It wasn't just a case of lifting a blindfold: there were a lot of pads and bandages. But, more importantly, I was scared to try. Over a week's complete blindness can do a lot to frighten you out of taking chances with your sight. It was true that they intended to remove the bandages to-day, but that would be done in a special, dim light, and they would only allow them to stay off if the inspection of my eyes were satisfactory. I did not know whether it would be. It might be that my sight was permanently impaired. Or that I would not be able to see at all. I did not know yet. . . .

I swore, and laid hold of the bell-push again. It helped to relieve my feelings a bit.

No one, it seemed, was interested in bells. I began to get as much annoyed as worried. It's humiliating to be dependent, anyway, but it's a still poorer pass to have no one to depend on. My patience was whittling down. Something, I decided, had got to be done about it.

If I were to bawl down the passage and generally raise hell, somebody ought to show up if only to tell me what they thought of me. I turned back the sheet, and got out of bed. I'd never seen the room I was in, and though I had a fairly good idea by ear of the position of the door, it wasn't all that easy to find. There seemed to be several puzzling and unnecessary obstacles, but I got across at the cost of a stubbed toe and minor damage to my shin. I shoved my head out into the passage.

'Hey!' I shouted. 'I want some breakfast. Room forty-eight!'

For a moment nothing happened. Then came voices all shouting together. It sounded like hundreds of them, and not a word coming through clearly. It was as though I'd put on a record of crowd noises—and an ill-disposed crowd at that. I had a nightmarish flash wondering whether I had been transferred to a mental home while I was sleeping, and that this was not St. Merryn's Hospital at all. Those voices simply didn't sound normal to me. I closed the door hurriedly on the babel, and groped my way back to bed. At that moment bed seemed to be the one safe, comforting thing in my whole baffling environment. As if to underline that there came a sound which checked me in the act of pulling up the sheets. From the street below rose a scream, wildly distraught and contagiously terrifying. It came three times, and when it had died away it seemed still to tingle in the air.

I shuddered. I could feel the sweat prickle my forehead under the bandages. I knew now that something fearful and horrible was happening. I could not stand my isolation and helplessness any longer. I had to know what was going on around me. I put my hands up to my bandages; then, with my fingers on the safety-pins, I stopped. . . .

Suppose the treatment had not been successful? Suppose that when I took the bandages off I were to find that I still could not see? That would be worse still—a hundred times worse. . . .

I lacked the courage to be alone and find out that they had not saved my sight. And even if they had, would it be safe yet to keep my eyes uncovered?

I dropped my hands, and lay back. I was wild at myself and the place, and I did some silly, weak cursing.

Some little while must have passed before I got a proper hold on things again, but after a bit I found myself churning round in my mind once more after a possible explanation. I did not find it. But I did become absolutely convinced that, come all the paradoxes of hell, it was Wednesday. For the previous day had been notable, and I could swear that no more than a single night had passed since then.

You'll find it in the records that on Tuesday, May 7th, the Earth's orbit passed through a cloud of comet debris. You can even believe it, if you like—millions did. Maybe it was so. I can't prove anything either way. I was in no state to see what happened; but I do have my own ideas. All that I actually know of the occasion is that I had to spend the

evening in my bed listening to eye-witness accounts of what
was constantly claimed to be the most remarkable celestial
spectacle on record.

And yet, until the thing actually began nobody had ever
heard a word about this supposed comet, or its debris. . . .

Why they broadcast it, considering that everyone who
could walk, hobble, or be carried was either out of doors or
at windows enjoying the greatest free firework display ever,
I don't know. But they did, and it helped to impress on me
still more heavily what it meant to be sightless. I got round
to feeling that if the treatment had not been successful I'd
rather end the whole thing than go on that way.

It was reported in the news-bulletins during the day that
mysterious bright green flashes had been seen in the Cali-
fornian skies the previous night. However, such a lot of
things did happen in California that no one could be expected to get greatly worked up over that, but as further
reports came in this comet-debris motif made its appearance,
and it stuck.

Accounts arrived from all over the Pacific of a night made
brilliant by green meteors said to be 'sometimes in such
numerous showers that the whole sky appeared to be
wheeling about us.' And so it was, when you come to think
of it.

As the night line moved westward the brilliance of the
display was in no way decreased. Occasional green flashes
became visible even before darkness fell. The announcer,
giving an account of the phenomenon in the six o'clock
news, advised everyone that it was an amazing scene, and
one not to be missed. He mentioned also that it seemed to
be interfering seriously with short-wave reception at long
distances, but that the medium waves on which there would
be a running commentary were unaffected, as, at present,
was television. He need not have troubled with the advice.

By the way everyone in the hospital got excited about it, it seemed to me that there was not the least likelihood of anybody missing it—except myself.

And, as if the radio's comments were not enough, the nurse who brought me my supper had to tell me all about it.

'The sky's simply full of shooting stars,' she said. 'All bright green. They make people's faces look frightfully ghastly. *Every*body's out watching them, and sometimes it's almost as light as day—only all the wrong colour. Every now and then there's a big one so bright that it hurts to look at it. It's a marvellous sight. They say there's never been anything like it before. It *is* such a pity you can't see it, isn't it?'

'It is,' I agreed, somewhat shortly.

'We've drawn back the curtains in the wards so that they can all see it,' she went on. 'If only you hadn't those bandages you'd have a wonderful view of it from here.'

'Oh,' I said.

'But it must be better still outside, though. They say thousands of people are out in the parks and on the Heath watching it all. And on all the flat roofs you can see people standing and looking up.'

'How long do they expect it to go on?' I asked, patiently.

'I don't know, but they say it's not so bright now as it was in other places. Still, even if you'd had your bandages off to-day I don't expect they'd have let you watch it. You'll have to take things gently at first, and some of the flashes are very bright. They—Ooooh!'

'Why "oooh"?' I inquired.

'That was such a brilliant one then—it made the whole room look green. What a pity you couldn't see it.'

'Isn't it?' I agreed. 'Now do go away, there's a good girl.'

I tried listening to the radio, but it was making the same 'ooohs' and 'aaahs' helped out by gentlemanly tones which blathered about this 'magnificent spectacle' and 'unique phenomenon' until I began to feel that there was a party for all the world going on, with me as the only person not invited.

I didn't have any choice of entertainment, for the hospital radio system gave only one programme, take it or leave it. After a bit I gathered that the show had begun to wane. The announcer advised everyone who had not yet seen it to hurry up and do so, or regret all his life that he had missed it.

The general idea seemed to be to convince me that I was passing up the very thing I was born for. In the end I got sick of it, and switched off. The last thing I heard was that the display was diminishing fast now, and that we'd probably be out of the debris area in a few hours.

There could be no doubt in my mind that all this had taken place the previous evening—for one thing, I should have been a great deal hungrier even than I was had it been longer ago. Very well, what *was* this then? Had the whole hospital, the whole city, made such a night of it that they'd not pulled round yet?

About which point I was interrupted as the chorus of clocks, near and far, started announcing nine.

For the third time I played hell with the bell. As I lay waiting I could hear a sort of murmurousness beyond the door. It seemed composed of whimperings, slitherings and shufflings, punctuated occasionally by a raised voice in the distance.

But still no one came to my room.

By this time I was slipping back. The nasty, childish fancies were on me again. I found myself waiting for the unseeable door to open, and horrible things to come padding in—in fact, I wasn't perfectly sure that somebody or something wasn't in already, and stealthily prowling round the room. . . .

Not that I'm given to that kind of thing, really. . . . It was those damned bandages over my eyes, the medley of voices that had shouted back at me down the corridor. But I certainly was getting the willies—and once you get 'em, they grow. Already they were past the stage where you can shoo them off by whistling or singing at yourself.

It came at last to the straight question: was I more scared of endangering my sight by taking off the bandages, or of staying in the dark with the willies growing every minute?

If it had been a day or two earlier I don't know what I'd have done—very likely the same in the end—but this day I could at least tell myself:

'Well, hang it, there can't be a lot of harm if I use common sense. After all, the bandages are due to come off to-day. I'll risk it.'

There's one thing I put to my credit. I was not far enough gone to tear them off wildly. I had the sense and the self-control to get out of bed and pull the blind down before I started on the safety-pins.

Once I had the coverings off, and had found out that I could see in the dimness, I felt a relief that I'd never known before. Nevertheless, the first thing I did after assuring myself that there were indeed no malicious persons or things lurking under the bed or elsewhere, was to slip a chair-back under the door-handle. I could, and did, begin to get a better grip on myself then. I made myself take a whole hour gradually getting used to full daylight. At the end of it I knew that thanks to swift first-aid, followed by good doctoring, my eyes were as good as ever.

But still no one came.

On the lower shelf of the bedside table I discovered a pair of dark glasses thoughtfully put ready against my need of them. Cautiously I put them on before I went right close to the window. The lower part of it was not made to open, so that the view was restricted. Squinting down and sideways I could see one or two people who appeared to be wandering in an odd, kind of aimless way further up the street. But what struck me most, and at once, was the sharpness, the clear definition of everything—even the distant housetops view across the opposite roofs. And then I noticed that no chimney, large or small, was smoking. . . .

I found my clothes hung tidily in a cupboard. I began to feel more normal once I had them on. There were some cigarettes still in the case. I lit one, and started to get into the state of mind where, though everything was still undeniably queer, I could no longer understand why I had been quite so near panic.

It is not easy to think oneself back to the outlook of those days. We have to be more self-reliant now. But then there was so much routine, things were so interlinked. Each one of us so steadily did his little part in the right place that it was easy to mistake habit and custom for the natural law—and all the more disturbing, therefore, when the routine was in any way upset.

When getting on for half a lifetime has been spent in one conception of order, reorientation is no five-minute business. Looking back at the shape of things then, the amount we did not know and did not care to know about our daily lives is not only astonishing, but somehow a bit shocking. I knew practically nothing, for instance, of such ordinary things as how my food reached me, where the fresh water came from, how the clothes I wore were woven and made, how the drainage of cities kept them healthy. Our life had become a complexity of specialists all attending to their own jobs with more or less efficiency, and expecting others to do the same. That made it incredible to me, therefore, that complete disorganization could have overtaken the hospital. Somebody somewhere, I was sure, must have it in hand—

unfortunately it was a somebody who had forgotten all about Room 48.

Nevertheless, when I did go to the door again and peer into the corridor I was forced to realize that whatever had happened it was affecting a great deal more than the single inhabitant of Room 48.

Just then there was no one in sight, though in the distance I could hear a pervasive murmur of voices. There was a sound of shuffling footsteps, too, and occasionally a louder voice echoing hollowly in the corridors, but nothing like the din I had shut out before. This time I did not shout. I stepped out cautiously—why cautiously? I don't know. There was just something that induced it.

It was difficult in that reverberating building to tell where the sounds were coming from, but one way the passage finished at an obscured french-window, with the shadow of a balcony rail upon it, so I went the other. Rounding a corner, I found myself out of the private-room wing and on a broader corridor.

When I first looked along it I thought it empty, then as I moved forward I saw a figure come out of a shadow. He was a man wearing a black jacket and striped trousers, with a white cotton coat over them. I judged him to be one of the staff doctors—but it was curious that he should be crouching against the wall and feeling his way along.

'Hullo, there,' I said.

He stopped suddenly. The face he turned towards me was grey and frightened.

'Who are you?' he asked, uncertainly.

'My name's Masen,' I told him. 'William Masen. I'm a patient—Room 48. And I've come to find out why——'

'You can see?' he interrupted, swiftly.

'Certainly I can. Just as well as ever,' I assured him. 'It's a wonderful job. Nobody came to unbandage my eyes, so

I did it myself. I don't think there's any harm done. I took——'

But he interrupted again.

'Please take me to my office. I must telephone at once.'

I was slow to catch on, but everything ever since I woke that morning had been bewildering.

'Where's that?' I asked.

'Fifth floor, west wing. The name's on the door—Doctor Soames.'

'All right,' I agreed, in some surprise. 'Where are we now?'

The man rocked his head from side to side, his face tense and exasperated.

'How the hell should I know?' he said, bitterly. 'You've got eyes, damn it. Use them. Can't you see I'm blind?'

There was nothing to show that he was blind. His eyes were wide open, and apparently looking straight at me.

'Wait here a minute,' I said. I looked round. I found a large '5' painted on the wall opposite the lift gate. I went back and told him.

'Good. Take my arm,' he directed. 'You turn right as you come out of the lift. Then take the first passage on the left, and it's the third door.'

I followed instructions. We met no one at all on the way. Inside the room I led him up to the desk, and handed him the telephone. He listened for some moments. Then he groped about until he found the rest, and rattled the bar impatiently. Slowly his expression changed. The irritability and the harassed lines faded away. He looked simply tired— very tired. He put the receiver down on the desk. For some seconds he stood silently, looking as though he was staring at the wall opposite. Then he turned.

'It's useless—dead. You *are* still here?' he added.

'Yes,' I told him.

His fingers felt along the edge of the desk.

'Which way am I facing? Where's the damned window?' he demanded, with a return of irritability.

'It's right behind you,' I said.

He turned, and stepped towards it, both hands extended. He felt the sill and the sides carefully, and stepped back a pace. Before I had realized what he was doing he had launched himself full at it, and crashed through. . . .

I didn't look to see. After all, it was the fifth floor.

When I moved, it was to sit down heavily in the chair. I took a cigarette from a box on the desk, and lit it shakily. I sat there for some minutes while I steadied up, and let the sick feeling subside. After a while it did. I left the room, and went back to the place where I had first found him. I still wasn't feeling too good when I got there.

At the far end of the wide corridor were the doors of a ward. The panels were frosted save for ovals of clear glass at face level. I reckoned there ought to be someone on duty there that I could report to about the doctor.

I opened the door. It was pretty dark in there. The curtains had evidently been drawn after the previous night's display was over—and they were still drawn.

'Sister?' I inquired.

'She ain't 'ere,' a man's voice said. 'What's more,' it went on, 'she ain't been 'ere for ruddy hours, neither. Can't you pull them ruddy curtains, mate, and let's 'ave some flippin' light? Don't know what's come over the bloody place this morning.'

'Okay,' I agreed.

Even if the whole place were disorganized, it didn't seem to be any good reason why the unfortunate patients should have to lie in the dark.

I pulled back the curtains on the nearest window, and let

in a shaft of bright sunlight. It was a surgical ward with about twenty patients, all bedridden. Leg injuries mostly, several amputations, by the look of it.

'Stop foolin' about with 'em, mate, and pull 'em back,' said the same voice.

I turned and looked at the man who spoke. He was a dark, burly fellow with a weatherbeaten skin. He was sitting up in bed, facing directly at me—and at the light. His eyes seemed to be gazing into my own, so did his neighbour's, and the next man's. . . .

For a few moments I stared back at them. It took that long to register. Then:

'I—they—they seem to be stuck,' I said. 'I'll find someone to see to them.'

And with that I fled from the ward.

I was shaky again, and I could have done with a stiff drink. The thing was beginning to sink in. But I found it difficult to believe that *all* the men in that ward could be blind, just like the doctor, and yet . . .

The lift wasn't working, so I started down the stairs. On the next floor I pulled myself together, and plucked up the courage to look into another ward. The beds there were all disarranged. At first I thought the place was empty, but it wasn't—not quite. Two men in nightclothes lay on the floor. One was soaked in blood from an unhealed incision, the other looked as if some kind of congestion had seized him. They were both quite dead. The rest had gone.

Back on the stairs once more, I realized that most of the background voices I had been hearing all the time were coming up from below, and that they were louder and closer now. I hesitated a moment, but there seemed to be nothing for it but to go on making my way down.

On the next turn I nearly tripped over a man who lay

across my way in the shadow. At the bottom of the flight lay somebody who actually had tripped over him—and cracked his head on the stone steps as he landed.

At last I reached the final turn where I could stand and look down into the main hall. Seemingly everyone in the place who was able to move must have made instinctively for that spot either with the idea of finding help or of getting outside. Perhaps some of them had got out. One of the main entrance doors was wide open, but most of them couldn't find it. There was a tight-packed mob of men and women, nearly all of them in their hospital nightclothes milling slowly and helplessly around. The motion pressed those on the outskirts cruelly against marble corners or ornamental projections. Some of them were crushed breathlessly against the walls. Now and then one would trip. If the press of bodies allowed him to fall, there was little chance that it would let him come up again.

The place looked—well, you'll have seen some of Doré's pictures of sinners in hell. But Doré couldn't include the sounds: the sobbing, the murmurous moaning, and occasionally a forlorn cry.

A minute or two of it was all I could stand. I fled back up the stairs.

There was the feeling that I ought to do something about it. Lead them out into the street, perhaps, and at least put an end to that dreadful slow milling. But a glance had been enough to show that I could not hope to make my way to the door to guide them there. Besides, if I were to, if I did get them outside—what then?

I sat down on a step for a while to get over it, with my head in my hands and that awful conglomerate sound in my ears all the time. Then I searched for, and found, another staircase. It was a narrow service flight which led me out by a back way into the yard.

Maybe I'm not telling this part too well. The whole thing was so unexpected and shocking that for a time I deliberately tried not to remember the details. Just then I was feeling much as though it were a nightmare from which I was desperately but vainly seeking the relief of waking myself. As I stepped out into the yard I still half-refused to believe what I had seen.

But one thing I was perfectly certain about. Reality or nightmare, I needed a drink as I had seldom needed one before.

There was nobody in sight in the little side street outside the yard gates, but almost opposite stood a pub. I can recall its name now—'The Alamein Arms.' There was a board bearing a reputed likeness of Viscount Montgomery hanging from an iron bracket, and below, one of the doors stood open.

I made straight for it.

Stepping into the public bar gave me for the moment a comforting sense of normality. It was prosaically and familiarly like dozens of others.

But although there was no one in that part, there was certainly something going on in the saloon bar, round the corner. I heard heavy breathing. A cork left its bottle with a pop. A pause. Then a voice remarked:

'Gin, blast it! T'hell with gin!'

There followed a shattering crash. The voice gave a sozzled chuckle.

'Thash the mirror. Wash good of mirrors, anyway?'

Another cork popped.

''S' damned gin again,' complained the voice, offended. 'T'*hell* with gin.'

This time the bottle hit something soft, thudded to the floor, and lay there gurgling away its contents.

'Hey!' I called. 'I want a drink.'

There was a silence. Then:

'Who're you?' the voice inquired, cautiously.

'I'm from the hospital,' I said. 'I want a drink.'

'Don' 'member y'r voice. Can you see?'

'Yes,' I told him.

'Well then, for God's sake get over the bar, Doc, and find me a bottle of whisky.'

'I'm doctor enough for that,' I said.

I climbed across, and went round the corner. A large-bellied, red-faced man with a greying walrus moustache stood there clad only in trousers and a collarless shirt. He was fairly drunk. He seemed undecided whether to open the bottle he held in his hand, or to use it as a weapon.

' 'F you're not a doctor, what are you?' he demanded, suspiciously.

'I was a patient—but I need a drink as much as any doctor,' I said. 'That's gin again you've got there,' I added.

'Oh, is it! B—— gin,' he said, and slung it away. It went through the window with a lively crash.

'Give me that corkscrew,' I told him.

I took down a bottle of whisky from the shelf, opened it, and handed it to him with a glass. For myself I chose a stiff brandy with very little soda, and then another. After that my hand wasn't shaking so much.

I looked at my companion. He was taking his whisky neat, out of the bottle.

'You'll get drunk,' I said.

He paused and turned his head towards me. I could have sworn that his eyes really saw me.

'Get drunk! Damn it, I *am* drunk,' he said, scornfully.

He was so perfectly right that I didn't comment. He brooded a moment before he announced:

'Gotta get drunker. Gotta get mush drunker.' He leaned closer. 'D'you know what?—I'm blind. Thash what I am—

blind's a bat. *Every*body's blind's a bat. 'Cept you. Why aren't you blind's a bat?'

'I don't know,' I told him.

' 'S that bloody comet, b—— it! Thash what done it. Green shootin' shtarsh—an' now everyone's blind's a bat. D'ju shee green shootin' shtarsh?'

'No,' I admitted.

'There you are. Proves it. You didn't see 'em: you aren't blind. Everyone else saw 'em'—he waved an expressive arm—'all's blind's bats. B—— comets, I say.'

I poured myself a third brandy, wondering whether there might not be something in what he was saying.

'*Every*one blind?' I repeated.

'Thash it. All of 'em. Prob'ly everyone in th' world—'cept you,' he added, as an afterthought.

'How do you know?' I asked.

' 'S easy. Listen!' he said.

We stood side by side leaning on the bar of the dingy pub, and listened. There was nothing to be heard—nothing but the rustle of a dirty newspaper blown down the empty street. Such a quietness held everything as cannot have been known in those parts for a thousand years and more.

'See what I mean? 'S obvious,' said the man.

'Yes,' I said slowly. 'Yes—I see what you mean.'

I decided that I must get along. I did not know where to. But I must find out more about what was happening.

'Are you the landlord?' I asked him.

'Wha' 'f I am?' he demanded, defensively.

'Only that I've got to pay someone for three double brandies.'

'Ah—forget it.'

'But, look here——'

'Forget it, I tell you. D'ju know why? 'Cause what's the

good 'f money to a dead man? An' thash what I am—'s good as. Jus' a few more drinks.'

He looked a pretty robust specimen for his age, and I said so.

'Wha's good of living blind's a bat?' he demanded, aggressively. 'Thash what my wife said. An' she was right—only she's more guts than I have. When she found as the kids was blind too, what did she do? Took 'em into our bed with her, and turned on the gas. Thash what she done. An' I hadn't the guts to stick with 'em. She's got pluck, my wife, more'n I have. But I will have soon. I'm goin' back up there soon—when I'm drunk enough.'

What was there to say? What I did say served no purpose, save to spoil his temper. In the end he groped his way to the stairs, and disappeared up them, bottle in hand. I didn't try to stop him, or follow him. I watched him go. Then I knocked back the last of my brandy, and went out into the silent street.

2. The Coming of the Triffids

THIS is a personal record. It involves a great deal that has vanished for ever, but I can't tell it in any other way than by using the words we used to use for those vanished things, so they have to stand. But even to make the setting intelligible I find that I shall have to go back further than the point at which I started:

When I was a child we lived, my father, my mother, and myself, in a southern suburb of London. We had a small house which my father supported by conscientious daily attendance at his desk in the Inland Revenue Department, and a small garden at which he worked rather harder during the summer. There was not a lot to distinguish us from the ten or twelve million other people who used to live in and around London in those days.

My father was one of those persons who could add a column of figures—even of the ridiculous coinage then in use locally—with a flick of the eye, so that it was natural for him to have in mind that I should become an accountant. As a result, my inability to make any column of figures reach the same total twice caused me to be something of a mystery as well as a disappointment to him. Still, there it was: just one of those things. And each of a succession of teachers who tried to show me that mathematical answers were derived logically and not through some form of esoteric inspiration was forced to give up with the assurance that I had no head for figures. My father would read my school reports with a gloom which in other respects they scarcely warranted. His mind worked, I think, this way: no head for figures = no idea of finance = no money.

'I really don't know what we shall do with you. What do you *want* to do?' he would ask.

And until I was thirteen or fourteen I would shake my head, conscious of my sad inadequacy, and admit that I did not know.

My father would then shake *his* head.

For him the world was divided sharply into desk-men who worked with their brains, and non-desk-men who didn't, and got dirty. How he contrived to maintain this view which was already a century or so out of date I do not know, but it pervaded my early years to such an extent that I was late in perceiving that a weakness in figures did not of necessity condemn me to the life of a street-sweeper or a scullion. It did not occur to me that the subject which interested me most could lead to a career—and my father failed either to notice, or, if he did, to care that reports on my biology were consistently good.

It was the appearance of the triffids which really decided the matter for us. Indeed, they did a lot more than that for me. They provided me with a job and comfortably supported me. They also on several occasions almost took my life. On the other hand, I have to admit that they preserved it, too, for it was a triffid sting that had landed me in hospital on the critical occasion of the 'comet debris.'

In the books there is quite a lot of loose speculation on the sudden occurrence of the triffids. Most of it is nonsense.

Certainly they were not spontaneously generated as many simple souls believed. Nor did most people endorse the theory that they were a kind of sample visitation—harbingers of worse to come if the world did not mend its ways and behave its troublesome self. Nor did their seeds float to us through space as specimens of the horrid forms life might assume upon other, less favoured worlds—at least, I am satisfied that they did not.

I learned more about it than most people because triffids were my job, and the firm I worked for was intimately, if not very gracefully, concerned in their public appearance. Nevertheless, their true origin still remains obscure. My own belief, for what it is worth, is that they were the outcome of a series of ingenious biological meddlings—and very likely accidental at that. Had they been evolved anywhere but in the region they were we should doubtless have had a well-documented ancestry for them. As it was, no authoritative statement was ever published by those who must have been best qualified to know. The reason for this lay, no doubt, in the curious political conditions then prevailing.

The world we lived in then was wide, and most of it was open to us with little trouble. Roads, railways and shipping lines laced it, ready to carry one thousands of miles safely and in comfort. If we wanted to travel more swiftly still, and could afford it, we travelled by aeroplane. There was no need for anyone to take weapons or even precautions in those days. You could go just as you were to wherever you wished, with nothing to hinder you—other than a lot of forms and regulations. A world so tamed sounds utopian now. Nevertheless, it was so over five-sixths of the globe—though the remaining sixth was something different again.

It must be difficult for young people who never knew it to

envisage a world like that. Perhaps it sounds like a golden age—though it wasn't quite that to those who lived in it. Or they may think that an Earth ordered and cultivated almost all over sounds dull—but it wasn't that, either. It was rather an exciting place—for a biologist, anyway. Every year we were pushing the northern limit of growth for food plants a little further back. New fields were growing quick crops on what had historically been simply tundra or barren land. Every season, too, stretches of desert both old and recent were reclaimed and made to grow grass or food. For food was then our most pressing problem, and the progress of the regeneration schemes and the advance of the cultivation lines on the maps was followed with almost as much attention as an earlier generation had paid to battle-fronts.

Such a swerve of interest from swords to plough-shares was undoubtedly a social improvement, but, at the same time, it was a mistake for the optimistic to claim it as showing a change in the human spirit. The human spirit continued much as before—ninety-five per cent. of it wanting to live in peace; and the other five per cent. considering its chances if it should risk starting anything. It was chiefly because no one's chances looked too good that the lull continued.

Meanwhile, with something like twenty-five million new mouths bawling for food every year the supply problem became steadily worse, and after years of ineffective propaganda a couple of atrocious harvests had at last made the people aware of its urgency.

The factor which had caused the militant five per cent. to relax a while from fomenting discord was the satellites. Sustained research in rocketry had at last succeeded in attaining one of its objectives. It had sent up a missile which stayed up. It was, in fact, possible to fire a rocket far enough up for it to fall into an orbit round the earth. Once there it would continue to circle like a tiny moon, quite inactive and innocuous—until the pressure on a button should give it the impulse to drop back, with devastating effect.

Great as was the public concern which followed the triumphant announcement of the first nation to establish a satellite weapon satisfactorily, a still greater concern was felt over the failure of others to make any announcement at all even when they were known to have had similar successes. It was by no means pleasant to realize that there was an unknown number of menaces up there over your head, quietly circling and circling until someone should arrange for them to drop—and that there was nothing to be done about them. Still, life has to go on—and novelty is a wonderfully short-lived thing. One became used to the idea perforce. From time to time there would be a panicky flare-up of expostulation when reports circulated that as well as satellites with atomic heads there were others with such things as crop diseases, cattle diseases, radio-active dusts, viruses, and infections not only of familiar kinds, but brand-new sorts recently thought up in laboratories, all floating around up there. Whether such uncertain and potentially back-firing weapons had actually been placed is hard to say. But then, the limits of folly itself—particularly of folly with fear on its heels—are not easy to define. A virulent organism, unstable enough to become harmless in the course of a few days (and who is to say that such could not be bred?) could be considered to have strategic uses if dropped in suitable spots.

At least the United States Government took the suggestion seriously enough to deny emphatically that it controlled any satellites designed to conduct biological warfare directly upon human beings. One or two minor nations, whom no one suspected of controlling any satellites at all, hastened to make similar declarations. Other, and major, powers did not. In the face of this ominous reticence the public began demanding to know why the United States had neglected to prepare for a form of warfare which others were ready to use—and just what did 'directly' mean, anyway? At this point all parties tacitly gave up denying or confirming anything about satellites, and an intensified effort was made to divert the public interest to the no less important, but far less acrimonious matter of food scarcity.

The laws of supply and demand should have enabled the more enterprising to organize commodity monopolies, but the world at large had become antagonistic to declared monopolies. However, the laced-company system really worked very smoothly without anything so imputable as Articles of Federation. The general public heard scarcely anything of such little difficulties within the pattern as had to be untangled from time to time. Hardly anyone heard of even the existence of Umberto Christoforo Palanguez, for instance. I only heard of him myself years later in the course of my work.

Umberto was of assorted Latin descent, and something South American by nationality. His first appearance as a possibly disruptive spanner in the neat machinery of the edible-oil interests occurred when he walked into the offices of the Arctic and European Fish-Oil Company, and produced a bottle of pale pink oil in which he proposed to interest them.

Arctic and European displayed no eagerness. The trade was pretty well tied up. However, they did in the course of time get around to analysing the sample he had left with them.

The first thing they discovered about it was that it was not a fish-oil, anyway: it was vegetable, though they could not identify the source. The second revelation was that it made most of their best fish-oils look like grease-box fillers. Alarmed, they sent out what remained of the sample for

intensive study, and put round hurried inquiries to know if
Mr. Palanguez had made other approaches.

When Umberto called again the managing-director
received him with flattering attention.

'That is a very remarkable oil you brought us, Mr.
Palanguez,' he said.

Umberto nodded his sleek, dark head. He was well aware
of the fact.

'I have never seen anything quite like it,' the managing-
director admitted.

Umberto nodded again.

'No?' he said, politely. Then, seemingly as an afterthought, he added: 'But I think you will, señor. A very great
deal of it.' He appeared to ponder. 'It will, I think, come
on the market seven, maybe eight, years from now.' He
smiled.

The managing-director thought that unlikely. He said,
with a frank air:

'It is better than our fish-oils.'

'So I am told, señor,' agreed Umberto.

'You are proposing to market it yourself, Mr. Palanguez?'

Umberto smiled again.

'Would I be showing it to you if I did?'

'We might reinforce one of our own oils synthetically,'
observed the managing-director, reflectively.

'With some of the vitamins—but it would be costly to
synthesize all of them: even if you could,' Umberto said
gently. 'Besides,' he added, 'I am told that this oil will easily
undersell your best fish-oils, anyway.'

'H'm,' said the managing-director. 'Well, I suppose you
have a proposition, Mr. Palanguez. Shall we come to it?'

Umberto explained: 'There are two ways of dealing with
such an unfortunate matter. The usual one is to prevent it
happening—or at least to delay it until the capital sunk in

present equipment has been paid off. That is, of course, the desirable way.'

The managing-director nodded. He knew plenty about that.

'But this time I am so sorry for you, because, you see, it is not possible.'

The managing-director had his doubts. His inclination was to say, 'You'd be surprised,' but he resisted it, and contented himself with a non-committal: 'Oh?'

'The other way,' suggested Umberto, 'is to produce the thing yourself before the trouble starts.'

'Ah!' said the managing-director.

'I think,' Umberto told him, 'I think that I might be able to supply you with seeds of this plant in, maybe, six months time. If you were to plant then you could begin production of oil in five years—or it might be six for full yield.'

'Just nicely in time, in fact,' observed the managing-director.

Umberto nodded.

'The other way would be simpler,' remarked the managing director.

'If it were possible at all,' Umberto agreed. 'But unfortunately your competitors are not approachable—or suppressible.'

He made the statement with a confidence which caused the managing-director to study him thoughtfully for some moments.

'I see,' he said at last. 'I wonder—er—you don't happen to be a Soviet citizen, Mr. Pelanguez?'

'No,' said Umberto. 'On the whole my life has been lucky—but I have very varied connections. . . .'

That brings us to considering the other sixth of the world—that part which one could not visit with such facility as the rest. Indeed, permits to visit the Union of Soviet

Socialist Republics were almost unobtainable, and the movements of those who did achieve them were strictly circumscribed. It had deliberately organized itself into a land of mystery. Little of what went on behind the veiling secrecy which was almost pathological in the region was known to the rest of the world. What was, was usually suspect. Yet, behind the curious propaganda which distributed the laughable while concealing all likely to be of the least importance, achievements undoubtedly went on in many fields. One was biology. Russia, who shared with the rest of the world the problem of increasing food supplies, was known to have been intensively concerned with attempts to reclaim desert, steppe, and the northern tundra. In the days when information was still exchanged she had reported some successes. Later, however, a cleavage of methods and views had caused biology there, under a man called Lysenko, to take a different course. It, too, then succumbed to the endemic secrecy. The lines it had taken were unknown, and thought to be unsound—but it was anybody's guess whether very successful, very silly, or very queer things were happening there—if not all three at once.

'Sunflowers,' said the managing-director, speaking absentmindedly out of his own reflections. 'I happen to know they were having another shot at improving the yield of sunflower-seed oil. But it isn't that.'

'No,' agreed Umberto. 'It is not that.'

The managing-director doodled.

'Seeds, you said. Do you mean that it is some new species? Because if it is merely some improved strain more easily processed——'

'I understand that it is a new species—something quite new.'

'Then you haven't actually seen it yourself? It may, in fact, be some modified kind of sunflower?'

'I have seen a picture, señor. I do not say there is *no* sunflower there at all. I do not say there is no turnip there. I do not say that there is no nettle, or even no orchid there. But I do say that if they were all fathers to it they would none of them know their child. I do not think it would please them greatly, either.'

'I see. Now what was the figure you had in mind for getting us the seeds of this thing?'

Umberto named a sum which stopped the managing-director's doodling quite abruptly. It made him take off his glasses to regard the speaker more closely. Umberto was unabashed.

'Consider, señor,' he said, ticking off points on his fingers. 'It is difficult. And it is dangerous—very dangerous. I do not fear—but I do not go to danger to amuse myself. There is another man, a Russian. I shall have to bring him away, and he must be paid well. There will be others that he must pay first. Also I must buy an aeroplane—a jet aeroplane, very fast. All these things cost money.

'And I tell you it is not easy. You must have seeds that are good. Many of the seeds of this plant are infertile. To make sure, I have to bring you seeds that have been sorted. They are valuable. And in Russia everything is a state secret and guarded. Certainly it will not be easy.'

'I believe that. But all the same——'

'Is it so much, señor? What will you say in a few years when these Russians are selling their oil all over the world—and your company is finished?'

'It will need thinking over, Mr. Palanguez.'

'But of course, señor?' Umberto agreed, with a smile. 'I can wait—a little while. But I am afraid I cannot reduce my price.'

Nor did he.

The discoverer and the inventor are the bane of business.

A little sand in the works is comparatively a mere nothing—
you just replace the damaged parts, and go on. But the
appearance of a new process, a new substance, when you
are all organized and ticking nicely is the very devil. Sometimes it is worse than that—it just cannot be allowed to
occur. Too much is at stake. If you can't use legal methods,
you must try others.

For Umberto had understated the case. It was not simply
that the competition of a cheap new oil would send Arctic
and European and their associates out of business. The
effects would be widespread. It might not be fatal to the
groundnut, the olive, the whale and a number of other oil
industries, but it would be a nasty knock. Moreover, there
would be violent repercussions in dependent industries, in
margarine, soap, and a hundred more products from face-
creams to house-paints, and beyond. Indeed, once a few
of the more influential concerns had grasped the quality
of the menace Umberto's terms came to seem almost
modest.

He got his agreement, for his samples were convincing, if
the rest was somewhat vague.

In point of fact it cost those interested quite a lot less than
they had undertaken to pay, for after Umberto went off
with his aeroplane and his advance he was never seen again.

But that is not to say he was altogether unheard of.

Some years later an indeterminate individual giving simply
the name Fedor turned up at the offices of Arctic and European Oils. (They had dropped 'Fish' from both their title
and activities then.) He was, he said, a Russian. He would
like, he said, some money, if the kind capitalists would be
good enough to spare some.

His story was that he had been employed in the first
experimental triffid station in the district of Elovsk in
Kamchatka. It was a forlorn place, and he greatly disliked

it. His desire to get away had caused him to listen to a suggestion from another worker there, to be specific, one Tovaritch Nikolai Alexandrovitch Baltinoff, and the suggestion had been backed up by several thousand roubles.

It did not require a great deal of earning. He had simply to remove a box of sorted fertile triffid seeds from its rack, and substitute a similar box of infertile seeds. The purloined box was to be left at a certain place at a certain time. There was practically no risk. It might be years before the substitution was discovered.

A further requirement, however, was a little more tricky. He was to see that a pattern of lights was laid out on a large field a mile or two from the plantation. He was to be there himself on a certain night. He would hear an aeroplane flying directly above. He would switch on the lights. The plane would land. The best thing he could do then would be to get away from the neighbourhood as soon as possible before anyone should arrive to investigate.

For these services he would receive not only the comfortable wad of roubles, but if he should succeed in leaving Russia he would find more money waiting for him at the offices of Arctic and European, in England.

By his account the operation had gone entirely to plan. Fedor had not waited once the plane was down. He had switched off the lights, and beat it.

The plane had stopped only a short time, perhaps not ten minutes, before it took off again. From the sound of the jets he judged that it was climbing steeply as it went. A minute or so after the noise had died away he heard the sound of engines again. Some more planes went over headed east, after the other. There might have been two, or more, he could not tell. But they were travelling very fast, with their jets shrieking. . . .

The next day Comrade Baltinoff was missing. There had been a lot of trouble, but in the end it was decided that Baltinoff must have been working alone. So it had all passed off safely for Fedor.

He had cautiously waited for a year before he made a move. It had cost him almost the last of his roubles by the time he had bought his way through the final obstacles. Then he had had to take various jobs to live, so that he had spent a long time in reaching England. But now he had, could he have some money, please?

Something had been heard about Elovsk by that time. And the date he gave for the plane landing was within probability. So they gave him some money. They also gave him a job, and told him to keep his mouth shut. For it was clear that though Umberto had not personally delivered the goods, he had at least saved the situation by broadcasting them.

Arctic-European had not at first connected the appearance of the triffids with Umberto, and the police of several countries went on keeping an eye open for him on their behalf. It was not until some investigator produced a specimen of triffid oil for their inspection that they realized that it corresponded exactly with the sample Umberto had shown them, and that it was the seeds of the triffid he had set out to bring.

What happened to Umberto himself will never be definitely known. It is my guess that over the Pacific Ocean, somewhere high up in the stratosphere, he and Comrade Baltinoff found themselves attacked by the planes that Fedor had heard in pursuit. It may be that the first they knew of it was when cannon-shells from Russian fighters started to break up their craft.

And I think, too, that one of those shells blew to pieces a certain twelve-inch cube of plywood—the receptacle like a small tea-chest in which, according to Fedor, the seeds were packed.

Perhaps Umberto's plane exploded, perhaps it just fell to pieces. Whichever it was, I am sure that when the fragments began their long, long fall towards the sea they left behind them something which looked at first like a white vapour.

It was not vapour. It was a cloud of seeds, floating, so infinitely light they were, even in the rarefied air. Millions of gossamer-slung triffid seeds, free now to drift wherever the winds of the world should take them. . . .

It might be weeks, perhaps months, before they would sink to earth at last, many of them thousands of miles from their starting-place.

That is, I repeat, conjecture. But I cannot see a more probable way in which that plant, intended to be kept secret could come, quite suddenly, to be found in almost every part of the world.

My introduction to a triffid came early. It so happened that we had one of the first in the locality growing in our own garden. The plant was quite well developed before any of us bothered to notice it, for it had taken root along with a number of other casuals behind the bit of hedge that screened the rubbish heap. It wasn't doing any harm there, and it wasn't in anyone's way. So when we did notice it later on we'd just take a look at it now and then to see how it was getting along, and let it be.

However, a triffid is certainly distinctive, and we couldn't help getting a bit curious about it after a time. Not, perhaps, very actively, for there are always a few unfamiliar things that somehow or other manage to lodge in the neglected corners of a garden, but enough to mention to one another that it was beginning to look a pretty queer sort of thing.

Nowadays when everyone knows only too well what a triffid looks like it is difficult to recall how odd and somehow *foreign* the first ones appeared to us. Nobody, as far as I know, felt any misgiving or alarm about them then. I imagine that most people thought of them—when they thought of them at all—in much the same way that my father did.

I have a picture in my memory of him examining ours and puzzling over it at a time when it must have been about a year old. In almost every detail it was a half-size replica of a fully-grown triffid—only it didn't have a name yet, and no one had seen one fully grown. My father leant over, peering at it through his horn-rimmed glasses, fingering its stalk, and blowing gently through his gingery moustache as was his habit when thoughtful. He inspected the straight stem, and the woody bole from which it sprang. He gave curious, if not very penetrative attention to the three small, bare sticks which grew straight up beside the stem. He smoothed the short sprays of leathery green leaves between his finger and thumb as if their texture might tell him something. Then he peered into the curious, funnel-like formation at the top of the stem, still puffing reflectively but inconclusively through his moustache. I remember the first time he lifted me up to look inside that conical cup and see the tightly-wrapped whorl within. It looked not unlike the new, close-rolled frond of a fern, emerging a couple of inches from a sticky mess in the base of the cup. I did not touch it, but I knew the stuff must be sticky because there were flies and other small insects struggling in it.

More than once my father ruminated that it was pretty queer, and observed that one of these days he really must try to find out what it was. I don't think he ever made the effort, nor, at that stage, was he likely to have learned much if he had tried.

The thing would be about four feet high then. There must have been plenty of them about, growing up quietly and inoffensively, with nobody taking any particular notice of them—at least, it seemed so, for if the biological or botanical experts were excited over them no news of their interest percolated to the general public. And so the one in our garden continued its growth peacefully, as did thousands like it in neglected spots all over the world.

It was some little time later that the first one picked up its roots, and walked.

That improbable achievement must, of course, have been known for some time in Russia where it was doubtless classified as a state secret, but as far as I have been able to confirm its first occurrence in the outside world took place in Indo-China—which meant that people went on taking practically no notice. Indo-China was one of those regions from which such curious and unlikely yarns might be expected to drift in, and frequently did—the kind of thing an editor might conceivably use if news were scarce and a touch of the 'mysterious East' would liven the paper up a bit. But in any case the Indo-Chinese specimen can have had no great lead. Within a few weeks reports of walking plants were pouring in from Sumatra, Borneo, Belgian Congo, Colombia, Brazil and most places in the neighbourhood of the equator.

This time they got into print, all right. But the much-handled stories written up with that blend of cautiously defensive frivolity which the Press habitually employed to cover themselves in matters regarding sea-serpents, elementals, thought-transference and other irregular phenomena prevented anyone from realizing that these accomplished plants at all resembled the quiet, respectable weed beside our rubbish heap. Not until the pictures began to appear did we realize that they were identical with it save in size.

The news-reel men were quickly off the mark. Possibly they got some good and interesting pictures for their trouble of flying to outlandish places, but there was a current theory among cutters that more than a few seconds of any one news-subject—except a boxing match—could not fail to paralyse an audience with boredom. My first view, therefore, of a development which was to play such an important part in my future, as well as in so many other people's, was a glimpse sandwiched between a hula contest in Honolulu, and the First Lady launching a battleship. (That is no anachronism. They were still building them; even admirals had to live.) I was permitted to see a few triffids sway across the screen to the kind of accompaniment supposed to be on the level of the great movie-going public:

'And now, folks, get a load of what our cameraman found in Ecuador. Vegetables on vacation! *You*'ve only seen this kind of thing after a party, but down in sunny Ecuador they see it any time—and no hangover to follow! Monster plants on the march! Say, now, that's given me a big idea! Maybe if we can educate our potatoes right we can fix it so they'll walk right into the pot. How'd that be, Momma?'

For the short time the scene was on, I stared at it, fascinated. There was our mysterious rubbish-heap plant grown to a height of seven feet or more. There was no mistaking it—and it was 'walking'!

The bole, which I now saw for the first time, was shaggy with little rootlet hairs. It would have been almost spherical but for three bluntly-tapered projections extending from the lower part. Supported on these, the main body was lifted about a foot clear of the ground.

When it 'walked' it moved rather like a man on crutches. Two of the blunt 'legs' slid forward, then the whole thing lurched as the rear one drew almost level with them, then the two in front slid forward again. At each 'step' the long stem whipped violently back and forth: it gave one a kind of seasick feeling to watch it. As a method of progress it looked both strenuous and clumsy—faintly reminiscent of young elephants at play. One felt that if it were to go on lurching for long in that fashion it would be bound to strip all its leaves if it did not actually break its stem. Nevertheless, ungainly though it looked, it was contriving to cover the ground at something like an average walking pace.

That was about all I had time to see before the battleship launching began. It was not a lot, but it was enough to incite an investigating spirit in a boy. For, if that thing in Ecuador could do a trick like that, why not the one in our garden? Admittedly ours was a good deal smaller, but it did *look* the same. . . .

About ten minutes after I got home I was digging round our triffid, carefully loosening the earth near it to encourage it to 'walk.'

Unfortunately there was an aspect of this self-propelled plant discovery which the news-reel people had either not experienced, or chosen for some reason of their own not to reveal. There was no warning, either. I was bending down, intent on clearing the earth without harming the plant, when something from nowhere hit me one terrific slam, and knocked me out. . . .

I woke up to find myself in bed, with my mother, my father, and the doctor watching me anxiously. My head felt as if it were split open, I was aching all over, and, as I later discovered, one side of my face was decorated with a blotchy-red raised weal. The insistent questions as to how I came to be lying unconscious in the garden were quite useless; I had no faintest idea what it was that had hit me. And some little time passed before I learned that I must have been one of the first persons in England to be stung

by a triffid and get away with it. The triffid was, of course,
immature. But before I had fully recovered my father had
found out what had undoubtedly happened to me, and by
the time I went into the garden again he had wreaked
stern vengeance on our triffid, and disposed of the remains
on a bonfire.

Now that walking plants were established facts the Press
lost its former tepidity, and bathed them in publicity. So a
name had to be found for them. Already there were botanists
wallowing after their custom in polysyllabic dog-Latin and
Greek to produce variants on *ambulans* and *pseudopodia*,
but what the newspapers and the public wanted was something easy on the tongue and not too heavy on the headlines
for general use. If you could see the papers of that time you
would find them referring to:

Trichots	Trinits
Tricusps	Tripedals
Trigenates	Tripeds
Trigons	Triquets
Trilogs	Tripods
Tridentates	Trippets

and a number of other mysterious things not even beginning
with 'tri'—though almost all centred on the feature of that
active, three-pronged root.

There was argument, public, private, and bar-parlour
with heated championship of one term or another on near-
scientific, quasi-etymological, and a number of other
grounds, but gradually one term began to dominate this
philological gymkhana. In its first form it was not quite
acceptable, but common usage modified the original long
first 'i,' and custom quickly wrote in a second 'f,' to leave
no doubt about it. And so emerged the standard term. A
catchy little name originating in some newspaper office as a

handy label for an oddity—but destined one day to be associated with pain, fear and misery—TRIFFID. . . .

The first wave of public interest soon ebbed away. Triffids were, admittedly, a bit weird—but that was, after all, just because they were novelties. People had felt the same about novelties of other days—about kangaroos, giant lizards, black swans. And, when you came to think of it, were triffids all that much queerer than mudfish, ostriches, tadpoles, and a hundred other things? The bat was an animal that had learned to fly: well, here was a plant that had learned to walk—what of that?

But there were features of it to be less casually dismissed. On its origins the Russians, true to type, lay low and said nuffin. Even those who had heard of Umberto did not yet connect him with it. Its sudden appearance, and even more, its wide distribution promoted very puzzled speculation. For though it matured more rapidly in the tropics, specimens in various stages of development were reported from almost any region outside the polar circles and the deserts.

People were surprised, and a little disgusted, to learn that the species was carnivorous, and that the flies and other insects caught in the cups were actually digested by the sticky substance there. We in temperate zones were not ignorant of insectivorous plants, but we were unaccustomed to find them outside special hothouses, and apt to consider them as in some way slightly indecent, or at least improper. But actually alarming was the discovery that the whorl topping a triffid's stem could lash out as a slender stinging weapon ten feet long, capable of discharging enough poison to kill a man if it struck squarely on his unprotected skin.

As soon as this danger was appreciated there followed a

nervous smashing and chopping of triffids everywhere until
it occurred to someone that all that was necessary to make
them harmless was the removal of the actual stinging
weapon. At this, the slightly hysterical assault upon the
plants declined, with their numbers considerably thinned.
A little later it began to be a fashion to have a safely-docked
triffid or two about one's garden. It was found that it took
about two years for the lost sting to be dangerously replaced,
so that an annual pruning assured that they were in a state
of safety where they could provide vast amusement for the
children.

In temperate countries, where man had succeeded in
putting most forms of nature save his own under a reasonable degree of restraint, the status of the triffid was thus
made quite clear. But in the tropics, particularly in the dense
forest areas, they quickly became a scourge.

The traveller very easily failed to notice one among the
normal bushes and undergrowth, and the moment he was
in range the venomous sting would slash out. Even the
regular inhabitant of such a district found it difficult to
detect a motionless triffid cunningly lurking beside a jungle
path. They were uncannily sensitive to any movement near
them, and it was hard to take them unawares.

Dealing with them became a serious problem in such
regions. The most favoured method was to shoot the top off
the stem, and the sting with it. The jungle natives took to
carrying long, light poles mounted with hooked knives
which they used effectively if they could get their blows in
first—but not at all if the triffid had a chance to sway
forward and increase its range by an unexpected four or five
feet. Before long, however, these pike-like devices were
mostly superseded by spring-operated guns of various types.
Most of them shot spinning discs, crosses, or small boomerangs of thin steel. As a rule they were inaccurate above

about twelve yards, though capable of slicing a triffid stem neatly at twenty-five if they hit it. Their invention pleased both the authorities—who had an almost unanimous distaste for the indiscriminate toting of rifles—and the users who found the missiles of razor-blade steel far cheaper and lighter than cartridges, and admirably adaptable to silent banditry.

Elsewhere immense research into the nature, habits, and constitution of the triffid went on. Earnest experimenters set out to determine in the interests of science how far and for how long it could walk; whether it could be said to have a front, or could perform its march in any direction with equal clumsiness; what proportion of its time it must spend with its roots in the ground; what reactions it showed to the presence of various chemicals in the soil; and a vast quantity of other questions, both useful and useless.

The largest specimen ever observed in the tropics stood nearly ten feet high. No European specimen over eight feet had been seen, and the average was little over seven. They appeared to adapt easily to a wide range of climate and soils. They had, it seemed, no natural enemies—other than man.

But there were a number of not unobvious characteristics which escaped comment for some little time. It was, for instance, quite a while before anyone drew attention to the uncanny accuracy with which they aimed their stings, and that they almost invariably struck for the head. Nor did anyone at first take notice of their habit of lurking near their fallen victims. The reason for that only became clear when it was shown that they fed upon flesh as well as upon insects. The stinging tendril did not have the muscular power to tear firm flesh, but it had strength enough to pull shreds from a decomposing body and lift them to the cup on its stem.

There was no great interest, either, in the three little leafless sticks at the base of the stem. There was a light notion that they might have something to do with the reproductive system—that system which tends to be a sort of botanical glory-hole for all parts of doubtful purpose until they can be sorted out and more specifically assigned later on. It was assumed, consequently, that their characteristic of suddenly losing their immobility and rattling a rapid tattoo against the main stem was some strange form of triffidian amatory exuberance.

Possibly my uncomfortable distinction of getting myself stung so early in the triffid era had the effect of stimulating my interest, for I seemed to have a sort of link with them from then on. I spent—or 'wasted,' if you look at me through my father's eyes—a great deal of fascinated time watching them.

One could not blame him for considering this a worthless pursuit, yet, later, the time turned out to have been better employed than either of us suspected, for it was just before I left school that the Arctic and European Fish-Oil Company reconstituted itself, dropping the word 'Fish' in the process. The public learned that it and similar companies in other countries were about to farm triffids on a large scale in order to extract valuable oils and juices, and to press highly nutritious oil-cake for stock feeding. Consequently, triffids moved into the realm of big business overnight.

Right away I decided my future. I applied to the Arctic and European where my qualifications got me a job on the production side. My father's disapproval was somewhat qualified by the rate of pay, which was good for my age. But when I spoke enthusiastically of the future he blew doubtfully through his moustache. He had real faith only in a type of work steadied by long tradition, but he let me have my way. 'After all, if the thing isn't a success you'll find out young enough to start in on something more solid,' he conceded.

There turned out to be no need for that. Before he and my mother were killed together in a holiday air-bus crash five years later they had seen the new companies drive all competing oils off the market, and those of us who had been in at the beginning apparently well set for life.

One of the early comers was my friend Walter Lucknor.

There had been some doubt at first about taking Walter on. He knew little of agriculture, less of business, and lacked the qualifications for lab. work. On the other hand, he did know a lot about triffids—he had a kind of inspired knack with them.

What happened to Walter that fatal May years later I do not know—though I can guess. It is a sad thing that he did not escape. He might have been immensely valuable later on. I don't think anybody really understands triffids, or ever will, but Walter came nearer to beginning to understand them than any man I have known. Or should I say that he was given to intuitive feelings about them?

It was a year or two after the job had begun that he first surprised me.

The sun was close to setting. We had knocked off for the day and were looking with a sense of satisfaction at three new fields of nearly fully-grown triffids. In those days we didn't simply corral them as we did later. They were arranged across the fields roughly in rows—at least the steel stakes to which each was tethered by a chain were in rows, though the plants themselves had no sense of tidy regimentation. We reckoned that in another month or so we'd be able to start tapping them for juice. The evening was peaceful, almost the only sounds that broke it were the occasional rattlings of the triffids, little sticks against their stems. Walter regarded them with his head slightly on one side. He removed his pipe.

'They're talkative to-night,' he observed.

I took that as anyone else would, metaphorically.

'Maybe it's the weather,' I suggested. 'I fancy they do it more when it's dry.'

He looked sidelong at me, with a smile.

'Do you talk more when it's dry?'

'Why should——?' I began, and then broke off. 'You don't really mean you think they're talking?' I said, noticing his expression.

'Well, why not?'

'But it's absurd. Plants talking!'

'So much more absurd than plants walking?' he asked.

I stared at them, and then back at him.

'I never thought——' I began, doubtfully.

'You try thinking of it a bit, and watching them—— I'd be interested to hear your conclusions,' he said.

It was a curious thing that in all my dealings with triffids such a possibility had never occurred to me. I'd been prejudiced, I suppose, by the love-call theory. But once he had put the idea into my mind, it stuck. I couldn't get away from the feeling that they might indeed be rattling out secret messages to one another.

Up to then I'd fancied I'd watched triffids pretty closely, but when Walter was talking about them I felt that I'd noticed practically nothing. He could, when he was in the mood, talk on about them for hours, advancing theories that were sometimes wild, but sometimes not impossible.

The public had by this time grown out of thinking triffids freakish. They were clumsily amusing, but not greatly interesting. The Company found them interesting, however. It took the view that their existence was a piece of benevolence for everyone—particularly for itself. Walter shared neither view. At times, listening to him, I began to have some misgivings myself.

He had become quite certain that they 'talked.'

'And that,' he argued, 'means that somewhere in them is intelligence. It can't be seated in a brain because dissection shows nothing like a brain—but that doesn't prove there isn't something there that does a brain's job.

'And there's certainly intelligence there, of a kind. Have you noticed that when they attack they always go for the unprotected parts? Almost always the head—but sometimes the hands? And another thing: if you look at the statistics of casualties, just take notice of the proportion that has been stung across the eyes, and blinded. It's remarkable— and significant.'

'Of what?' I asked.

'Of the fact that they know what is the surest way to put a man out of action—in other words, they know what they're doing. Look at it this way. Granted that they do have intelligence; then that would leave us with only one important superiority—sight. We can see, and they can't. Take away our vision, and the superiority is gone. Worse than that—our position becomes inferior to theirs because they are adapted to a sightless existence, and we are not.'

'But even if that were so, they can't *do* things. They can't handle things. There's very little muscular strength in that sting lash,' I pointed out.

'True, but what's the good of our ability to handle things if we can't see what to do with them? Anyway, they don't need to handle things—not in the way we do. They can get their nourishment direct from the soil, or from insects and bits of raw meat. They don't have to go through all the complicated business of growing things, distributing them,

53   THE COMING OF THE TRIFFIDS

and usually cooking them as well. In fact, if it were a choice
for survival between a triffid and a blind man, I know which
I'd put my money on.'

'You're assuming equal intelligence,' I said.

'Not at all. I don't need to. I should imagine it's likely to
be an altogether different type of intelligence, if only because
their needs are so much simpler. Look at the complex pro-
cesses we have to use to get an assimilable extract from a
triffid. Now reverse that. What does the triffid have to do?
Just sting us, wait a few days, and then begin to assimilate
us. The simple, natural course of things.'

He would go on like that by the hour until listening to
him would have me getting things out of proportion, and
I'd find myself thinking of the triffids as though they were
some kind of competitor. Walter himself never pretended to
think otherwise. He had, he admitted, thought of writing a
book on that very aspect of the subject when he had
gathered more material.

'Had?' I repeated. 'What's stopping you?'

'Just this.' He waved his hand to include the farm
generally. 'It's a vested interest now. It wouldn't pay anyone
to put out disturbing thoughts about it. Anyway, we have
the triffids controlled well enough so it's an academic point,
and scarcely worth raising.'

'I never can be quite sure with you,' I told him. 'I'm
never certain how far you are serious, and how far beyond
your facts you allow your imagination to lead you. Do you
honestly think there is a danger in the things?'

He puffed a bit at his pipe before he answered.

'That's fair enough,' he admitted, 'because—well, I'm by
no means sure myself. But I'm pretty certain of one thing,
and that is that there *could* be danger in them. I'd feel a lot
nearer giving you a real answer if I could get a line on what
it means when they patter. Somehow I don't care for that.

There they sit, with everyone thinking no more of them than they might of a pretty odd lot of cabbages, yet half the time they're pattering and clattering away at one another? Why? What is it they patter about? That's what I want to know.'

I think Walter rarely gave a hint of his ideas to anyone else, and I kept them confidential, partly because I knew no one who wouldn't be more sceptical than I was myself, and partly because it wouldn't do either of us any good to get a reputation in the firm as crackpots.

For a year or so more we were working fairly close together. But with the opening of new nurseries and the need for studying methods abroad I began to travel a lot. He gave up field work, and went into the research department. It suited him there, doing his own searching as well as the Company's. I used to drop in to see him from time to time. He was for ever making experiments with his triffids, but the results weren't clearing his general ideas as much as he had hoped. He had proved, to his own satisfaction at least, the existence of a well-developed intelligence —and even I had to admit that his results seemed to show something more than instinct. He was still convinced that the pattering of the sticks was a form of communication. For public consumption he had shown that the sticks were something more, and that a triffid deprived of them gradually deteriorated. He had also established that the infertility rate of triffid seeds was something like ninety-five per cent.

'Which,' he remarked, 'is a damned good thing. If they all germinated there'd soon be standing room only for triffids only on this planet.'

With that, too, I agreed. Triffid seed time was quite a sight. The dark green pod just below the cup was glistening and distended, about half as big again as a large apple.

When it burst, it did it with a pop that was audible twenty yards away. The white seeds shot into the air like steam, and began drifting away on the lightest of breezes. Looking down on a field of triffids late in August you could well get the idea that some kind of desultory bombardment was in progress.

It was Walter's discovery again that the quality of the extracts was improved if the plants retained their stings. In consequence, the practice of docking was discontinued on farms throughout the trade, and we had to wear protective devices when working among the plants.

At the time of the accident that had landed me in hospital I was actually with Walter. We were examining some specimens which were showing unusual deviations. Both of us were wearing wire-mesh masks. I did not see exactly what happened. All I know is that as I bent forward a sting slashed viciously at my face and smacked against the wire of the mask. Ninety-nine times in a hundred it would not have mattered; that was what the masks were for. But this one came with such force that some of the little poison sacs were burst open, and a few drops from them went into my eyes.

Walter got me back into his lab. and administered the antidote in a few seconds. It was entirely due to his quick work that they had the chance of saving my sight at all. But even so, it had meant over a week in bed, in the dark.

While I lay there I had quite decided that when—and if—I had my sight back I was going to apply for a transfer to another side of the business. And if that did not go through, I'd quit the job altogether.

I had built up a considerable resistance to triffid poison since my first sting in the garden. I could take, and had taken, without very much harm, stings which would have laid an inexperienced man out very cold indeed. But an old

saying about a pitcher and a well kept on recurring to me.
I was taking my warning.

I spent, I remember, a good many of my enforcedly dark
hours deciding what kind of job I would try for if they
would not give me that transfer.

Considering what was just around the corner for us all, I
could scarcely have found a contemplation more idle.

3. The Groping City

I LEFT the pub door swinging behind me as I made my way to the corner of the main road. There I hesitated.

To the left, through miles of suburban streets, lay the open country; to the right, the West End of London, with the City beyond. I was feeling somewhat restored, but curiously detached now, and rudderless. I had no glimmering of a plan, and, in the face of what I had at last begun to perceive as a vast and not merely local catastrophe, I was still too stunned to begin to reason one out. What plan could there be to deal with such a thing? I felt forlorn, cast into desolation, and yet not quite real, not quite myself here and now.

In no direction was there any traffic, nor any sound of it. The only signs of life were a few people here and there cautiously groping their ways along the shop-fronts.

The day was perfect for early summer. The sun poured down from a deep blue sky set with tufts of white woolly clouds. All of it was clean and fresh save for a smear made by a single column of greasy smoke coming from somewhere behind the houses to the north.

I stood there indecisively for a few minutes. Then I turned east, Londonwards. . . .

To this day I cannot say quite why. Perhaps it was an instinct to seek familiar places, or the feeling that if there were authority anywhere it must be somewhere in that direction.

The brandy had made me more hungry than ever, but I did not find the problem of feeding as easy to deal with as it should have been. And yet, there were the shops, untenanted and unguarded, with food in the windows—and here was I, with hunger and the means to pay—or, if I did not wish to pay, I had only to smash a window and take what I wanted.

Nevertheless, it was hard to persuade oneself to do that. I was not yet ready to admit, after nearly thirty years of a reasonably right-respecting existence and law-abiding life, that things had changed in any fundamental way. There was, too, a feeling that as long as I remained *my* normal self, things might even yet in some inconceivable way return to *their* normal. Absurd it undoubtedly was, but I had a very strong sense that the moment I should stove-in one of those sheets of plate-glass I would leave the old order behind me for ever: I should become a looter, a sacker, a low scavenger upon the dead body of the system that had nourished me. Such a foolish niceness of sensibility in a stricken world!— and yet it still pleases me to remember that civilized usage did not slide off me at once, and that for a time at least I wandered along past displays which made my mouth water while my already obsolete conventions kept me hungry.

The problem resolved itself in a sophistical way after perhaps half a mile. A taxi, after mounting the pavement, had finished up with its radiator buried in a pile of deli-catessen. That made it seem different from doing my own breaking in. I climbed past the taxi, and collected the makings of a good meal. But even then, something of the

old standards still clung: I conscientiously left a fair price
for what I had taken lying on the counter.

Almost across the road there was a garden. It was the
kind that had once been the graveyard of a vanished church.
The old headstones had been taken up and set back against
the surrounding brick wall, the cleared space turfed over
and laid out with gravelled paths. It looked pleasant under
the freshly-leafed trees, and to one of the seats there I took
my lunch.

The place was withdrawn and peaceful. No one else came
in, though occasionally a figure would shuffle past the railings at the entrance. I threw some crumbs to a few sparrows,
the first birds I had seen that day, and felt all the better for
watching their perky indifference to calamity.

When I had finished eating I lit a cigarette. While I sat
there smoking it, wondering where I should go, and what
I should do, the quiet was broken by the sound of a piano
played somewhere in a block of apartments that overlooked
the garden. Presently a girl's voice began to sing. The song
was Byron's ballad:

> So, we'll go no more a-roving
> So late into the night,
> Though the heart be still as loving,
> And the moon be still as bright.
>
> For the sword outwears its sheath,
> And the soul wears out the breast
> And the heart must pause to breathe,
> And love itself have rest.
>
> Though the night was made for loving,
> And the day returns too soon,
> Yet we'll go no more a-roving
> By the light of the moon.

I listened, looking up at the pattern that the tender young leaves and the branches made against the fresh blue sky. The song finished. The notes of the piano died away. Then there was a sound of sobbing. No passion: softly, helplessly, forlorn, heartbroken. Who she was, whether it was the singer or another weeping her hopes away, I do not know. But to listen longer was more than I could endure. I went quietly back into the street, seeing it only mistily for a while.

Even Hyde Park Corner, when I reached it, was almost deserted. A few derelict cars and lorries stood about on the roads. Very little, it seemed, had gone out of control when it was in motion. One bus had run across the path and come to rest in the Green Park; a runaway horse with shafts still attached to it lay beside the artillery memorial against which it had cracked its skull. The only moving things were a few men and a lesser number of women feeling their way carefully with hands and feet where there were railings, and shuffling forward with protectively outstretched arms where there were not. Also, and rather unexpectedly, there were one or two cats, apparently intact visually, and treating the whole situation with that self-possession common to cats. They had poor luck prowling through the eerie quietness— the sparrows were few, and the pigeons had vanished.

Still magnetically drawn towards the old centre of things, I crossed in the direction of Piccadilly. I was just about to start along it when I noticed a sharp new sound—a steady tapping not far away, and coming closer. Looking up Park Lane, I discovered its source. A man, more neatly dressed than any other I had seen that morning, was walking rapidly towards me, hitting the wall beside him with a white stick. As he caught the sound of my steps he stopped, listening alertly.

'It's all right,' I told him. 'Come on.'

I felt relieved to see him. He was, so to speak, normally blind. His dark glasses were much less disturbing than the staring but useless eyes of the others.

'Stand still, then,' he said. 'I've already been bumped into by God knows how many fools to-day. What the devil's happened? Why is it so quiet? I know it isn't night—I can feel the sunlight. What's gone wrong with everything?'

I told him as much as I knew.

When I had finished he said nothing for almost a minute, then he gave a short, bitter laugh.

'There's one thing,' he said. 'They'll be needing all their damned patronage for themselves now.'

With that he straightened up, a little defiantly.

'Thank you. Good luck,' he said to me, and set off westwards wearing an exaggerated air of independence.

The sound of his briskly confident tapping gradually died away behind me as I made my way up Piccadilly.

There were more people to be seen now, and I walked among the scatter of stranded vehicles in the road. Out there I was much less disturbing to the people feeling their way along the fronts of the buildings, for every time they heard a step close by they would stop and brace themselves against a possible collision. Such collisions were taking place every now and then all down the street, but there was one that I found significant. The subjects of it had been groping along a shop front from opposite directions until they met with a bump. One was a young man in a well-cut suit, but wearing a tie obviously selected by touch alone: the other, a woman who carried a small child. The child whined something inaudible. The young man had started to edge his way past the woman. He stopped abruptly.

'Wait a minute,' he said. 'Can your child see?'

'Yes,' she said. 'But I can't.'

The young man turned. He put one finger on the plate-glass window, pointing.

'Look, Sonny, what's in there?' he asked.

'Not Sonny,' the child objected.

'Go on, Mary. Tell the gentleman,' her mother encouraged her.

'Pretty ladies,' said the child.

The man took the woman by the arm, and felt his way to the next window.

'And what's in here?' he asked, again.

'Apples and fings,' the child told him.

'Fine!' said the young man.

He pulled off his shoe, and hit the window a smart smack with the heel of it. He was inexperienced: the first blow did not do it, but the second did. The crash reverberated up and down the street. He restored his shoe, put an arm cautiously through the broken window, and felt about until he found a couple of oranges. One he gave to the woman and one to the child. He felt about again, found one for himself, and began to peel it. The woman fingered hers.

'But——' she began.

'What's the matter? Don't like oranges?' he asked.

'But it isn't right,' she said. 'We didn't ought to take 'em. Not like this.'

'How else are you going to get food,' he inquired.

'I suppose—well, I don't know,' she admitted, doubtfully.

'Very well. That's the answer. Eat it up now, and we'll go and find something more substantial.'

She still held the orange in her hand, head bent down as though she were looking at it.

'All the same, it don't seem right,' she said again, but there was less conviction in her tone.

Presently she put the child down, and began to peel the orange. . . .

Piccadilly Circus was the most populous place I had found so far. It seemed crowded after the rest, though there were probably less than a hundred people there, all told. Mostly they were wearing queer, ill-assorted clothes, and were prowling restlessly around as though still semi-dazed. Occasionally a mishap would bring an outburst of profanity and futile rage—rather alarming to hear because it was itself the product of fright, and childish in temper. But with one exception there was little talk and little noise. It seemed as though their blindness had shut people into themselves.

The exception had found himself a position out on one of the traffic-islands. He was a tall, elderly, gaunt man with a bush of wiry grey hair, and he was holding forth emphatically about repentance, the wrath to come, and the uncomfortable prospects for sinners. Nobody was paying him any attention: for most of them the day of wrath had already arrived

Then, from a distance, came a sound which caught everyone's attention: a gradually swelling chorus:

> *And when I die,*
> *Don't bury me at all,*
> *Just pickle my bones*
> *In alcohol.*

Dreary and untuneful, it slurred through the empty streets, echoing dismally back and forth. Every head in the Circus was turning now left, now right, trying to place its direction. The prophet of doom raised his voice against the competition. The song wailed discordantly closer:

> *Put a bottle of booze*
> *At my head and my feet,*
> *And then, I'm sure*
> *My bones will keep.*

And as an accompaniment to it there was the shuffle of feet more or less in step.

From where I stood I could see them come in single file out of a side street into Shaftesbury Avenue, and turn towards the Circus. The second man had his hands on the shoulders of the leader, the third on his, and so on, to the number of twenty-five or thirty. At the conclusion of that song somebody started *Beer, Beer, Glorious Beer!* pitching it in such a high key that it petered out in confusion.

They trudged steadily on until they reached the centre of the Circus, then the leader raised his voice. It was a considerable voice, with parade-ground quality:

'Companee-ee-ee—*HALT!*'

Everybody else in the Circus was now struck motionless, all with their faces turned towards him, all trying to guess what was afoot. The leader raised his voice again, mimicking the manner of a professional guide:

' 'Ere we are, gents one an' all. Piccabloodydilly Circus. The Centre of the World. The 'Ub of the Universe. Where all the nobs had their wine, women and song.'

He was not blind, far from it. His eyes were ranging round, taking stock as he spoke. His sight must have been saved by some such accident as mine, but he was pretty drunk, and so were the men behind him.

'An' *we*'ll 'ave it, too,' he added. 'Next stop, the well-known Caffy Royal—an' all drinks on the house.'

'Yus—but what abaht the women?' asked a voice, and there was a laugh.

'Oh, women. 'S that what you want?' said the leader.

He stepped forward, and caught a girl by the arm. She screamed as he dragged her towards the man who had spoken, but he took no notice of that.

'There y'are, chum. An' don't say I don't treat you right.

It's a peach, a smasher—if that makes any difference to you.'

'Hey, what about me?' said the next man.

'You, mate? Well, let's see. Like 'em blonde or dark?'

Considered later, I suppose I behaved like a fool. My head was still full of standards and conventions that had ceased to apply. It did not occur to me that if there was to be any survival anyone adopted by this gang would stand a far better chance than she would on her own. Fired with a mixture of schoolboy heroics and noble sentiments, I waded in. He didn't see me coming until I was quite close, and then I slogged for his jaw. Unfortunately, he was a little quicker. . . .

When I next took an interest in things I found myself lying in the road. The sound of the gang was diminishing into the distance, and the prophet of doom, restored to eloquence, was sending threatful bolts of damnation, hell-fire, and a brimstone gehenna hurtling after them.

With a bit of sense knocked into me, I became thankful that the affair had not fallen out worse. Had the result been reversed, I could scarcely have escaped making myself responsible for the men he had been leading. After all, and whatever one might feel about his methods, he was the eyes of that party, and they'd be looking to him for food as well as for drink. And the women would go along, too, on their own account as soon as they got hungry enough. And now I came to look around me I felt doubtful whether any of the women hereabouts would seriously mind, anyway. What with one thing and another, it looked as if I might have had a lucky escape from promotion to gang leader-ship.

Remembering that they had been headed for the Café Royal, I decided to revive myself and clear my head at the

C

Regent Palace Hotel. Others appeared to have thought of that before me, but there were quite a lot of bottles they had not found.

I think it was while I was sitting there comfortably with a brandy in front of me and a cigarette in my hand that I at last began to admit that what I had seen was all real—and decisive. There would be no going back—ever. It was finish to all I had known. . . .

Perhaps it had needed that blow to drive it home. Now I came face to face with the fact that my existence simply had no focus any longer. My way of life, my plans, ambitions, every expectation I had had, they were all wiped out at a stroke, along with the conditions that had formed them. I suppose that had I had any relatives or close attachments to mourn I should have felt suicidally derelict at that moment. But what had seemed at times a rather empty existence turned out now to be lucky. My mother and father were dead, my one attempt to marry had miscarried some years before, and there was no particular person dependent on me. And, curiously, what I found that I did feel—with a consciousness that it was against what I ought to be feeling— was release. . . .

It wasn't just the brandy, for it persisted. I think it may have come from the sense of facing something quite fresh and new to me. All the old problems, the stale ones, both personal and general, had been solved by one mighty slash. Heaven alone knew as yet what others might arise—and it looked as though there would be plenty of them—but they would be *new*. I was emerging as my own master, and no longer a cog. It might well be a world full of horrors and dangers that I should have to face, but I could take my own steps to deal with it—I would no longer be shoved hither and thither by forces and interests that I neither understood nor cared about.

No, it wasn't altogether the brandy, for even now, years afterwards, I can still feel something of it—though possibly the brandy did over-simplify things a little just then.

Then there was, too, the little question of what to do next; how and where to start on this new life. But I did not let that worry me a lot for the present. I drank up, and went out of the hotel to see what this strange world had to offer.

4. Shadows Before

IN order to give a reasonable berth to the Café Royal
mob I struck up a side street into Soho, intending to cut
back to Regent Street higher up.

Perhaps hunger was driving more people out of their
homes. Whatever the reason, I found that the parts I now
entered were more populous than any I'd seen since I left
the hospital. Constant collisions took place on the pavements and in the narrow streets, and the confusion of those
who were trying to get along was made worse by knots of
people clustering in front of the now frequently broken shop
windows. None of those who crowded there seemed to be
quite sure what kind of shop they were facing. Some in the
front sought to find out by groping for any recognizable
object; others, taking the risk of disembowelling themselves
on standing splinters of glass, more enterprisingly climbed
inside.

I felt that I ought to be showing these people where to
find food. But should I? If I were to lead them to a food
shop still intact there would be a crowd which would not
only have swept the place bare in five minutes, but have
crushed a number of its weaker members in the process.
Soon, anyway, all the food would be gone, then what was

to be done with the thousands clamouring for more? One might collect a small party and keep it alive somehow for an uncertain length of time—but who was to be taken, and who left? No obviously right course presented itself, however I tried to look at it.

What was going on was a grim business without chivalry, with no give and all take about it. A man bumping into another and feeling that he carried a parcel would snatch it and duck away on the chance that it contained something to eat, while the loser clutched furiously at the air or hit out indiscriminately. Once, I had to step hurriedly aside to avoid being knocked down by an elderly man who darted into the roadway with no care for possible obstacles. His expression was vastly cunning, and he clutched avariciously to his chest two cans of red paint. On a corner my way was blocked by a group almost weeping with frustration over a bewildered child who could see, but was just too young to understand what they wanted of it.

I began to become uneasy. Fighting with my civilized urge to be of some help to these people was an instinct that told me to keep clear. They were already fast losing ordinary restraints. I felt, too, an irrational sense of guilt at being able to see while they could not. It gave me an odd feeling that I was hiding from them even while I moved among them. Later on, I found how right the instinct was.

Close to Golden Square I began to think of turning left and working back to Regent Street where the wider roadway would offer easier going. I was about to take a corner that would lead me that way when a sudden, piercing scream stopped me. It stopped everyone else, too. All along the street they stood still, turning their heads this way and that, apprehensively trying to guess what was happening. The alarm coming on top of their distress and nervous tension started a number of the women whimpering: the men's nerves weren't in any too good a state, either, they showed it mostly in short curses at being startled. For it was an ominous sound, one of the kinds of thing they had been subconsciously expecting. They waited for it to come again.

It did. Frightened, and dying into a gasp. But less alarming now that one was ready for it. This time I was able to place it. A few steps took me to an alley entrance. As I turned the corner a cry that was half a gasp came again.

The cause of it was a few yards down the alley. A girl was crouched on the ground while a burly man laid into her with a thin brass rod. The back of her dress was torn, and the flesh beneath showed red weals. As I came closer I saw why she did not run away—her hands were tied together behind her back, and a cord tethered them to the man's left wrist.

I reached the pair as his arm was raised for another stroke. It was easy to snatch the rod from his unexpecting hand and bring it down with some force upon his shoulder. He promptly lashed a heavy boot out in my direction, but I had dodged back quickly, and his radius of action was limited by the cord on his wrist. He made another swiping kick at the air while I was feeling in my pocket for a knife. Finding nothing there, he turned and kicked the girl for good measure, instead. Then he swore at her and pulled on the cord to bring her to her feet. I slapped him on the side of his head, just hard enough to stop him, and make it sing for a bit—somehow I could not bring myself to lay out a blind man, even this type. While he was steadying himself from that I stooped swiftly and cut the cord which joined them. A slight shove on his chest sent him staggering back, and half turned him so that he lost his bearings. With his freed left hand he let out a fine raking swing. It missed me, but ultimately reached the brick wall. After that he lost interest in pretty well everything but the pain of his cracked knuckles. I helped the girl up, loosed her hands, and led her away down the alley while he was still blistering the air behind us.

As we turned into the street she began to come out of her daze. She turned a smeary, tear-stained face, and looked up at me.

'But you can *see!*' she said, incredulously.

'Certainly I can,' I told her.

'Oh, thank God! Thank God! I thought I was the only one,' she said, and burst into tears again.

I looked around us. A few yards away there was a pub with a gramophone playing, glasses smashing, and a high old time being had by all. A few yards beyond that was a smaller pub, still intact. A good heave with my shoulder broke in the door to the saloon bar. I half carried the girl in, and put her in a chair. Then I dismembered another chair and put two of its legs through the handles of the swing doors for the discouragement of further visitors before I turned my attention to the restoratives at the bar.

There was no hurry. She sipped at, and snuffled over, the first drink. I gave her time to get sorted out, twiddling the stem of my glass, and listening to the gramophone in the other pub churning out the currently popular if rather lugubrious ditty:

> *My love's locked up in a frigidaire,*
> *And my heart's in a deep-freeze pack.*
> *She's gone with a guy, I'd not know where,*
> *But she wrote that she'd never come back.*
> *Now she don't care for me no more*
> *I'm just a one-man frozen store,*
>   *And it ain't nice*
>   *To be on ice*
> *With my love locked up in a frigidaire,*
> *And my heart in a deep-freeze pack.*

While I sat I stole an occasional covert look at the girl.
Her clothes, or the remnants of them, were good quality.
Her voice was good, too—probably not stage or movie
acquired, for it had not deteriorated under stress. She was
blonde, but quite a number of shades sub-platinum. It
seemed likely that beneath the smudges and smears she was
good-looking. Her height was three or four inches less than
mine, her build slim, but not thin. She looked as if she had
strength if it were necessary, but strength which, in her
approximately twenty-four years, had most likely not been
applied to anything more important than hitting balls,
dancing, and, probably, restraining horses. Her well-
shaped hands were smooth, and the finger-nails that were
still unbroken showed a length more decorative than
practical.

The drink gradually did good work. By the end of it she
was sufficiently recovered for habit of mind to assert itself.

'God, I must look awful,' she remarked.

It did not seem that anyone but me was like to be in a
position to notice that, but I left it.

She got up, and walked over to a mirror.

'I certainly do,' she confirmed. 'Where——?'

'You might try through there,' I suggested.

Twenty minutes or so passed before she came back. Considering the limited facilities there must have been, she'd
made a good job: morale was much restored. She approxi-
mated now to the film-director's idea of the heroine after a
rough-house rather than the genuine thing.

'Cigarette?' I inquired, as I slid another fortifying glass
across.

While the pulling round process was completing itself we
swapped stories. To give her time I let her have mine first.
Then she said:

'I'm damned ashamed of myself. I'm not a bit like that,

really—like you found me, I mean. In fact, I'm reasonably self-reliant, though you might not think it. But somehow the whole thing had got too big for me. What has happened is bad enough, but the awful prospect suddenly seemed too much to bear, and I panicked. I began to think that perhaps I was the only person left in the whole world who could see. It got me down, and all at once I was frightened and silly, I cracked, and howled like a girl in a Victorian melodrama. I'd never, never have believed it of me.'

'Don't let it worry you,' I said. 'We'll probably be learning a whole lot of surprising things about ourselves soon.'

'But it does worry me. If I start off by slipping my gears like that——' she left the sentence unfinished.

'I was near enough to panic in that hospital,' I said. 'We're human beings, not calculating machines.'

Her name was Josella Playton. There seemed to be something not unfamiliar about that, but I could not place it. Her home was in Dene Road, St. John's Wood. The district fitted in more or less with my surmises. I remembered Dene Road. Detached, comfortable houses, mostly ugly, but all expensive. Her escape from the general affliction had been no less a matter of luck than mine—well, perhaps more. She had been at a party on the Monday night—a pretty considerable party, it seemed.

'I reckon somebody who thinks that kind of thing funny must have been fooling with the drinks,' she said. 'I've never felt so ill as I did at the end of it—and I didn't take a lot.'

Tuesday she recollected as a day of blurred misery and record hangover. About four in the afternoon she had had more than enough of it. She rang the bell and gave instructions that come comets, earthquakes or the day of judgement itself, she was not to be disturbed. Upon that ultimatum she had taken a strong dose of sleeping-draught which on an empty stomach had worked with the efficiency of a knock-out drop.

From then on she had known nothing until this morning when she had been awakened by her father stumbling into her room.

'Josella,' he was saying, 'for God's sake get Doctor Mayle. Tell him I've gone blind—stone blind.'

She had been amazed to see that it was already almost nine o'clock. She got up and dressed hurriedly. The servants had answered neither her father's bell nor her own. When she went to rouse them, she had found to her horror that they, too, were blind.

With the telephone out of order, the only course seemed to be for her to take the car and fetch the doctor herself. The quiet streets and absence of traffic had seemed queer, but she had already driven almost a mile before it came to her what had happened. When she realized, she had all but turned back in panic—but that wasn't going to do anyone any good. There still was the chance that the doctor might have escaped the malady, whatever it was, just as she had herself. So, with a desperate but waning hope, she had driven on.

Half-way down Regent Street the engine started to miss and sputter; finally it stopped. In her hurried start she had not looked at the gauge: it was the reserve tank she had run dry.

She sat there for a moment, dismayed. Every face in sight was now turned towards her, but she had realized by this time that not one of those she saw could see or help her. She got out of the car, hoping to find a garage somewhere nearby or, if there was none, prepared to walk the rest of the way. As she slammed the door behind her, a voice called:

'Hey! Just a minute, mate!'

She turned, and saw a man groping towards her.

'What is it?' she asked. She was by no means taken with the look of him.

His manner changed on hearing her voice.

'I'm lost. Dunno where I am,' he said.

'This is Regent Street. The New Gallery cinema's just behind you,' she told him, and turned to go.

'Just show me where the kerb is, miss, will you?' he said.

She hesitated, and in that moment he came close. The outstretched hand sought and touched her sleeve. He lunged forward, and caught both her arms in a painful grip.

'So you can *see*, can you!' he said. 'Why the hell should you be able to see when I can't—nor anyone else?'

Before she could realize what was happening he had turned her and tripped her, and she was lying in the road with his knee in her back. He caught both her wrists in the grasp of one large hand, and proceeded to tie them together with a piece of string from his pocket. Then he stood up, and pulled her on to her feet again.

'All right,' he said. 'From now on you can do your seeing for me. I'm hungry. Take me where there's a bit of good grub. Get on with it.'

Josella dragged away from him.

'I won't. Undo my hands at once. I——'

He cut that short with a smack across her face.

'That'll be enough o' that, my girl. Come on now. Get cracking. Food, d'yer hear?'

'I won't, I tell you.'

'You bloody well will, my girl,' he assured her.

And she had.

She'd done it watching all the time for a chance to get away. And he'd been expecting just that. Once she almost brought it off, but he had been too quick. Even as she had pulled free he had put out a foot to trip her, and before she could get up he had a grip on her again. After that he had found the strong cord and tethered her to his wrist.

She had led him first to a café, and directed him to a refrigerator. The machine was no longer working, but it was stored with food that was still fresh. The next call was a bar where he wanted Irish whisky. She could see it, perched up on a shelf beyond his reach.

'If you'd untie my hands——' she suggested.

'What, and have you crown me with a bottle? I wasn't born yesterday, my girl. No, I'll have the Scotch. Which is it?'

She told him what was in the various bottles as he laid his hand on them.

'I think I must have been dazed,' she explained. 'I can see now half a dozen ways I could have outwitted him. Probably I'd have killed him later on if you hadn't come along. But you can't change and turn brutal all at once—at least, I can't. I didn't seem to be able to think properly at first. I'd a sort of feeling that things like that didn't happen nowadays, and that somebody would come along and stop it soon.'

There had been a row in that bar before they left. Another party of men and women discovered the open door and came in. Incautiously her captor instructed her to tell them what was in the bottle they found. At that they all stopped talking, and turned their sightless eyes towards her. There was a whisper, then two men stepped warily forward. They had a purposeful look on their faces. She jerked at the cord.

'Look out!' she cried.

Without the least hesitation her captor swung out his boot. It was a lucky kick. One of the men folded up with a yell of pain. The other jumped forward, but she side-stepped and he brought up against the counter with a crash.

'You bloody well leave her alone,' roared the man who

held her. He turned his face menacingly this way and that. 'She's mine, blast you. I found her.'

But it was clear that the rest were not intending to give up that easily. Even had they been able to see the danger in her companion's expression it would not have been likely to stop them. Josella started to realize that the gift of sight, even at second hand, was now something vastly surpassing all riches, and the chance of it not to be released without bitter contest. The others began to close in, with their hands questing in front of them. Reaching out with one foot, she hooked the leg of a chair, and overturned it in their way.

'Come on!' she cried, dragging the other man back.

Two men tripped over the fallen chair, and a woman fell on top of them. Swiftly the place became a struggling confusion. She steered a way through it, and they escaped into the street.

She scarcely knew why she did it save that the prospect of being enslaved to act as the eyes of that group had seemed even worse than her present plight. Nor did the man give her any thanks. He merely directed her to find another bar: an empty one.

'I think,' she said judicially, 'that though you wouldn't have guessed it to look at him, he wasn't perhaps too bad a man really. Only he was frightened. Deep down inside him he was much more frightened than I was. He gave me some food and something to drink. He only started beating me like that because he was drunk, and I wouldn't go into his house with him. I don't know what would have happened if you hadn't come along.' She paused. Then she added: 'But I am pretty ashamed of myself. Shows you what a modern young woman can come to after all, doesn't it? Screaming, and collapsing with the vapours—— Hell!'

She was looking, and obviously feeling, rather better, though she winced as she reached for her glass.

'I think,' I said, 'that I've been fairly dense over this business—and pretty lucky. I ought to have made more of the implications when I saw that woman with the child in Piccadilly. It's only been chance that's stopped me from falling into the same kind of mess that you did.'

'Anybody who has had a great treasure has always led a precarious existence,' she said, reflectively.

'I'll go on bearing that in mind, henceforth,' I told her.

'It's already very well impressed on mine,' she remarked.

We sat listening to the uproar from the other pub for a few minutes.

'And what,' I said at last, 'just what do we propose to do now?'

'I must get back home. There's my father. It's obviously no good going on to try to find the doctor now—even if he has been one of the lucky ones.'

She seemed about to add something, but hesitated.

'Do you mind if I come, too?' I asked. 'This doesn't seem to me the sort of time when anyone like us should be wandering about on his or her own.'

She turned with a grateful look.

'Thank you. I almost asked, but I thought there might be somebody you'd be wanting to look for.'

'There isn't,' I said. 'Not in London, at any rate.'

'I'm glad. It's not so much that I'm afraid of getting caught again—I'll be much too careful for that. But, to be honest, it's the loneliness I'm afraid of. I'm beginning to feel so—so cut off and stranded.'

I was starting to see things in another new light. The sense of release was tempered with a growing realization of the grimness that might lie ahead of us. It had been impossible at first not to feel some superiority, and, therefore, confidence. Our chances of surviving the catastrophe were a million times greater than those of the rest. Where they must fumble, grope, and guess, we had simply to walk in and take. But there were going to be a lot of things beyond that. . . .

I said: 'I wonder just how many of us have escaped and can still see? I've come across one other man, a child, and a baby: you've met none. It looks to me as if we are going to find out that sight is very rare indeed. Some of the others have evidently grasped already that their only chance of survival is to get hold of someone who can see. When they all understand that, the outlook's going to be none too good.'

The future seemed to me at that time a choice between a lonely existence, always in fear of capture, or of gathering together a selected group which we could rely on to protect us from other groups. We'd be filling a kind of leader-cum-prisoner rôle—and along with it went a nasty picture of bloody gang wars being fought for possession of us. I was still uncomfortably elaborating these possibilities when Josella recalled me to the present by getting up.

'I must go,' she said. 'Poor father. It's after four o'clock.'

Back in Regent Street again, a thought suddenly struck me.

'Come across,' I said. 'I fancy I remember a shop somewhere here . . .'

The shop was still there. We equipped ourselves with a couple of useful-looking sheath knives, and belts to carry them.

'Makes me feel like a pirate,' said Josella, as she buckled hers on.

'Better, I imagine, to be a pirate than a pirate's moll,' I told her.

A few yards up the street we came upon a large, shiny saloon car. It looked the kind of craft that should simply have purred. But the noise when I started it up sounded louder in our ears than all the normal traffic of a busy street. We made our way northward, zigzagging to avoid derelicts and wanderers stricken into immobility in the middle of the road by the sound of our approach. All the way heads turned hopefully towards us as we came; and faces fell as we went past. One building on our route was blazing fiercely, and a cloud of smoke rose from another fire somewhere along Oxford Street. There were more people about in Oxford Circus, but we got through them neatly, then passed the B.B.C., and so north to the carriageway in Regent's Park.

It was a relief to get out of the streets and reach an open space—and one where there were no unfortunate people wandering and groping. The only moving things we could see on the broad stretches of grass were two or three little groups of triffids lurching southwards. Somehow or other they had contrived to pull up their stakes and were dragging them along behind them on their chains. I remembered that there were some undocked specimens, a few tethered, but most of them double-fenced, in an enclosure beside the zoo, and wondered how they had got out. Josella noticed them, too.

'It's not going to make much difference to them,' she said.

For the rest of the way there was little to delay us. Within a few minutes I was pulling up at the house she pointed out. We got out of the car, and I pushed open the gate. A short drive curved round a bed of bushes which hid most of the house front from the road. As we turned the corner Josella gave a cry, and ran forward. A figure was lying on the gravel, chest downwards, but with the head turned to show one side of its face. The first glance at it showed me the bright red streak across the cheek.

'Stop!' I shouted at her.

There was enough alarm in my voice to check her.

I had spotted the triffid now. It was lurking among the bushes, well within striking range of the sprawled figure.

'Back! Quick!' I said.

Still looking at the man on the ground, she hesitated.

'But I must——' she began, turning towards me. Then she stopped. Her eyes widened, and she screamed.

I whipped round to find a triffid towering only a few feet behind me.

In one automatic movement I had my hands over my eyes. I heard the sting whistle as it slashed out at me—but there was no knockout, no agonized burning, even. One's mind can move like lightning at such a moment: nevertheless, it was more instinct than reason which sent me leaping at it before it had time to strike again. I collided with it, over-turning it, and even as I went down with it my hands were on the upper part of its stem, trying to pull off the cup and the sting. Triffid stems do not snap—but they can be mangled. This one was mangled thoroughly before I stood up.

Josella was standing in the same spot, transfixed.

'Come here,' I told her. 'There's another in the bushes behind you.'

She glanced fearfully over her shoulder, and came.

'But it *hit* you!' she said, incredulously. 'Why aren't you——?'

'I don't know. I ought to be,' I said.

I looked down at the fallen triffid. Suddenly remembering the knives that we'd acquired with quite other enemies in mind, I used mine to cut off the sting at its base. I examined it.

'That explains it,' I said, pointing to the poison-sacs. 'See, they're collapsed, exhausted. If they'd been full, or even part full . . .' I turned a thumb down.

I had that, and my acquired resistance to the poison to

thank. Nevertheless, there was a pale red mark across the backs of my hands and my neck that was itching like the devil. I rubbed it while I stood looking at the sting.

'It's queer——' I murmured, more to myself than to her, but she heard me.

'What's queer?'

'I've never seen one with the poison-sacs quite empty like this before. It must have been doing a hell of a lot of stinging.'

But I doubt if she heard me. Her attention had reverted to the man who was lying in the drive, and she was eyeing the triffid standing by.

'How can we get him away?' she asked.

'We can't—not till that thing's been dealt with,' I told her. 'Besides—well, I'm afraid we can't help him now.'

'You mean, he's dead?'

I nodded. 'Yes. There's not a doubt of it—I've seen others who have been stung. Who was he?' I added.

'Old Pearson. He did gardening for us, and chauffering for my father. Such a dear old man—I've known him all my life.'

'I'm sorry——' I began, wishing I could think of something more adequate, but she cut me short.

'Look!—oh, look!' She pointed to a path which ran round the side of the house. A black-stockinged leg with a woman's shoe on it protruded round the corner.

We prospected carefully, and then moved safely to a spot which gave a better view. A girl in a black dress lay half on the path and half in a flower-bed. Her pretty, fresh face was scarred with a bright red line. Josella choked. Tears came into her eyes.

'Oh!—oh, it's Annie! Poor little Annie,' she said.

I tried to console her a little.

'They can scarcely have known it, either of them,' I

told her. 'When it is strong enough to kill, it's mercifully quick.'

We did not see any other triffid in hiding there. Possibly it was the same one that had attacked them both. Together we crossed the path and got into the house by the side-door. Josella called. There was no answer. She called again. We both listened in the complete silence that wrapped the house. She turned to look at me. Neither of us said anything. Quietly she led the way along a passage to a baize-covered door. As she opened it there was a swish, and something slapped across door and frame, an inch or so above her head. Hurriedly she pulled the door shut again, and turned wide-eyed to me.

'There's one in the hall,' she said.

She spoke in a frightened half-whisper, as though it might be listening.

We went back to the outer door, and into the garden once more. Keeping to the grass for silence we made our way round the house until we could look into the lounge-hall. The french window which led from the garden was open, and the glass of one side was shattered. A trail of muddy blobs led over the step and across the carpet. At the end of it a triffid stood in the middle of the room. The top of its stem almost brushed the ceiling, and it was swaying ever so slightly. Close beside its damp, shaggy bole lay the body of an elderly man clad in a bright silk dressing-gown. I took hold of Josella's arm. I was afraid she might rush in there.

'Is it—your father?' I asked, though I knew it must be.

'Yes,' she said, and put her hands over her face. She was trembling slightly.

I stood still, keeping an eye on the triffid inside lest it should move our way. Then I thought of a handkerchief, and handed her mine. There wasn't much anyone could do.

After a little while she took more control of herself. Remembering the people we had seen that day, I said:

'You know, I think I would rather *that* had happened to me than be like those others.'

'Yes,' she said, after a pause.

She looked up into the sky. It was a soft, depthless blue, with a few little clouds floating like white feathers.

'Oh, yes,' she repeated with more conviction. 'Poor Daddy He couldn't have stood blindness. He loved all this too much.' She glanced inside the room again. 'What shall we do? I can't leave——'

At that moment I caught the reflection of movement in the remaining window-pane. I looked behind us quickly to see a triffid break clear of the bushes and start across the lawn. It was lurching on a line that led straight towards us. I could hear the leathery leaves rustling as the stem whipped back and forth.

There was no time for delay. I had no idea how many more there might be round the place. I grabbed Josella's arm again, and ran her back by the way we had come. As we scrambled safely into the car, she burst into real tears at last.

She would be the better for having her cry out. I lit a cigarette, and considered the next move. Naturally, she was not going to care for the idea of leaving her father as we had found him. She would wish that he should have a proper burial—and, by the looks of it, that would be a matter of the pair of us digging the grave and effecting the whole business. And before that could even be attempted it would be necessary to fetch the means to deal with the triffids that were already there, and keep off any more that might appear. On the whole, I would be in favour of dropping the whole thing—but then, it was not my father. . . .

The more I considered this new aspect of things, the less

I liked it. I had no idea how many triffids there might be in London. Every park had a few at least. Usually they kept some docked ones that were allowed to roam about as they would, often there were others, with stings intact, either staked, or safely behind wire-netting. Thinking of those we had seen crossing Regent's Park, I wondered just how many they had been in the habit of keeping in the pens by the zoo, and how many had escaped. There'd be a number in private gardens, too; you'd expect all those to be safely docked—but you never can tell what fool carelessness may go on. And then there were several nurseries of the things, and experimental stations a little further out. . . .

While I sat there pondering, I was aware of something nudging at the back of my mind; some association of ideas that didn't quite join up. I sought it for a moment or two: then, suddenly, it came. I could almost hear Walter's voice speaking, saying:

'I tell you, a triffid's in a damn sight better position to survive than a blind man.'

Of course, he had been talking about a man who had been blinded by a triffid sting. All the same, it was a jolt. More than a jolt. It scared me a bit.

I thought back. No, it had just arisen out of general speculation—nevertheless, it seemed a bit uncanny now. . . .

'Take away our sight,' he had said. 'And our superiority to them is gone.'

Of course, coincidences are happening all the time—but it's just now and then you happen to notice them. . . .

A crunch on the gravel brought me back to the present. A triffid came swaying down the drive towards the gate. I leant across, and screwed up the window.

'Drive on! Drive on!' said Josella, hysterically.

'We're all right here,' I told her. 'I want to see what it does.'

Simultaneously I realized that one of my questions was solved. Being accustomed to triffids, I had forgotten how most people felt about an undocked one. I suddenly understood that there would be no question of coming back here. Josella's feeling about an armed triffid was the general idea —get well away from it, and stay away.

The thing paused by the gatepost. One could have sworn that it was listening. We sat perfectly still and quiet, Josella staring at it with horror. I expected it to lash out at the car, but it didn't. Probably the muffling of our voices inside had misled it into thinking we were out of range.

The little bare stalks began abruptly to clatter against its stem. It swayed, lumbered clumsily off to the right, and disappeared into the next driveway.

Josella gave a sigh of relief.

'Oh, let's get away before it comes back,' she implored.

I started the car, turned it round, and we drove off Londonwards again.

5. A Light in the Night

JOSELLA began to recover her self-possession. With the deliberate and obvious intention of taking her mind off what lay behind us she asked:

'Where are we going now?'

'Clerkenwell first,' I told her. 'After that we'll see about getting you some more clothes. Bond Street for them, if you like, but Clerkenwell first.'

'But why Clerkenwell——? Good heavens!'

She might well exclaim. We had turned a corner to see the street seventy yards ahead of us filled with people. They were coming towards us at a stumbling run, with their arms outstretched before them. A mingled crying and screaming came from them. Even as we turned into sight of them, a woman at the front tripped and fell; others tumbled over her, and she disappeared beneath a kicking, struggling heap. Beyond the mob, we had a glimpse of the cause of it all: three dark-leaved stalks swaying over the panic-stricken heads. I accelerated, and swung off into a by-road.

Josella turned a terrified face.

'Did—did you see what that was? They were *driving* them.'

'Yes,' I said. 'That's why we are going to Clerkenwell.

There's a place there that makes the best triffid-guns and masks in the world.'

We worked back again, and picked up our intended route, but we did not find the clear run I had hoped for. Near King's Cross Station there were many more people on the streets. Even with a hand on the horn it was increasingly difficult to get along. In front of the station itself it became impossible. Why there should have been such crowds in that place I don't know. All the people in the district seemed to have converged upon it. We could not get through the people, and a glance behind showed that it would be almost as hopeless to try to go back. Those we had passed had already closed in on our track.

'Get out, quick!' I said. 'I think they're after us.'

'But——' Josella began.

'Hurry!' I said shortly.

I blew a final blast on the horn, and slipped out after her, leaving the engine running. We were not many seconds too soon. A man found the handle of the rear door. He pulled it open, and pawed inside. We were all but pushed over by the pressure of others making for the car. There was a shout of anger when somebody opened the front door and found the seats there empty, too. By that time we had ourselves safely become members of the crowd. Somebody grabbed the man who had opened the rear door under the impression that it was he who had just got out. Around that the confusion began to thrive. I took a firm grip of Josella's hand, and we started to worm our way out as unobviously as possible.

Clear of the crowd at last, we kept on foot for a while, looking out for a suitable car. After a mile or so we found it—a station-waggon, likely to be more useful than an ordinary body for the plan that was beginning to form vaguely in my mind.

In Clerkenwell they had been accustomed for two or three

centuries to make fine, precise instruments. The small factory I had dealt with professionally at times had adapted the old skill to new needs. I found it with little difficulty, nor was it hard to break in. When we set off again there was a comforting sense of support to be derived from several excellent triffid-guns, some thousands of little steel boomerangs for them and some wire-mesh helmets that we had loaded into the back.

'And now—clothes?' suggested Josella, as we started.

'Provisional plan, open to criticism and correction,' I told her. 'First what you might call a *pied-à-terre:* i.e. somewhere to pull ourselves together and discuss things.'

'Not another bar,' she protested. 'I've had quite enough of bars for one day.'

'Improbable though my friends might think it—with everything free; so have I,' I agreed. 'What I was thinking of was an empty flat. That shouldn't be difficult to find. We could ease up there awhile, and settle the rough plan of campaign. Also, it would be convenient for spending the night—or, if you find that the trammels of convention still defy the peculiar circumstances, well, maybe we could make it two flats.'

'I think I'd be happier to know there was someone close at hand.'

'Okay,' I agreed. 'Then operation Number Two will be ladies' and gents' outfitting. For that perhaps we had better go our separate ways—both taking exceedingly good care not to forget which flat it was that we decided on.'

'Y-es,' she said, but a little doubtfully.

'It'll be all right,' I assured her. 'Make a rule for yourself not to speak to anyone, and nobody's going to guess you can see. It was only being quite unprepared that landed you in that mess before. "In the country of the blind the one-eyed man is king." '

'Oh, yes—Wells said that, didn't he?—Only in the story it turned out not to be true.'

'The crux of the difference lies in what you mean by the word "country"—*patria* in the original,' I said. '*Cæcorum in patria luscus rex imperat omnis*—a classical gentleman called Fullonius said it first: it's all anyone seems to know about him. But there's no organized *patria*, no State, here—only chaos. Wells imagined a people who had adapted themselves to blindness. I don't think that is going to happen here—I don't see how it can.'

'What do you think *is* going to happen?'

'My guess would be no better than yours. And soon we shall begin to know, anyway. Better get back to matters in hand. Where were we?'

'Choosing clothes.'

'Oh, yes. Well, it's simply a matter of slipping into a shop, adopting a few trifles, and slipping out again. You'll not meet any triffids in Central London—at least, not yet.'

'You talk so lightly about taking things,' she said.

'I don't feel quite so lightly about it,' I admitted. 'But I'm not sure that that's virtue—it's more likely merely habit. And an obstinate refusal to face facts isn't going to bring anything back, or help us at all. I think we'll have to try to see ourselves not as the robbers of all this, but more as—well, the unwilling heirs to it.'

'Yes. I suppose it is something like that,' she agreed, in a qualified way.

She was silent for a time. When she spoke again she reverted to the earlier question.

'And after the clothes?' she asked.

'Operation Number Three,' I told her, 'is, quite definitely, dinner.'

There was, as I had expected, no great difficulty about the flat. We left the car locked up in the middle of the road in front of an opulent-looking block, and climbed to the third storey. Quite why we chose the third I can't say, except that it seemed a bit more out of the way. The process of selection was simple. We knocked or we rang, and if anyone answered, we passed on. After we had passed on three times we found a door where there was no response. The socket of the rim-lock tore off to one good heft of the shoulder, and we were in.

I had not, myself, been one of those addicted to living in a flat with a rent of some £2,000 a year, but I found that there were decidedly things to be said in favour of it. The interior decorators had been, I guessed, elegant young men with just that ingenious gift for combining taste with advanced topicality which is so expensive. Consciousness of fashion was the mainspring of the place. Here and there were certain unmistakable *derniers cris*, some of them undoubtedly destined—had the world pursued its expected course—to become the rage of to-morrow: others, I would say, a dead loss from their very inception. The overall effect was all Trade Fair in its neglect of human foibles—a book left a few inches out of place, or with the wrong colour on its jacket would ruin the whole carefully considered balance and tone—so, too, would the person thoughtless enough to wear the wrong clothes when sitting upon the wrong luxurious chair or sofa. I turned to Josella who was staring wide-eyed at it all.

'Will this little shack serve—or do we go further?' I asked.

'Oh, I guess we'll make out,' she said. And together we waded through the delicate cream carpet to explore.

It was quite uncalculated, but I could scarcely have hit upon a more satisfactory method of taking her mind off the events of the day. Our tour was punctuated with a series of exclamations in which admiration, envy, delight, contempt, and, one must confess, malice, all played their parts. Josella paused on the threshold of a room rampant with all the most aggressive manifestations of femininity.

'I'll sleep here,' she said.

'My God!' I remarked. 'Well, each to her taste.'

'Don't be nasty. I probably won't have another chance to be decadent. Besides, don't you know there's a bit of the dumbest film-star in every girl? So I'll let it have its final fling.'

'You shall,' I said. 'But I hope they keep something quieter around here. Heaven preserve me from having to sleep in a bed with a mirror set in the ceiling over it.'

'There's one above the bath, too,' she said, looking into an adjoining room.

'I don't know whether that would be the zenith or nadir of decadence,' I said. 'But anyway, you'll not be using it. No hot water.'

'Oh, I'd forgotten that. What a shame!' she exclaimed, disappointedly.

We completed our inspection of the premises, finding the rest less sensational. Then she went out to deal with the matter of clothes. I made an inspection of the apartment's resources and limitations, and then set out on an expedition of my own.

As I stepped outside, another door further down the passage opened. I stopped, and stood still where I was. A young man came out, leading a fair-haired girl by the hand. As she stepped over the threshold he released his grasp.

'Wait just a minute, darling,' he said.

He took three or four steps on the silencing carpet. His outstretched hands found the window which ended the passage. His fingers went straight to the catch and opened it. I had a glimpse of a fire-escape outside.

'What are you doing, Jimmy?' she asked.

'Just making sure,' he said, stepping quickly back to her, and feeling for her hand again. 'Come along, darling.'

She hung back.

'Jimmy—I don't like leaving here. At least we know where we are in our own flat. How are we going to feed? How are we going to live?'

'In the flat, darling, we shan't feed at all—and therefore not live long. Come along, sweetheart. Don't be afraid.'

'But I am, Jimmy—I am.'

She clung to him, and he put one arm round her.

'We'll be all right, darling. Come along.'

'But Jimmy, that's the wrong way——'

'You've got it twisted round, dear. It's the right way.'

'Jimmy—I'm so frightened. Let's go back.'

'It's too late, darling.'

By the window he paused. With one hand he felt his position very carefully. Then he put both arms round her, holding her to him.

'Too wonderful to last, perhaps,' he said, softly. 'I love you, my sweet. I love you so very, very much.'

She turned her lips up to be kissed.

As he lifted her he turned, and stepped out of the window. . . .

'You've got to grow a hide,' I told myself. '*Got to.* It's either that or stay permanently drunk. Things like that must be happening all around. They'll go on happening. You can't help it. Suppose you'd given them food to keep them alive for another few days? What after that? You've got to learn to take it, and come to terms with it. There's nothing else but the alcoholic funk-hole. If you don't fight to live your own life in spite of it, there won't be any survival. . . .

Only those who can make their minds tough enough to stick it are going to get through. . . .

It took me longer than I had expected to collect what I wanted. Something like two hours had passed before I got back. I dropped one or two things from my armful in negotiating the door. Josella's voice called with a trace of nervousness from that over-feminine room.

'Only me,' I reassured her, as I advanced down the passage with the load.

I dumped the things in the kitchen, and went back for those I'd dropped. Outside her door I paused.

'You can't come in,' she said.

'That wasn't quite my intended angle,' I protested. 'What I want to know is, can you cook?'

'Boiled egg standard,' said her muffled voice.

'I was afraid of that. There's an awful lot of things we're going to have to learn,' I told her.

I went back to the kitchen. I erected the oil-stove I had brought on top of the useless electric cooker, and got busy.

When I'd finished laying the places at the small table in the sitting-room, the effect seemed to me fairly good. I fetched a few candles and candlesticks to complete it, and set them ready. Of Josella there was still no visible sign, though there had been sounds of running water some little time ago. I called her.

'Just coming,' she answered.

I wandered across to the window, and looked out. Quite consciously I began saying good-bye to it all. The sun was low. Towers, spires, and façades of Portland stone were white or pink against the dimming sky. More fires had broken out here and there. The smoke climbed in big black smudges, sometimes with a lick of flame at the bottom of them. Quite likely, I told myself, I would never in my life

again see any of these familiar buildings after to-morrow.
There might be a time when one would be able to come
back—but not to the same place. Fires and weather would
have worked on it: it would be visibly dead and abandoned.
But now, at a distance, it could still masquerade as a living
city.

My father once told me that before Hitler's war he used
to go round London with his eyes more widely open than
ever before, seeing the beauties of buildings that he had
never noticed before—and saying good-bye to them. And
now I had a similar feeling. But this was something worse.
Much more than anyone could have hoped for had survived
that war—but this was an enemy they would not survive.
It was not wanton smashing and wilful burning that they
waited for this time: it was simply the long, slow, inevitable
course of decay and collapse.

Standing there, and at that time, my heart still resisted
what my head was telling me. Even yet I had the feeling that
it was all something too big, too unnatural really to happen.
Yet I knew that it was by no means the first time that it had
happened. The corpses of other great cities are lying buried
in deserts, and obliterated by the jungles of Asia. Some of
them fell so long ago that even their names have gone with
them. But to those who lived there their dissolution can have
seemed no more probable or possible than the necrosis of a
great modern city seemed to me. . . .

It must be, I thought, one of the race's most persistent
and comforting hallucinations to trust that 'it can't happen
here'—that one's own little time and place is beyond
cataclysms. And now it *was* happening here. Unless there
should be some miracle I was looking on the beginning of
the end of London—and very likely, it seemed, there were
other men, not unlike me, who were looking on the beginning of the end of New York, Paris, San Francisco, Buenos

Aires, Bombay, and all the rest of the cities that were destined to go the way of those others under the jungles.

I was still looking out when a sound of movement came from behind me. I turned, and saw that Josella had come into the room. She was wearing a long, pretty frock of palest blue georgette with a little jacket of white fur. In a pendant on a simple chain a few blue-white diamonds flashed, the stones that gleamed in her ear-clips were smaller but as fine in colour. Her hair and her face might have been fresh from a beauty parlour. She crossed the floor with a flicker of silver slippers and a glimpse of gossamer stockings. As I went on staring without speaking, her mouth lost its little smile.

'Don't you like it?' she asked, with childish half-disappointment.

'It's lovely—you're beautiful,' I told her. 'I—well, I just wasn't expecting anything like this. . . .'

Something more was needed. I knew that it was a display which had little or nothing to do with me. I added:

'You're saying good-bye?'

A different look came into her eyes.

'So you do understand. I hoped you would.'

'I think I do. I'm glad you've done it. It'll be a lovely thing to remember,' I said.

I stretched out my hand to her and led her to the window.

'I was saying good-bye, too—to all this.'

What went on in her mind as we stood there side by side is her secret. In mine there was a kind of kaleidoscope of the life and ways that were now finished—or perhaps it was more like flipping through a huge volume of photographs with one, all-comprehensive 'do-you-remember?'

We looked for a long time, lost in our thoughts. Then she sighed. She glanced down at her dress, fingering the delicate silk.

'Silly?—Rome burning?' she said, with a rueful little smile.

'No—sweet,' I said. 'Thank you for doing it. A gesture—and a reminder that with all the faults there was so much beauty. You couldn't have done—or looked—a lovelier thing.'

Her smile lost its ruefulness.

'Thank you, Bill.' She paused. Then she added: 'Have I said thank you before? I don't think I have. If you hadn't helped me when you did——'

'But for you,' I told her, 'I should probably by now be lying maudlin and sozzled in some bar. I have just as much to thank you for. This is no time to be alone.' Then, to change the trend, I added: 'And speaking of drink, there's an excellent Amontillado here, and some pretty good things to follow. This is a very well-found flat.'

I poured out the sherry, and we raised our glasses.

'To health, strength—and luck,' I said.

She nodded. We drank.

'What,' Josella asked, as we started on an expensive-tasting paté, 'what if the owner of all this suddenly comes back?'

'In that case we will explain—and he or she should be only too thankful to have someone here to tell him which bottle is which, and so on—but I don't think that is very likely to happen.'

'No,' she agreed, considering. 'No. I'm afraid that's not very likely. I wonder——' She looked round the room. Her eyes paused at a fluted white pedestal. 'Did you try the radio—I suppose that thing *is* a radio, isn't it?'

'It's a television projector, too,' I told her. 'But no good. No power.'

'Of course. I forgot. I suppose we'll go on forgetting things like that for quite a time.'

D

'But I did try one when I was out,' I said. 'A battery affair. Nothing doing. All broadcast bands as silent as the grave.'

'That means it's like this everywhere?'

'I'm afraid so. There was something pip-pipping away around forty-two metres. Otherwise nothing. Not even carriers. I wonder who and where he was, poor chap.'

'It's—it's going to be pretty grim, Bill, isn't it?'

'It's—no, I'm not going to have my dinner clouded,' I said. 'Pleasure before business—and the future is definitely business. Let's talk about something interesting like how many love-affairs you have had and why somebody hasn't married you long before this—or has he? You see how little I know. Life story, please.'

'Well,' she said, 'I was born about three miles from here. My mother was very annoyed about it at the time.'

I raised my eyebrows.

'You see, she had quite made up her mind that I should be an American. But when the car came to take her to the airport it was just too late. Full of impulses, she was—I think I inherited some of them.'

She prattled on. There was not much remarkable about her early life, but I think she enjoyed herself in summarizing it, and forgetting where we were for a while. I enjoyed listening to her babble of the familiar and amusing things that had all vanished from the world outside. We worked lightly through childhood, schooldays, and 'coming out'— in so far as the term still meant anything.

'I did nearly get married when I was nineteen,' she admitted, 'and aren't I glad now it didn't happen. But I didn't feel like that at the time. I had a frightful row with Daddy who'd broken the whole thing up because he saw right away that Lionel was a spizzard and . . .'

'A what?' I interrupted.

'A spizzard. A sort of cross between a spiv and a lizard—

the lounge kind. So then I cut my family off and went and lived with a girl I knew who had a flat. And my family cut off my allowance, which was a very silly thing to do because it might have had just the opposite effect from what they intended. As it happened, it didn't, because all the girls I knew who were making out that way seemed to me to have a very wearing sort of time of it. Not much fun, an awful lot of jealousy to put up with—and so much planning. You'd never believe how much planning it needs to keep one or two second strings in good condition—or do I mean two or three spare strings——?' She pondered.

'Never mind,' I told her. 'I get the general idea. You just didn't want the strings at all.'

'Intuitive, you are. All the same, I couldn't just sponge on the girl who had the flat. I did have to have some money, so I wrote the book.'

I did not think I'd heard quite aright.

'You made a book?' I suggested.

'I *wrote* the book.' She glanced at me, and smiled. 'I must look awfully dumb—that's just the way *they* all used to look at me when I told them I was writing a book. Mind you, it wasn't a very good book—I mean, not like Aldous or Charles or people of that kind, but it worked.'

I refrained from inquiring which of many possible Charles's this referred to. I simply asked:

'You mean it did get published?'

'Oh, yes. And it really brought in quite a lot of money. The film rights——'

'What was this book?' I asked, curiously.

'It was called *Sex is My Adventure*.'

I stared, and then smote my forehead.

'Josella Playton, of course. I couldn't think why that name kept on nearly ringing bells. You wrote that thing?' I added, incredulously.

I couldn't think why I had not remembered before. Her photograph had been all over the place—not a very good photograph now I could look at the original, and the book had been all over the place, too. Two large circulating libraries had banned it, probably on the title alone. After that, its success had been assured, and the sales went rocketing up into the hundred thousands. Josella chuckled. I was glad to hear it.

'Oh, dear,' she said. 'You look just like all my relatives did.'

'I can't blame them,' I told her.

'Did you read it?' she asked.

I shook my head. She sighed.

'People are funny. All you know about it is the title and the publicity, and you're shocked. And it's such a harmless little book, really. Mixture of green-sophisticated and pink-romantic, with patches of school-girly-purple. But the title was a good idea.'

'All depends what you mean by good,' I suggested. 'And you put your own name to it, too.'

'That,' she agreed, 'was a mistake. The publishers persuaded me that it would be so much better for publicity. From their point of view they were right. I became quite notorious for a bit—it used to make me giggle inside when I saw people looking speculatively at me in restaurants and places—they seemed to find it so hard to tie up what they saw with what they thought. Lots of people I didn't care for took to turning up regularly at the flat, so to get rid of them, and because I'd proved that I didn't *have* to go home, I went home again.

'The book rather spoiled things, though. People would be so literal-minded about that title. I seem to have been keeping up a permanent defensive ever since against people I don't like—and those I wanted to like were either scared or shocked. What's so annoying is that it wasn't even a wicked book—it was just silly-shocking, and sensible people ought to have seen that.'

She paused contemplatively. It occurred to me that the sensible people had probably decided that the author of *Sex is My Adventure* would be silly-shocking, too, but I forebore to suggest it. We all have our youthful follies embarrassing to recall—but people somehow find it hard to dismiss as a youthful folly anything that has happened to be a financial success.

'It sort of twisted everything,' she complained. 'I was writing another book to try to balance things up again. But I'm glad I'll never finish it—it was rather bitter.'

'With an equally alarming title?' I asked.

She shook her head: 'It was to be called *Here the Foresaken*.'

'H'm—well, it certainly lacks the snap of the other,' I said. 'Quotation?'

'Yes.' She nodded. 'Mr. Congreve: "Here the forsaken Virgin rests from Love." '

'Er—oh,' I said, and thought that one over for a bit.

'And now,' I suggested, 'I think it's about time we began to rough out a plan of campaign. Shall I throw around a few observations first?'

We lay back in two superbly comfortable armchairs. On the low table between us stood the coffee apparatus and two glasses. Josella's was the small one with the Cointreau. The plutocratic-looking balloon with the puddle of unpriceable brandy was mine. Josella blew out a feather of smoke, and took a sip of her drink. Savouring the flavour, she said:

'I wonder whether we shall ever taste fresh oranges again? Okay, shoot.'

'Well, it's no good blinking facts. We had better clear out soon. If not to-morrow, then the day after. You can begin to see already what's going to happen here. At present there's still water in the tanks. Soon there won't be. The whole city will begin to stink like a great sewer. There are already some bodies lying about—every day there will be more.' I noticed her shudder. I had for the moment, in taking the general view, forgotten the particular application it would have for her. I hurried on: 'That may mean typhus, or cholera, or God knows what. It's important to get away before anything of that kind starts.'

She nodded agreement to that.

'Then the next question seems to be, where do we go? Have you any ideas?' I asked her.

'Well—I suppose, roughly, somewhere out of the way. A place with a good water supply we can be sure of, a well, perhaps. And I should think it would be best to be as high up as we reasonably can—some place where there'll be a nice clean wind.'

'Yes,' I said, 'I'd not thought of the clean wind part, but you're right. A hilltop with a good water supply—that's not so easy offhand.' I thought a moment. 'The Lake District? No, too far. Wales, perhaps? Or maybe Exmoor or Dartmoor—or right down in Cornwall? Around Land's End we'd have the prevailing south-west wind coming in untainted over the Atlantic. But that, too, was a long way. We should be dependent on towns when it became safe to visit them again.

'What about the Sussex Downs?' Josella suggested. 'I know a lovely old farmhouse on the north side, looking right across towards Pulborough. It's not on the top of hills, but it's well up the side. There's a wind-pump for water, and I think they make their own electricity. It's all been converted and modernized.'

'Desirable residence, in fact. But it's a bit near populous places. Don't you think we ought to get further away?'

'Well, I was wondering. How long is it going to be before it'll be safe to go into the towns again?'

'I've no real idea,' I admitted. 'I'd something like a year in mind—surely that ought to be a safe enough margin?'

'I see. But if we do go too far away, it isn't going to be at all easy to get supplies later on.'

'That is a point, certainly,' I agreed.

We dropped the matter of our final destination for the moment, and got down to working out details for our removal. In the morning, we decided, we would first of all acquire a lorry—a capacious lorry—and between us we made a list of the essentials we would put into it. If we could finish the stocking up, we would start on our way the next evening, if not—and the list was growing to a length which made this appear much the more likely—we would risk another night in London, and get away the following day.

It was close on midnight when we had finished adding our own secondary wants to the list of musts. The result resembled a department-store catalogue. But if it had done no more than serve to take our minds off ourselves for the evening it would have been worth the trouble.

Josella yawned, and stood up.

'Sleepy,' she said. '—And silk sheets waiting on an ecstatic bed.'

She seemed to float across the thick carpet. With her hand on the door-knob she stopped and turned to regard herself solemnly in a long mirror.

'Some things were fun,' she said, and kissed her hand to her reflection.

'Good night, you vain, sweet vision,' I said.

She turned with a small smile, and then vanished through the door like a mist drifting away.

I poured out a final drop of the superb brandy, warmed it in my hands, and sipped it.

'Never—never again now will you see a sight like that,' I told myself. '*Sic transit . . .*'

And then, before I should become utterly morbid, I took myself to my more modest bed.

I was stretched in comfort on the edge of sleep when there came a knocking at the door.

'Bill,' said Josella's voice. 'Come quickly. There's a light!'

'What sort of a light?' I inquired, struggling out of bed.

'Outside. Come and look.'

She was standing in the passage wrapped in the sort of garment that could have belonged only to the owner of that remarkable bedroom.

'Good God!' I said, nervously.

'Don't be a fool,' she told me, irritably. 'Come and look at that light.'

A light there certainly was. Looking out of her window towards what I judged to be the north-east, I could see a bright beam like that of a searchlight pointed unwaveringly upwards.

'That must mean there's somebody else there who can see,' she said.

'It must,' I agreed.

I tried to locate the source of it, but in the surrounding darkness I was unable to decide. No great distance away, I was sure, and seeming to start in mid-air—which probably meant that it was mounted on a high building. I hesitated.

'Better leave it till to-morrow,' I decided.

The idea of trying to find our way to it through the dark streets was far from attractive. And it was just possible—highly unlikely, but just possible—that it was a trap. Even a blind man who was clever and desperate enough *might* be able to wire such a thing up by touch.

I found a nail-file and squatted down with my eye on the level of the window-sill. With the point of the file I drew a careful line in the paint, marking the exact direction of the beam's source. Then I went back to my room.

I lay awake for an hour or more. Night magnified the quiet of the city, making the sounds which broke it the more desolate. From time to time voices rose from the street, edgy and brittle with hysteria. Once there came a freezing scream which seemed to revel horribly in its release from sanity. Somewhere not far away a sobbing went on endlessly, hopelessly. Twice I heard the sharp reports of single pistol shots. . . . I gave heartfelt thanks to whatever it was that had brought Josella and me together for companionship.

Complete loneliness was the worst state I could imagine just then. Alone one would be nothing. Company meant purpose, and purpose helped to keep the morbid fears at bay.

I tried to shut out the sounds by thinking of all the things I must do the next day, the day after, and the days after that; by guessing what the beam of light might mean, and how it might affect us. But the sobbing in the background went on and on and on, reminding me of the things I had seen that day, and would see to-morrow. . . .

The opening of the door brought me sitting up in sudden alarm. It was Josella, carrying a lighted candle. Her eyes were wide and dark, and she had been crying.

'I can't sleep,' she said. 'I'm frightened—horribly frightened. Can you hear them—all those poor people? I can't stand it. . . .'

She came like a child for comfort. I'm not sure that her need of it was much greater than mine.

She fell asleep before I did, with her head resting on my shoulder.

Still the memories of the day would not leave me in peace. But, in the end, one does sleep. My last recollection was of the sweet, sad voice of the girl who had sung:

So we'll go no more a-roving . . .

6. Rendezvous

WHEN I awoke I could hear Josella already moving around in the kitchen. My watch said nearly seven o'clock. By the time I had shaved uncomfortably in cold water and dressed myself, there was a smell of toast and coffee drifting through the apartment. I found her holding a pan over the oilstove. She had an air of self-possession which was hard to associate with the frightened figure of the night before. Her manner was practical, too.

'Canned milk, I'm afraid. The fridge stopped. Everything else is all right, though,' she said.

It was difficult for a moment to believe that the expediently dressed form before me had been the ballroom vision of the previous evening. She had chosen a dark-blue skiing suit with white-topped socks rolled above sturdy shoes. On a dark leather belt she wore a finely-made hunting knife to replace the mediocre weapon I had found the day before. I have no idea how I expected to find her dressed, nor whether I had given the matter any thought, but the practicality of her choice was by no means the only impression I received as I saw her.

'Will I do, do you think?' she asked.

'Eminently,' I assured her. I looked down at myself. 'I

107

wish I'd had as much forethought. Gents' lounge-suiting isn't quite the rig for the job,' I added.

'You could do better,' she agreed, with a candid glance at my crumpled suit.

'That light last night,' she went on, 'came from the University Tower—at least, I'm pretty sure it did. There's nothing else noticeable exactly on that line. It seems about the right distance, too.'

I went into her room, and looked along the scratch I had drawn on the sill. It did, as she said, point directly at the tower. And I noticed something more. The tower was flying two flags on the same mast. One might have been left hoisted by chance, but two must be a deliberate signal; the daytime equivalent of the light. We decided over breakfast that we would postpone our planned programme and make investigation of the tower our first job for the day.

We left the flat about half an hour later. As I had hoped, the station waggon by standing out in the middle of the street had escaped the attentions of prowlers, and was intact. Without delaying further, we dropped the suitcases that Josella had acquired into the back among the triffid gear, and started off.

Few people were about. Presumably weariness and the chill in the air had made them aware that night had fallen, and not many had yet emerged from whatever sleeping-places they had found. Those who were to be seen were keeping more to the gutters and less to the walls than they had on the previous day. Most of them were now holding sticks or bits of broken wood with which they tapped their way along the kerb. It made for easier going than by the housefronts with their entrances and projections, and the tapping had decreased the frequency of collisions.

We threaded our way with little difficulty, and after a time

turned into Store Street to see the University Tower at the
end of it rising straight before us.

'Steady,' said Josella, as we turned into the empty road.
'I think there's something happening at the gates.'

She was right. As we came nearer we could see a not
inconsiderable crowd beyond the end of the street. The
previous day had given us a distaste for crowds. I swung
right down Gower Street, ran on for fifty yards or so, and
stopped.

'What do you reckon's going on there? Do we investigate
or clear out?' I asked.

'I'd say investigate,' Josella replied promptly.

'Good. Me too,' I agreed.

'I remember this part,' she added. 'There's a garden
behind these houses. If we can get in there we ought to be
able to see what's happening without mixing ourselves up
in it.'

We left the car, and started peering hopefully into base-
ment areas. In the third we found an open door. A passage
straight through the house led into the garden. The place
was common to a dozen or so houses, and curiously laid out,
being for the most parts at the level of the basements, and
thus below that of the surrounding streets, but on the far
side, that closest to the University Building, it rose to a
kind of terrace separated from the road by tall iron gates
and a low wall. We could hear the sound of the crowd
beyond it as a kind of composite murmur. We crossed the
lawn, made our way up a sloped gravel path and found a
place behind a screen of bushes whence we could watch.

The crowd that stood in the road outside the University
gates must have numbered several hundred men and women.
It was larger than the sound of it had led us to expect, and
for the first time I realized how much quieter and more
inactive a crowd of blind people is than a comparably-sized

crowd of the sighted. It is natural, of course, for they must depend almost entirely on their ears to know what is happening so that the quietness of each is to the advantage of all, but it had not been obvious to me until that moment.

Whatever was going on was right at the front. We managed to find a slightly higher mound which gave us a view of the gates across the heads of the crowd. A man in a cap was talking volubly through the bars. He did not appear to be making a lot of headway, for the part taken in the conversation by the man on the other side of the gates consisted almost entirely of negative headshakes.

'What is it?' Josella asked, in a whisper.

I helped her up beside me. The talkative man turned so that we had a glimpse of his profile. He was, I judged, about thirty, with a straight, narrow nose, and rather bony features. What showed of his hair was dark, but it was the intensity of his manner that was more noticeable than his appearance.

As the colloquy through the gates continued to get nowhere his voice became louder and more emphatic—though without visible effect on the other. There could be no doubt that the man beyond the gates was able to see; he was doing so watchfully, through horn-rimmed glasses. A few yards behind him stood a little knot of three more men about whom there was equally little doubt. They, too, were regarding the crowd and its spokesman with careful attention. The man on our side grew more heated. His voice rose as if he were talking as much for the benefit of the crowd as for those behind the railings.

'Now listen to me,' he said, angrily. 'These people here have got just as much bloody right to live as you have, haven't they? It's not their fault they're blind, is it? It's nobody's fault—but it's going to be your fault if they starve, and you know it.'

His voice was a curious mixture of the rough and the

educated so that it was hard to place him—as though neither style seemed quite natural to him, somehow.

'I've been showing them where to get food. I've been doing what I can for them, but, Christ, there's only one of me, and there's thousands of them. *You* could be showing 'em where to get food, too—but are you?—hell! What *are* you doing about it? Damn all, that's what. Just sweet effay but look after your own lousy skins. I've met your kind before. It's "Damn you, Jack, I'm all right"—that's your motto.'

He spat with contempt, and raised a long, oratorical arm.

'Out there,' he said, waving his hand towards London at large, '—out there there are thousands of poor devils only wanting someone to show them how to get the food that's there for the taking. —And you could do it. All you've got to do is *show* them. But do you? Do you, you buggers? No, what you do is shut yourselves in here and let them bloody well starve when each one of you could keep hundreds alive by doing no more than coming out and *showing* the poor sods where to get the grub. God almighty, aren't you people human?'

The man's voice was violent. He had a case to put, and he was putting it passionately. I felt Josella's hand unconsciously clutching my arm, and I put my hand over hers. The man on the far side of the gate said something that was inaudible where we stood.

'How long?' shouted the man on our side. 'How in hell would I know how long the food's going to last? What I do know is that if bastards like you don't muck in and help, there ain't going to be many left alive by the time they come to clear this bloody mess up.' He stood glaring for a moment. 'Fact of it is, you're scared—scared to show 'em where the food is. And why? Because the more these poor devils get to eat, the less there's going to be for your lot. That's the way of it, isn't it? That's the truth—if you had the guts to admit it.'

Again we failed to hear the answer of the other man, but, whatever it was, it did nothing to mollify the speaker. He stared back grimly through the bars for a moment. Then he said:

'All right—if that's the way you want it!'

He made a lightning snatch between the bars, and caught the other's arm. In one swift movement he dragged it through, and twisted it. He grabbed the hand of a blind man standing beside him, and clamped it on the arm.

'Hang on there, mate,' he said, and jumped towards the main fastening of the gates.

The man inside recovered from his first surprise. He struck wildly through the bars behind him with his other hand. A chance swipe took the blind man in the face. It made him give a yell, and tighten his grip. The leader of the crowd was wrenching at the gate fastening. At that moment a rifle cracked. The bullet pinged against the railings, and whirred off on a ricochet. The leader checked suddenly, undecided. Behind him there was an outbreak of curses, and a scream or two. The crowd swayed back and forth as though uncertain whether to run or to charge the gates. The decision was made for them by those in the courtyard. I saw a youngish-looking man tuck something under his arm, and I dropped down, pulling Josella with me as the clatter of a sub-machine gun began.

It was obvious that the shooting was deliberately high, nevertheless, the rattle of it and the whizz of glancing bullets was alarming. One short burst was enough to settle the matter. When we raised our heads the crowd had lost entity and its components were groping their ways to safer parts in all three possible directions. The leader paused only to shout something unintelligible, then he turned away, too.

He made his way northwards up Malet Street, doing his best to rally his following behind him.

I sat where we were, and looked at Josella. She looked thoughtfully back at me, and then down at the ground before her. It was some minutes before either of us spoke.

'Well?' I asked, at last.

She raised her head to look across the road, and then at the last stragglers from the crowd pathetically fumbling their ways.

'He was right,' she said. 'You know he was right, don't you?'

I nodded.

'Yes, he was right. . . . And yet he was quite wrong, too. You see, there is no "they" to come to clear up this mess— I'm quite sure of that now. It won't be cleared up. We could do as he says. We *could* show some, though only some, of these people where there is food. We could do that for a few days, maybe for a few weeks, but after that—what?'

'It seems so awful, so callous . . .'

'If we face it squarely, there's a simple choice,' I said. 'Either we can set out to save what can be saved from the wreck—and that has to include ourselves: or we can devote ourselves to stretching the lives of these people a little longer. That is the most objective view I can take.

'But I can see, too, that the more obviously humane course is also, probably, the road to suicide. Should we spend our time in prolonging misery when we believe that there is no chance of saving the people in the end? Would that be the best use to make of ourselves?'

She nodded slowly.

'Put like that, there doesn't seem to be much choice, does there? And even if we could save a few, which are we going to choose?—and who are *we* to choose?—and how long could we do it, anyway?'

'There's nothing easy about this,' I said. 'I've no idea what proportion of semi-disabled persons it may be possible for us to support when we come to the end of handy supplies, but I don't imagine it could be very high.'

'You've made up your mind,' she said, glancing at me. There might or might not have been a tinge of disapproval in her voice.

'My dear,' I said. 'I don't like this any more than you do. I've put the alternatives baldly before you. Do we help those who have survived the catastrophe to rebuild some kind of life?—or do we make a moral gesture which, on the face of it, can scarcely be more than a gesture? The people across the road there evidently intend to survive.'

She dug her fingers into the earth, and let the soil trickle out of her hand.

'I suppose you're right,' she said. 'But you're right when you say I don't like it.'

'Our likes and dislikes as decisive factors have now pretty well disappeared,' I suggested.

'Maybe, but I can't help feeling that there must be something wrong about anything that starts with shooting.'

'He shot to miss—and it's very likely he saved fighting,' I pointed out.

The crowd had all gone now. I climbed over the wall, and helped Josella down on the other side. A man at the gate opened it to let us in.

'How many of you?' he asked.

'Just two of us. We saw your signal last night,' I told him.

'Okay. Come along, and we'll find the colonel,' he said, leading us across the forecourt.

The man whom he called the Colonel had set himself up in a small room not far from the entrance, and intended, seemingly, for the porters. He was a chubby man just turned fifty or thereabouts. His hair was plentiful but well-trimmed, and grey. His moustache matched it, and looked as if no single hair would dare to break the ranks. His complexion was so pink, healthy and fresh that it might have belonged to a much younger man; his mind, I discovered later, had never ceased to do so. He was sitting behind a table with quantities of paper arranged on it in mathematically exact blocks, and an unsoiled sheet of pink blotting-paper placed squarely before him.

As we came in he turned upon us, one after the other, an intense, steady look, and held it a little longer than was necessary. I recognized the technique. It is intended to convey that the user is a percipient judge accustomed to taking summarily the measure of his man; the receiver should feel that he now faces a reliable type with no nonsense about him—or, alternatively, that he has been seen through and had all his weaknesses noted. The right response is to return it in kind, and be considered a 'useful fella.' I did. The Colonel picked up his pen.

'Your names, please?'

We gave them.

'And addresses?'

'In the present circumstances I fear they won't be very useful,' I said. 'But if you really feel you must have them——' We gave them, too.

He murmured something about system, organization, and relatives, and wrote them down. Age, occupation, and all the rest of it followed. He bent his searching look upon us again, scribbled a note upon each piece of paper, and put them in a file.

'Need good men. Nasty business this. Plenty to do here, though. Plenty. Mr. Beadley'll tell you what's wanted.'

We came out into the hall again. Josella giggled.

'He forgot to ask for references in triplicate—but I gather we've got the job,' she said.

Michael Beadley, when we discovered him, turned out to be in decided contrast. He was lean, tall, broad-shouldered, and slightly stooping with something the air of an athlete run to books. In repose his face took on an expression of mild gloom from the darkness of his large eyes, but it was seldom that one had a glimpse of it in repose. The occasional streaks of grey in his hair helped very little in judging his age. He might have been anything between thirty-five and fifty. His obvious weariness just then made an estimate still more difficult. By his looks he must have been up all night, nevertheless he greeted us cheerfully and waved an introductory hand towards a young woman who took down our names again as we gave them.

'Sandra Telmont,' he explained. 'Sandra is our professional remembrancer—continuity is her usual work, so we regard it as particularly thoughtful of providence to contrive her presence here just now.'

The young woman nodded to me, and looked harder at Josella.

'We've met before,' she said, thoughtfully. She glanced down at the pad on her knee. Presently a faint smile passed across her pleasant though unexotic countenance.

'Oh, yes, of course,' she said, in recollection.

'What did I tell you? The thing clings like a flypaper,' Josella observed to me.

'What's this about?' inquired Michael Beadley.

I explained. He turned a more careful scrutiny on Josella. She sighed.

'Please forget it,' she suggested. 'I'm a bit tired of living it down.'

That appeared to surprise him agreeably.

'All right,' he said, and dismissed the matter with a nod. He turned back to the table. 'Now to get on with things. You've seen Jaques?'

'If that is the Colonel who is playing at Civil Service, we have,' I told him.

He grinned.

'Got to know how we stand. Can't get anywhere without knowing your ration-strength,' he said, in a fair imitation of the Colonel's manner. 'But it's quite true, though,' he went on. 'I'd better give you just a rough idea of how things do stand. Up to the present there are about thirty-five of us. All sorts. We hope and expect that some more will come in during the day. Out of those here now, twenty-eight can see. The others are wives or husbands—and there are two or three children—who cannot. At the moment the general idea is that we move away from here sometime to-morrow if we can be ready in time—to be on the safe side, you understand.'

I nodded. 'We'd decided to get away this evening for the same reason,' I told him.

'What have you for transport?'

I explained the present position of the station-waggon. 'We were going to stock up to-day,' I added. 'So far we've practically nothing except a quantity of anti-triffid gear.'

He raised his eyebrows. The girl Sandra also looked at me curiously.

'That's a queer thing to make your first essential,' he remarked.

I told them the reasons. Possibly I made a bad job of it, for they neither of them looked much impressed. He nodded casually, and went on:

'Well, if you're coming in with us, here's what I suggest. Bring in your car, dump your stuff, then drive off and swap it for a good big lorry. Then—oh, does either of you know anything about doctoring?' he broke off to ask.

We shook our heads.

He frowned a little. 'That's a pity. So far we've got no one who does. It'll surprise me if we're not needing a doctor before long—and anyway, we ought all of us to have inoculations . . . Still, it's not much good sending you two off on a medical supplies scrounge. What about food and general stores? Suit you?'

He flipped through some pages on a clip, detached one of them, and handed it to me. It was headed No. 15, and below was a typed list of canned goods, pots and pans, and some bedding.

'Not rigid,' he said, 'but keep reasonably close to it, and we'll avoid too many duplications. Stick to best quality. With the food, concentrate on value for bulk—I mean, even if cornflakes are your leading passion in life, forget 'em. I suggest you keep to warehouses and big wholesalers.' He took back the list, and scribbled two or three addresses on it. 'Cans and packets are your food line—don't get led away by sacks of flour, for instance; there's another party on that sort of stuff.' He looked thoughtfully at Josella. 'Heavyish work, I'm afraid, but it's the most useful job we can give you at present. Do as much as you can before dark. There'll be a general meeting and discussion here about nine-thirty this evening.'

As we turned to go:

'Got a pistol?' he asked.

'I didn't think of it,' I admitted.

'Better—just in case. Quite effective simply fired into the air,' he said. He took two pistols from a drawer in the table, and pushed them across. 'Less messy than that,' he added, with a look at Josella's handsome knife. 'Good scrounging to you.'

Even by the time we set out after unloading the station-waggon we found that there were still fewer people about than on the previous day. The ones that were showed an

inclination to get on the pavements at the sound of the
engine rather than to molest us.

The first lorry to take our fancy proved useless, being
filled with wooden cases too heavy for us to remove. Our
next find was luckier—a five-tonner, almost new, and empty.
We transhipped, and left the station-waggon to its fate.

At the first address on my list the shutters of the loading-
bay were down, but they gave way without much difficulty
to the persuasions of a crowbar from a neighbouring shop,
and rolled up easily. Inside, we made a find. Three lorries
stood backed up to the platform. One of them was fully
loaded with cases of canned meat.

'Can you drive one of these things?' I asked Josella.

She looked at it.

'Well, I don't see why not. The general idea's the same,
isn't it? And there's certainly no traffic problem.'

We decided to come back and fetch it later, and took the
empty lorry on to another warehouse where we loaded
parcels of blankets, rugs and quilts, and then went on further
to acquire a noisy miscellany of pots, pans, cauldrons and
kettles. When we had it filled we felt we'd put in a good
morning's work on a job that was heavier than we had
thought. We satisfied the appetite it had given us at a small
pub hitherto untouched.

The mood which filled the business and commercial
districts was gloomy—though it was a gloom that still had
more the style of a normal Sunday or public holiday than of
collapse. Very few people at all were to be seen in those
parts. Had the catastrophe come by day, instead of by night
after the workers had gone home, it would have been a
hideously different scene.

When we had refreshed ourselves we collected the already
loaded lorry from the food warehouse, and drove the two
of them slowly and uneventfully back to the University. We

parked them in the forecourt there, and set off again. About six-thirty we returned once more with another pair of well-loaded lorries, and a feeling of useful accomplishment.

Michael Beadley emerged from the building to inspect our contributions. He approved of it all, save half a dozen cases that I had added to my second load.

'What are they?' he asked.

'Triffid guns, and bolts for them,' I told him.

He looked at me thoughtfully.

'Oh, yes. You arrived with a lot of anti-triffid stuff,' he remarked.

'I think it's likely we'll need it,' I said.

He considered. I could see that I was being put down as a bit unsound on the subject of triffids. Most likely he was accounting for that by the bias my job might be expected to give—aggravated by a phobia resulting from my recent sting—and he was wondering whether it might connote other, perhaps less harmless, unsoundnesses.

'Look here,' I suggested, 'we've brought in four full loads between us. I just want enough space in one of them for these cases. If you think we can't spare that, I'll go out and find a trailer, or another lorry.'

'No, leave 'em where they are. They don't take a lot of room,' he decided.

We went into the building and had some tea at an improvised canteen that a pleasant-faced, middle-aged woman had competently set up there.

'He thinks,' I said to Josella, 'that I've got a bee in my bonnet over triffids.'

'He'll learn—I'm afraid,' she replied. 'It's queer that no one else seems to have seen them about.'

'These people have all been keeping pretty much to the centre, so it's not very surprising. After all, we've seen none ourselves to-day.'

'Do you think they'll come right down here among the streets?'

'I couldn't say. Maybe lost ones would.'

'How do you think they got loose?' she asked.

'If they worry at a stake hard enough and long enough, it'll usually come in the end. The breakouts we used to get sometimes on the farms were due as a rule to their all crowding up against one section of the fence until it gave way.'

'But couldn't you make the fences stronger?'

'We could have done, but we didn't want them fixed quite permanently. It didn't happen very often, and when it did it was usually simply from one field to another, so we'd just drive them back, and put up the fence again. I don't think any of them will intentionally make this way. From a triffid point of view a city must be much like a desert, so I should think they'll be moving outwards towards the open country on the whole. Have you ever used a triffid-gun?' I added.

She shook her head.

'After I've done something about these clothes I was thinking of putting in a bit of practice, if you'd like to try,' I suggested.

I got back an hour or so later feeling more suitably clad as a result of having infringed on her idea of a ski-suit and heavy shoes, to find that she had changed into a becoming dress of spring-green. We took a couple of the triffid-guns, and went out into the garden of Russell Square, close by. We had spent about half an hour snipping the topmost shoots off convenient bushes when a young woman in a brick-red lumber jacket and an elegant pair of green trousers strolled across the grass and levelled a small camera at us.

'Who are you—the Press?' inquired Josella.

'More or less,' said the young woman, '—at least, I'm the official record. Elspeth Cary.'

'So soon?' I remarked. 'I trace the hand of our order-conscious Colonel.'

'You're quite right,' she agreed. She turned to look at Josella. 'And you are Miss Playton. I've often wondered——'

'Now look here,' interrupted Josella. 'Why should the one static thing in a collapsing world be my reputation? Can't we forget it?'

'Um,' said Miss Cary, thoughtfully. 'Uh-huh.' She turned to another subject. 'What's all this about triffids?' she asked.

We told her.

'They think,' added Josella, 'that Bill here is either scary or scatty on the subject.'

Miss Cary turned a straight look at me. Her face was interesting rather than good-looking, with a complexion browned by stronger suns than ours. Her eyes were steady, observant, and dark brown.

'Are you?' she asked.

'Well, I think they're troublesome enough to be taken seriously when they get out of hand,' I told her.

She nodded. 'True enough. I've been in places where they are out of hand. Quite nasty. But in England—well, it's hard to imagine that here.'

'There'll not be a lot to stop them here now,' I said.

Her reply, if she had been about to make one, was forestalled by the sound of an engine overhead. We looked up and presently saw a helicopter come drifting across the roof of the British Museum.

'That'll be Ivan,' said Miss Cary. 'He thought he might manage to find one. I must go and get a picture of him landing. See you later.' And she hurried off across the grass.

Josella lay down, clasped her hands behind her head, and gazed up into the depths of the sky. When the helicopter's engine ceased it sounded very much quieter than before we had heard it.

'I can't believe it,' she said. 'I try, but I still can't *really* believe it. It can't all be going . . . going . . . going . . . This *is* some kind of dream. To-morrow this garden will be full of noise. The red buses will be roaring along over there, crowds of people will be scurrying along the pavements, the traffic-lights will be flashing. . . . A world doesn't just end like this—it can't—it isn't possible . . .'

I was feeling like that, too. The houses, the trees, the absurdly grandiose hotels on the other side of the Square were all too normal—too ready to come to life as a touch . . .

'And yet,' I said, 'I suppose that if they had been able to think at all the dinosaurs would have thought much the same thing. It just does happen from time to time, you see.'

'But why to us? It's like reading in the papers about the astonishing things that have happened to other people—but always to *other* people. There's nothing special about us.'

'Isn't there always a "why me?" Whether it's the soldier who's untouched when all his pals are killed, or the fellow who gets run in for fiddling his accounts? Just plain blind chance, I'd say.'

'Chance that it happened?—or chance that it happened now?'

'Now, I mean. It was bound to happen some time in some way. It's an unnatural thought that one type of creature should dominate perpetually.'

'I don't see why.'

'Why, is a heck of a question. But it is an inescapable conclusion that life has to be dynamic and not static. Change is bound to come one way or another. Mind you, I don't think it's quite done with us this time, but it has had a damned good try.'

'Then you don't think it really is the end—of people, I mean?'

'It might be. But—well, I don't think so—this time.'

It *could* be the end. I had no doubt of that. But there would be other little groups like ours. I saw an empty world with a few scattered communities trying to fight their way back to control of it. I had to believe that some, at least, of them would succeed.

'No,' I repeated, 'it need not be the end. We're still very adaptable, and we've a flying start compared with our ancestors. As long as there are any of us left sound and healthy we've got a chance—a thundering good chance.'

Josella made no answer. She lay facing upwards with a faraway look in her eyes. I thought perhaps I could guess something of what was passing in her mind, but I said nothing. She did not speak for a little while, then she said:

'You know, one of the most shocking things about it is to realize how *easily* we have lost a world that seemed so safe and certain.'

She was quite right. It was that simplicity that seemed somehow to be the nucleus of the shock. From very familiarity one forgets all the forces which keep the balance, and thinks of security as normal. It is not. I don't think it had ever before occurred to me that man's supremacy is not primarily due to his brain, as most of the books would have one think. It is due to the brain's capacity to make use of the information conveyed to it by a narrow band of visible light rays. His civilization, all that he has achieved or might achieve hangs upon his ability to perceive that range of vibrations from red to violet. Without that, he is lost. I saw for a moment the true tenuousness of his hold on his power, the miracles that he had wrought with such a fragile instrument. . . .

Josella had been pursuing her own line of thought.

'It's going to be a very queer sort of world—what's left of it. I don't think we're going to like it a lot,' she said, reflectively.

It seemed to me an odd view to take—rather as if one should protest that one did not *like* the idea of dying or being born. I preferred the notion of finding out first how it would be, and then doing what one could about the parts of it one disliked most, but I let it pass.

From time to time we had heard the sound of lorries driving up to the far side of the building. It was evident that most of the foraging parties must have returned by this hour. I looked at my watch, and reached for the triffid-guns lying on the grass beside me.

'If we're going to get any supper before we hear what other people feel about all this, it's time we went in,' I said.

7. Conference

I FANCY all of us had expected the meeting to be simply a kind of briefing talk. Just times, course instructions, the day's objective—that kind of thing. Certainly I had no expectation of the food for thought that we received.

It was held in a small lecture-theatre lit for the occasion by an arrangement of car headlamps and batteries. When we went in, some half-dozen men and two women who appeared to have constituted themselves a committee were conferring behind the lecturer's desk. To our surprise we found nearly a hundred people seated in the body of the hall. Young women predominated at a ratio of about four to one. I had not realized until Josella pointed it out to me how few of them were able to see.

Michael Beadley dominated the consulting group by his height. I recognized the Colonel beside him. The other faces were new to me, save that of Elspeth Cary who had now exchanged her camera for a notebook, presumably for the benefit of posterity. Most of their interest was centred round an elderly man of ugly but benign aspect who wore gold-rimmed spectacles, and fine white hair trimmed to a rather political length. They all had an air of being a little worried about him.

The other woman in the party was little more than a girl—perhaps twenty-two or three. She did not appear happy at finding herself where she was. She cast occasional looks of nervous uncertainty at the audience.

Sandra Telmont came in, carrying a sheet of foolscap. She studied it a moment, then briskly broke the group up, and sorted it into chairs. With a wave of her hand she directed Michael to the desk, and the meeting began.

He stood there a little bent, watching the audience from sombre eyes as he waited for the murmuring to die down. When he spoke, it was in a pleasant, practised voice, and with a fireside manner.

'Many of us here,' he began, 'must still be feeling numbed under this catastrophe. The world we knew has ended in a flash. Some of us may be feeling that it is the end of everything. It is not. But to all of you I will say at once that it *can* be the end of everything—*if we let it.*

'Stupendous as this disaster is, there is still a margin of survival. It may be worth remembering just now that we are not unique in looking upon vast calamity. Whatever the myths that have grown up about it, there can be no doubt that somewhere far back in our history there was a Great Flood. Those who survived that must have looked upon a disaster comparable in scale with this, and, in some ways, more formidable. But they cannot have despaired: they must have begun again—as we can begin again.

'Self-pity and a sense of high tragedy are going to build nothing at all. So we had better throw them out at once, for it is builders that we must become.

'And further to deflate any romantic dramatization I would like to point out to you that this, even now, is not the worst that could have happened. I, and quite likely many of you, have spent most of our lives in expectation of something worse. And I still believe that if this had not happened to us, that worse thing would.

'From August 6th, 1945, the margin of survival has narrowed appallingly. Indeed, two days ago it was narrower than it is at this moment. If you need to dramatize, you could well take for your material the years succeeding 1945 when the path of safety started to shrink to a tight-rope along which we had to walk with our eyes deliberately closed to the depths beneath us.

'In any single moment of the years since then the fatal slip might have been made. It is a miracle that it was not. It is a double miracle that can go on happening for years.

'But sooner or later that slip must have occurred. It would not have mattered whether it came through malice, carelessness, or sheer accident: the balance would have been lost, and the destruction let loose.

'How bad it would have been, we cannot say. How bad it *could* have been—well, there might have been no survivors: there might possibly have been no planet. . . .

'And now contrast our situation. The Earth is intact, unscarred, still fruitful. It can provide us with food and raw materials. We have repositories of knowledge that can teach us to do anything that has been done before—though there are some things that may be better unremembered. And we have the means, the health, and the strength to begin to build again.'

He did not make a long speech, but it had effect. It must have made quite a number of the members of his audience begin to feel that perhaps they were at the beginning of something after all, rather than at the end of everything. In spite of his offering little but generalities there was a more alert air in the place when he sat down.

The Colonel, who followed him, was practical and factual. He reminded us that for reasons of health it would be

advisable for us to get away from all built-up areas as soon
as practicable—which was expected to be at about 12.00
hours on the following day. Almost all the primary necessities as well as extras enough to give a reasonable standard
of comfort had now been collected. In considering our stocks
our aim must be to make ourselves as nearly independent of
outside sources as possible for a minimum of one year. We
should spend that period in virtually a state of siege. There
were, no doubt, many things we should all like to take
besides those on our lists, but they would have to wait until
the medical staff (and here the girl on the committee blushed
deeply) considered it safe for parties to leave isolation and
fetch them. As for the scene of our isolation, the committee
had given it considerable thought, and, bearing in mind the
desiderata of compactness, self-sufficiency, and detachment
had come to the conclusion that a country boarding-school
or, failing that, some large country mansion would best
serve our purposes.

Whether the committee had in fact not yet decided on any
particular place, or whether the military notion that secrecy
has some intrinsic value persisted in the Colonel's mind, I
cannot say, but I have no doubt that his failure to name the
place, or even the probable locality, was the gravest mistake
made that evening. At the time, however, his practical
manner had a further reassuring effect.

As he sat down, Michael rose again. He spoke encourag-
ingly to the girl, and then introduced her. It had, he said,
been one of our greatest worries that we had no one among
us with medical knowledge, therefore, it was with great
relief that he welcomed Miss Berr. It was true that she did
not hold medical degrees with impressive letters, but she did
have high nursing qualifications. For himself he thought
that knowledge recently attained might be worth more than
degrees acquired years ago.

E

The girl, blushing again, said a little piece about her determination to carry the job through, and ended a trifle abruptly with the information that she would inoculate us all against a variety of things before we left the hall.

A small, sparrow-like man whose name I did not catch rubbed it in that the health of each was the concern of all, and that any suspicion of illness should be reported at once since the effects of a contagious disease among us would be serious.

When he had finished Sandra rose and introduced the last speaker of the group: Dr. E. H. Vorless, D.Sc., of Edinburgh, Professor of Sociology at the University of Kingston.

The white-haired man walked to the desk. He stood there a few moments with his finger-tips resting upon it, and his head bent down as if he were studying it. Those behind regarded him carefully, with a trace of anxiety. The Colonel leaned over to whisper something to Michael who nodded without taking his eyes off the Doctor. The old man looked up. He passed a hand over his hair.

'My friends,' he said, 'I think I may claim to be the oldest among you. In nearly seventy years I have learned, and had to unlearn, many things—though not nearly so many as I could have wished. But if, in the course of a long study of man's institutions, one thing has struck me more than their stubbornness, it is their variety.

'Well indeed do the French say *autres temps, autres mœurs*. We must all see, if we pause to think, that one kind of community's virtue may well be another kind of community's crime: that what is frowned upon here may be considered laudable elsewhere; that customs condemned in one century are condoned in another. And we must also see that in each community and each period there is a wide-spread belief in the moral rightness of its own customs.

'Now, clearly, since many of these beliefs conflict they cannot all be "right" in an absolute sense. The most judgment one can pass on them—if one has to pass judgments at all—is to say that they have at some period been "right" for those communities that hold them. It may be that they still are, but it frequently is found that they are not, and that the communities who continue to follow them blindly without heed to changed circumstances do so to their own disadvantage—perhaps to their ultimate destruction.'

The audience did not perceive where the introduction might be leading. It fidgeted. Most of it was accustomed when it encountered this kind of thing to turn the radio off at once. Now it felt trapped. The speaker decided to make himself clearer.

'Thus,' he continued, 'you would not expect to find the same manners, customs, and forms in a penurious Indian village living on the edge of starvation as you would in, say, Mayfair. Similarly the people in a warm country where life is easy are going to differ quite a deal from the people of an overcrowded, hardworking country as to the nature of the principal virtues. In other words, different environments set different standards.

'I point this out to you because the world we knew is gone—finished.

'The conditions which framed and taught us our standards have gone with it. Our needs are now different, and our aims must be different. If you want an example, I would suggest to you that we have all spent the day indulging with perfectly easy consciences in what two days ago would have been housebreaking and theft. With the old pattern broken, we have now to find out what mode of life is best suited to the new. We have not simply to start building again: we have to start *thinking* again—which is much more difficult, and far more distasteful.

'Man remains physically adaptable to a remarkable degree. But it is the custom of each community to form the minds of its young in a mould, introducing a binding agent of prejudice. The result is a remarkably tough substance capable of withstanding successfully even the pressure of many innate tendencies and instincts. In this way it has been possible to produce a man who against all his basic sense of self-preservation will voluntarily risk death for an ideal—*but* also in this way is produced the dolt who is sure of everything and knows what is "right."

'In the time now ahead of us a great many of these prejudices we have been taught will have to go, or be radically altered. We can accept and retain only one primary prejudice, and that is that *the race is worth preserving*. To that consideration all else will for a time at least be subordinate. We must look at all we do, with the question in mind: "Is this going to help our race survive—or will it hinder us?" If it will help, we must do it, whether or not it conflicts with the ideas in which we were brought up. If not, we must avoid it even though the omission may clash with our previous notions of duty, and even of justice.

'It will not be easy: old prejudices die hard. The simple rely on a bolstering mass of maxim and precept, so do the timid, so do the mentally lazy—and so do all of us, more than we imagine. Now that the organization has gone, our ready-reckoners for conduct within it no longer give the right answers. We *must* have the moral courage to think and to plan for ourselves.'

He paused to survey his audience thoughtfully. Then he said:

'There is one thing to be made quite clear to you before you decide to join our community. It is that those of us who start on this task will all have our parts to play. The men must work—the women must have babies. Unless you can agree to that there can be no place for you in our community.'

After an interval of dead silence, he added:

'We can afford to support a limited number of women who cannot see, because they will have babies who can see. We cannot afford to support men who cannot see. In our new world, then, babies become very much more important than husbands.'

For some seconds after he stopped speaking silence continued, then isolated murmurs grew quickly into a general buzz.

I looked at Josella. To my astonishment she was grinning impishly.

'What do you find funny about this?' I asked, a trifle shortly.

'People's expressions mostly,' she replied.

I had to admit it as a reason. I looked round the place, and then across at Michael. His eyes were moving from one section to another of the audience as he tried to sum up the reaction.

'Michael's looking a bit anxious,' I observed.

'He should worry,' said Josella. 'If Brigham Young could bring it off in the middle of the nineteenth century, this ought to be a pushover.'

'What a crude young woman you are at times,' I said. 'Were you in on this before?'

'Not exactly, but I'm not quite dumb, you know. Besides, while you were away someone drove in a bus with most of these blind girls on board. They all came from some institution. I said to myself, why collect them from there when you could gather up thousands in a few streets round here? The answer obviously was that (a) being blind before this happened they had been trained to do work of some kind, and (b) they were all girls. The deduction wasn't terribly difficult.'

'H'm,' I said. 'Depends on one's outlook, I suppose. I must say, it wouldn't have struck me. Do you——?'

'Sh-sh,' she told me, as a quietness came over the hall.

A tall, dark, purposeful-looking, youngish woman had risen. While she waited, she appeared to have a mouth not made to open, but later it did.

'Are we to understand,' she inquired, using a kind of carbon-steel voice, 'are we to understand that the last speaker is advocating free love?' And she sat down, with spine-jarring decision.

Doctor Vorless smoothed back his hair as he regarded her.

'I think the questioner must be aware that I never mentioned love, free, bought, or bartered. Will she please make her question clearer?'

The woman stood up again.

'I think the speaker understood me. I am asking if he suggests the abolition of the marriage law?'

'The laws we knew have been abolished by circumstances. It now falls to us to make laws suitable to the conditions, and to enforce them if necessary.'

'There is still God's law, and the law of decency.'

'Madam. Solomon had three hundred—or was it five hundred?—wives, and God did not apparently hold that against him. A Mohammedan preserves rigid respectability with three wives. These are matters of local custom. Just what our laws in these matters, and in others, will be is for us all to decide later for the greatest benefit of the community.

'This committee, after discussion, has decided that if we are to build a new state of things and avoid a relapse into barbarism—which is an appreciable danger—we must have certain undertakings from those who wish to join us.

'Not one of us is going to recapture the conditions we

have lost. What we offer is a busy life in the best conditions we can contrive, and the happiness which will come of achievement against odds. In return we ask willingness and fruitfulness. There is no compulsion. The choice is yours. Those to whom our offer does not appeal are at perfect liberty to go elsewhere, and start a separate community on such lines as they prefer.

'But I would ask you to consider very carefully whether or not you do hold a warrant from God to deprive any woman of the happiness of carrying out her natural functions.'

The discussion which followed was a rambling affair descending frequently to points of detail and hypothesis on which there could as yet be no answers. But there was no move to cut it short. The longer it went on, the less strangeness the idea would have.

Josella and I moved over to the table where Nurse Berr had set up her paraphernalia. We took several shots in our arms, and then sat down again to listen to the wrangling.

'How many of them will decide to come, do you think?' I asked her.

She glanced round.

'Nearly all of them—by the morning,' she said.

I felt doubtful. There was a lot of objecting and questioning going on. Josella said:

'If you were a woman who was going to spend an hour or two before you went to sleep to-night considering whether you would choose babies and an organization to look after you, or adherence to a principle which might quite likely mean no babies and no one to look after you. You'd not really be very doubtful, you know. And after all, most women want babies, anyway—the husband's just what Doctor Vorless might call the local means to the end.'

'That's rather cynical of you.'

'If you really think that's cynical you must be a very sentimental character. I'm talking about real women, not those in the magazine-movie-make-believe world.'

'Oh,' I said.

She sat pensively awhile, and gradually acquired a frown. At last she said:

'The thing that worries me is how many will they expect? I like babies, all right, but there are limits.'

After the debate had gone on raggedly for an hour or so, it was wound up. Michael asked that the names of all those willing to join in his plan should be left in his office by ten o'clock the next morning. The Colonel requested all who could drive a lorry to report to him by 7.00 hours, and the meeting broke up.

Josella and I wandered out of doors. The evening was mild. The light on the tower was again stabbing hopefully into the sky. The moon had just risen clear of the Museum roof. We found a low wall, and sat on it, looking into the shadows of the Square garden, and listening to the faint sound of the wind in the branches of the trees there. We smoked a cigarette each almost in silence. When I reached the end of mine, I threw it away, and drew a breath.

'Josella,' I said.

'M'm?' she replied, scarcely emerging from her thoughts.

'Josella,' I said again. 'Er—those babies. I'd—er—I'd be sort of terribly proud and happy if they could be mine as well as yours.'

She sat quite still for a moment, saying nothing. Then she turned her head. The moonlight was glinting on her fair hair, but her face and eyes were in shadow. I waited, with a hammered, and slightly sick feeling inside me. She said, with surprising calm:

'Thank you, Bill, dear. I think I would, too.'

I sighed. The hammering did not ease up much, and I saw that my hand was trembling as it reached for hers. I didn't have any words, for the moment. Josella, however, did. She said:

'But it isn't quite as easy as that, now.'

I was jolted.

'What do you mean?' I asked.

She said, consideringly: 'I think that if I were those people in there'—she nodded in the direction of the tower—'I think that I should make a rule. I should divide us up into lots. I should say every man who marries a sighted girl must take on two blind girls as well. I'm pretty sure that's what I should do.'

I stared at her face in the shadow.

'You don't mean that,' I protested.

'I'm afraid I do, Bill.'

'But, look here——'

'Don't you think they may have some idea like that in their minds—from what they've been saying?'

'Not unlikely,' I conceded. 'But if *they* make the rule, that's one thing. I don't see——'

'You mean you don't love me enough to take on two other women as well?'

I swallowed. I also objected:

'Look here. This is all crazy. It's unnatural. What you're suggesting——'

She put up a hand to stop me.

'Just listen to me, Bill. I know it sounds a bit startling at first, but there's nothing crazy about it. It's all quite clear—and it's not very easy.

'All this'—she waved her hand around—'it's done something to me. It's like suddenly seeing everything differently. And one of the things I think I see is that those of us who get through are going to be much nearer to one another, more dependent on one another, more like—well, more like a *tribe* than we ever were before.

'All day long as we went about I've been seeing unfortunate people who are going to die very soon. And all the time I've been saying to myself: "There, but for the grace of God . . ." And then I've told myself: "This is a miracle! I don't deserve anything better than any of these people. But it has happened. Here I still am—so now it's up to me to justify it." Somehow it's made me feel closer to other people than I have ever done before. That's made me keep wondering all the time what I can do to help some of them.

'You see, we *must* do something to justify that miracle, Bill. I might have been any of these blind girls; you might have been any of these wandering men. There's nothing big we can do. But if we try to look after just a few and give them what happiness we can, we shall be paying back a little—just a tiny part of what we owe. You do see that, don't you, Bill?'

I turned it over in my mind for a minute or more.

'I think,' I said, 'that that's the queerest argument I've heard to-day—if not ever. And yet——'

'And yet it's *right*, isn't it, Bill? I know it's right. I've tried to put myself in the place of one of those blind girls, and I *know*. We hold the chance of as full a life as they can have, for some of them. Shall we give it them as a part of our gratitude—or shall we simply withhold it on account of the prejudices we've been taught? That's what it amounts to.'

I sat silently for a time. I had not a moment's doubt that Josella meant every word she said. I ruminated a little on the ways of purposeful, subversive-minded women like Florence Nightingale and Elizabeth Fry. You can't do anything with such women—and they so often turn out to have been right after all.

'Very well,' I said at last. 'If that's the way you think it ought to be. But I hope——'

She cut me short.

'Oh, Bill, I knew you'd understand. Oh, I'm glad—so very glad. You've made me so happy.'

After a time:

'I hope——' I began again.

Josella patted my hand.

'You won't need to worry at all, my dear. I shall choose two nice, sensible girls.'

'Oh,' I said.

We went on sitting there on the wall hand in hand, looking at the dappled trees—but not seeing them very much, at least, I wasn't. Then in the building behind us someone started up a gramophone, playing a Strauss waltz. It was painfully nostalgic as it lilted through the empty courtyard. For an instant the road before us became the ghost of a ballroom; a swirl of colour, with the moon for a crystal chandelier.

Josella slid off the wall. With her arms outstretched, her wrists and fingers rippling, her body swaying, she danced, light as a thistledown, in a big circle in the moonlight. She came round to me, her eyes shining and her arms beckoning.

And we danced, on the brink of an unknown future, to an echo from a vanished past.

8. Frustration

I WAS walking through an unknown, deserted city where a bell rang dismally and a sepulchral, disembodied voice called in the emptiness: 'The Beast is Loose! Beware! The Beast is Loose!' when I woke to find that a bell really was ringing. It was a handbell that jangled with a brassy double clatter so harsh and startling that for a moment I could not remember where I was. Then, as I sat up still bemused, there came a sound of voices calling 'Fire!' I jumped just as I was from my blankets, and ran into the corridor. There was a smell of smoke there, a noise of hurried feet, doors banging. Most of the sound seemed to come from my right where the bell kept on clanging and the frightened voices were calling, so it was that way I turned and ran. A little moonlight filtered in through tall windows at the end of the passage, relieving the dimness just enough for me to keep to the middle of the way and avoid the people who were feeling their way along the walls.

I reached the stairs. The bell was still clanging in the hall below. I made my way down as fast as I could through smoke that grew thicker. Near the bottom I tripped and fell forward. The dimness became a sudden darkness in which a light burst like a cloud of needles, and that was all. . . .

The first thing was an ache in my head. The next was a glare when I opened my eyes. At the first blink it was as dazzling as a klieg light, but when I started again and edged the lids up more cautiously it turned out to be only an ordinary window, and grimy, at that. I knew I was lying on a bed, but I did not sit up to investigate further; there was a piston pounding away in my head that discouraged any kind of movement. So I lay there quietly, and studied the ceiling—until I discovered that my wrists were tied together.

That snapped me out of my lethargy, in spite of the thumping head. I found it a very neat job. Not painfully tight, but perfectly efficient. Several turns of insulated wire on each wrist, and a complex knot on the far side where it was impossible for me to reach it with my teeth. I swore a bit, and looked around. The room was small and, save for the bed on which I lay, empty.

'Hey!' I called. 'Anybody around here?'

After half a minute or so there was a shuffle of feet outside. The door was opened, and a head appeared. It was a small head with a tweed cap on the top of it. It had a stringy-looking choker beneath, and a dark unshavenness across its face. It was not turned straight at me, but in my general direction.

' 'Ullo, cock,' it said, amiably enough. 'So you've come to, 'ave yer? 'Ang on a bit, an' I'll get you a cup o' char.' And it vanished again.

The instruction to hang on was superfluous, but I did not have to wait long. In a few minutes he returned, carrying a wire-handled can with some tea in it.

'Where are yer?' he said.

'Straight ahead of you, on the bed,' I told him.

He groped forward with his left hand until he found the foot of the bed, then he felt his way round it, and held out the can.

' 'Ere, y'are, chum. It'll taste a bit funny-like 'cause ol' Charlie put a shot of rum in it, but I reckon you'll not mind that.'

I took it from him, holding it with some difficulty between my bound hands. It was strong and sweet, and the rum hadn't been stinted. The taste might be queer, but it worked like the elixir of life itself.'

'Thanks,' I said. 'You're a miracle worker. My name's Bill.'

His, it seemed, was Alf.

'What's the line, Alf? What goes on here?' I asked him.

He sat down on the side of the bed, and held out a packet of cigarettes with a box of matches. I took one, lit his first, then my own, and gave him back the box.

'It's this way, mate,' he said. 'You know there was a bit of a shindy up at the University yesterday morning—maybe you was there?'

I told him I'd seen it.

'Well, after that lark, Coker—he's the chap that did the talking—he got kinda peeved. "Hokay," 'e says, nasty-like. "The—— ——s've asked for it. I put it to 'em fair and square in the first place. Now they can take what's comin' to them." Well, we'd met up with a couple of other fellers and one old girl what can still see, an' they fixed it all up between them. He's a lad, that Coker.'

'You mean—he framed the whole business—there wasn't any fire or anything?' I asked.

'Fire—my aunt fanny! What they done was fix up a trip-wire or two, light a lot of paper and sticks in the hall, an' start in ringing the ol' bell. We reckoned that them as could see 'ud be the first along, on account of there bein' a bit of light still from the moon. And sure enough they was. Coker an' another chap was givin' them the k.o. as they tripped, an' passin' them along to some of us chaps to carry out to the lorry. Simple as kiss your 'and.'

'H'm,' I said, ruefully. 'Sounds efficient, that Coker. How many of us mugs fell into that little trap?'

'I d say we got a couple of dozen—though it turned out as five or six of 'em was blinded. When we'd loaded up about all we'd room for in the lorry, we beat it, and left the rest to sort theirselves out.'

Whatever view Coker took of us, it was clear that Alf bore us no animosity. He appeared to regard the whole affair as a bit of sport. I found it a little too painful to class it so, but I mentally raised my hat to Alf. I'd a pretty good idea that in his position I'd be lacking the spirit to think of anything as a bit of sport. I finished the tea, and accepted another cigarette from him.

'And what's the programme now?' I asked him.

'Coker's idea is to make us all up into parties, an' put one of you with each party. You to look after the scrounging, and kind of act as the eyes of the rest, like. Your job'll be to help us keep goin' until somebody comes along to straighten this perishin' lot out.'

'I see,' I said.

He cocked his head towards me. There weren't any flies on Alf. He had caught more in my tone than I had realized was there.

'You reckon that's goin' to be a long time?' he said.

'I don't know. What's Coker say?'

Coker, it seemed, had not been committing himself to details. Alf had his own opinion, though.

' 'F you ask me, I reckon there ain't nobody goin' to come. If there was, they'd've been 'ere before this. Different if we was in some little town in the country. But London! Stands to reason they'd come 'ere afore anywhere else. No, the way I see it, they ain't come yet—an' that means they ain't *never* goin' to come—an' *that* means there ain't nobody to come. Cor, blimey, 'oo'd ever've thought it could 'appen like this!'

I didn't say anything. Alf wasn't the sort to be jollied with facile encouragements.

'Reckon that's the way you see it, too?' he said, after a bit.

'It doesn't look so good,' I admitted. 'But there still is a chance, you know—people from somewhere abroad . . .'

He shook his head.

'They'd've come before this. They'd've had loud-speaker cars round the streets tellin' us what to do, before this. No, chum, we've 'ad it: there ain't nobody nowhere *to* come. That's the fact of it.'

We were silent for a while, then:

'Ah, well, 't'weren't a bad ole life while it lasted,' he said.

We talked a little about the kind of life it had been for him. He'd had various jobs, each of which seemed to have included some interesting under-cover work. He summed it up:

'One way an' another I didn't do so bad. What was your racket?'

I told him. He wasn't impressed.

'Triffids, huh! Nasty damn things, I reckon. Not natcheral as you might say.'

We left it at that.

Alf went away, leaving me to my cogitations and a packet of his cigarettes. I surveyed the outlook, and thought little of it. I wondered how the others would be taking it. Particularly what would be Josella's view.

I got off the bed, and went across to the window. The prospect was poor. An interior well with sheer, white-tiled sides for four storeys below me, and a glass skylight at the bottom. There wasn't much to be done that way. Alf had locked the door after him, but I tried it, just in case. Nothing in the room gave me inspiration. It had the look of belonging in a third-rate hotel, except that everything save the bed had been thrown out.

I sat down again on the bed, and pondered. I could perhaps tackle Alf successfully, even with my hands tied— providing he had no knife. But probably he had a knife, and that would be unpleasant. It would be no good a blind man threatening me with a knife; he would have to use it to disable me. Besides, there would be the difficulty of dis- covering what others I would have to pass before I could find my way out of the building. Moreover, I did not wish Alf any harm. It seemed wiser to wait for an opportunity— one was bound to come to a sighted man among the sightless.

An hour later Alf came back with a plate of food, a spoon, and more tea.

'Bit rough-like,' he apologized. 'But they said no knife and fork, so there it is.'

While I was tackling it I asked about the others. He couldn't tell me much, and didn't know any names, but I found out that there had been women as well as men among those that had been brought here. After that I was left alone for some hours which I spent doing my best to sleep off the headache.

When Alf reappeared with more food and the inevitable can of tea, he was accompanied by the man he had called Coker. He looked more tired now than when I had seen him before. Under his arm he carried a bundle of papers. He gave me a searching look.

'You know the idea?' he asked.

'What Alf's told me,' I admitted.

'All right, then.' He dropped his papers on the bed, picked up the top one and unfolded it. It was a street-plan of Greater London. He pointed to an area covering part of Hampstead and Swiss Cottage, heavily outlined in blue pencil.

'That's your beat,' he said. 'Your party works inside that area, and not in anyone else's area. You can't have each lot going after the same pickings. Your job is to find the food in that area, and see that your party gets it—that, and anything else they need. Got that?'

'Or what?' I said, looking at him.

'Or they'll get hungry. And if they do, it'll be just too bad for you. Some of the boys are tough, and we're not any of us doing this for fun. So watch your step. To-morrow morning we'll run you and your lot up there in lorries. After that it'll be your job to keep 'em going until somebody comes along to tidy things up.'

'And if nobody does come?' I asked.

'Somebody's *got* to come,' he said grimly. 'Anyway, there's your job—and mind you keep to your area.'

I stopped him as he was on the point of leaving.

'Have you got a Miss Playton here?' I asked.

'I don't know any of your names,' he said.

'Fair-haired, about five-foot six or seven, grey-blue eyes,' I persisted.

'There's a girl about that size, and blonde. But I haven't looked at her eyes. Got something more important to do,' he said, as he left.

I studied the map. I was not greatly taken with the district allotted to me. Some of it was a salubrious enough suburb, indeed, but in the circumstances a location that included docks and warehouses would have had more to offer. It was doubtful whether there would be any sizeable storage depots in this part. Still, 'can't all 'ave a prize' as Alf would doubtless express it—and anyway, I had no intention of staying there any longer than was strictly necessary.

When Alf showed up again I asked him if he would take a note to Josella. He shook his head.

'Sorry, mate. Not allowed.'

I promised him it should be harmless, but he remained firm. I couldn't altogether blame him. He had no reason to trust me, and would not be able to read the note to know that it was as harmless as I claimed. Anyway, I'd neither pencil nor paper, so I gave that up. After pressing, he did consent to let her know that I was here, and to find out the district to which she was being sent. He was not keen on doing that much, but he had to allow that if there were to be any straightening out of the mess it would be a lot easier for me to find her again if I knew where to start looking.

After that I had simply my thoughts for company for a bit.

The trouble was that I was not wholeheartedly set on any course. There was a damnable ability to see the points on both sides. I knew that commonsense and the long-term view backed up Michael Beadley and his lot. If they had started, Josella and I would doubtless have gone with them and worked with them—and yet I knew I would have been uneasy. I'd never be quite convinced that nothing could have been done for the sinking ship, never quite sure that I had not rationalized my own preference. If, indeed, there was *no* possibility of organized rescue, then their proposal to salvage what we could was the intelligent course. But, unfortunately, intelligence is by no means the only thing that makes the human wheels go round. I was up against the very conditioning that the old Doctor had said was so hard to break. He was dead right about the difficulty of adopting new principles. If, for instance, some kind of relief should miraculously arrive, I knew just what kind of a louse I'd feel to have cleared out, whatever the motives—and just how much I'd despise myself and the rest for not having stayed here in London to help for as long as it was possible.

But if, on the other hand, help did not come, how would

I have felt about having wasted my time and frittered my efforts away when stronger-minded people had started getting on with the salvage while the going was good?

I knew I ought to make my mind up once and for all on the right course, and stick to it. But I could not. I see-sawed. Some hours later when I fell asleep I was still see-sawing.

There was no means of knowing which way Josella had made up her mind. I'd had no personal message from her. But Alf had put his head in once during the evening. His communication had been brief.

'Westminster,' he said. 'Cor! Don't reckon that lot's goin' to find much grub in the 'Ouses o' Parliament.'

I was woken by Alf coming in early the following morning. He was accompanied by a bigger, shifty-eyed man who fingered a butcher's knife with unnecessary ostentation. Alf advanced, and dropped an armful of clothes on the bed. His companion shut the door, and leaned against it, watching with a crafty eye, and toying with the knife.

'Give us yer mitts, mate,' said Alf.

I held my hands out towards him. He felt for the wires on my wrists, and snipped them with a cutter.

'Now just you put on that there clobber, chum,' he said, stepping back.

I got myself dressed while the knife-fancier followed every movement I made, like a hawk. When I'd finished, Alf produced a pair of handcuffs. 'There's just these,' he mentioned.

I hesitated. The man by the door ceased to lean on it, and brought his knife forward a little. For him this was evidently the interesting moment. I decided maybe it was not the time to try anything, and held my wrists out. Alf felt around, and clicked on the cuffs. After that he went and fetched me my breakfast.

Nearly two hours later the other man turned up again, his knife well in evidence. He waved it at the door.

'C'mon,' he said. It was the only remark I ever heard him make.

With the consciousness of the knife producing an uncomfortable feeling in my back, we went down a number of flights of stairs, and across a hall. In the street two loaded lorries were waiting. Coker, with two companions, stood by the tailboard of one. He beckoned me over. Without saying anything he passed a chain between my arms. At each end of it was a strap. One was fastened already round the left wrist of a burly blind man beside him; the other he attached to the right wrist of a similar tough case, so that I was between them. They weren't taking any unavoidable chances.

'I'd not try any funny business, if I were you,' Coker advised me. 'You do right by them, and they'll do right by you.'

The three of us climbed awkwardly on to the tailboard, and the two lorries drove off.

We stopped somewhere near Swiss Cottage, and piled out. There were perhaps twenty people in sight, prowling with apparent aimlessness along the gutters. At the sound of the engines every one of them had turned towards us with an incredulous expression on his face, and as if they were parts of a single mechanism they began to close hopefully towards us, calling out as they came. The drivers shouted to us to get clear. They backed, turned, and rumbled off by the way we had come. The converging people stopped. One or two of them shouted after the lorries; most turned hopelessly and silently back to their wandering. There was one woman about fifty yards away; she broke into hysterics, and began to bang her head against a wall. I felt sick.

I turned towards my companions.

'Well, what do you want first?' I asked them.

'A billet,' said one. 'We got to 'ave some place to doss down.'

I reckoned I'd have to find that at least for them. I couldn't just dodge out and leave them stranded right where we were. Now we'd come this far, I couldn't do less than find them a centre, a kind of headquarters, and put them on their feet. What was wanted was a place where the receiving, storing, and feeding could be done, and the whole lot keep together. I counted them. There were fifty-two; fourteen of them women. The best course seemed to be to find a hotel. It would save the trouble of fitting out with beds and bedding.

The place we found was a kind of glorified boarding-house made up of four Victorian terrace-houses knocked together, giving more than the accommodation we needed. There were already half a dozen people in the place when we got there. Heaven knows what had happened to the rest. We found the remnant huddled together and scared in one of the lounges—an old man, an elderly woman (who turned out to have been the manageress) a middle-aged man, and three girls. The manageress had the spirit to pull herself together and hand out some quite high-sounding threats, but the ice, even of her most severe boarding-house manner, was thin. The old man tried to back her up by blustering a bit. The rest did nothing but keep their faces turned nervously towards us.

I explained that we were moving in. If they did not like it, they could go; if, on the other hand, they preferred to stay and share equally what there was, they were free to do so. They were not pleased. The way they reacted suggested that somewhere in the place they had a cache of stores that they were not anxious to share. When they grasped that the intention was to build up bigger stores their attitude modified perceptibly, and they prepared to make the best of it.

I decided I'd have to stay on a day or two just to get the party set up. I guessed Josella would be feeling much the same about her lot. Ingenious man, Coker—the trick is called holding the baby. But after that I'd dodge out and join her.

During that next couple of days we worked systematically, tackling the bigger stores nearby—mostly chain-stores, and not very big, at that. Nearly everywhere there had been others before us. The fronts of the shops were in a bad way. The windows were broken in, the floors were littered with half-opened cans and spilt packages which had disappointed the finders, and now lay in a sticky, stinking mass among the fragments of window-glass. But as a rule the loss was small and the damage superficial, and we'd find the larger cases in and behind the shop untouched.

It was far from easy for blind men to carry and manoeuvre heavy cases out of the place and load them on handcarts. Then there was the job of getting them back to the billet, and stowing them. But practice began to give them a knack with it.

The most hampering factor was the necessity for my presence. Little or nothing could go on unless I was there to direct. It was impossible to use more than one working party at a time, though we could have made up a dozen. Nor could much go on back at the hotel while I was out with foraging squads. Moreover, such time as I had to spend investigating and prospecting the district was pretty much wasted for everyone else. Two sighted men could have got through a lot more than twice the work.

Once we had started I was too busy during the day to

spend much thought beyond the actual work in hand, and too tired at night to do anything but sleep the moment I lay down. Now and again I'd say to myself, 'by to-morrow night I'll have them pretty well fixed up—enough to keep them going for a bit, anyway. Then I'll light out of this, and find Josella.'

That sounded all right—but every day it was to-morrow that I'd be able to do it, and each day it became more difficult. Some of them had begun to learn a bit, but still practically nothing, from foraging to can-opening, could go on without my being around. It seemed, the way things were going, that I became less, instead of more dispensable.

None of it was their fault. That was what made it difficult. Some of them were trying so damned hard. I just had to watch them making it more and more impossible for me to play the skunk and walk out on them. A dozen times a day I cursed the man Coker for contriving me into the situation —but that didn't help to solve it: it just left me wondering how it could end. . . .

I had my first inkling of that, though I scarcely recognized it as such, on the fourth morning—or maybe it was the fifth —just as we were setting out. A woman called down the stairs that there were two sick up there; pretty bad, she thought.

My two watchdogs did not like it.

'Listen,' I told them. 'I've had about enough of this chain-gang stuff. We'd be doing a lot better than we are now without it, anyway.'

'An' have you slinkin' off to join your old mob?' said someone.

'I'd not fool yourself,' I said. 'I could have slugged this pair of amateur gorillas any hour of the day or night. I've not done it because I've got nothing against them other than their being a pair of dim-witted nuisances. . . .'

' 'Ere——' one of my attachments began to expostulate.

'But,' I went on, 'if they don't let me see what's wrong with these people, they can begin expecting to be slugged any minute from now.'

The two saw reason, but when we reached the room, they took good care to stand as far back as the chain allowed. The casualties turned out to be two men, one young, one middle-aged. Both had high temperatures and complained of agonized pain in the bowels. I didn't know much about such things then, but I did not need to know much to feel worried. I could think of nothing but to direct that they should be carried to an empty house nearby, and to tell one of the women to look after them as best she could.

That was the beginning of a day of setbacks. The next, of a very different kind, happened around noon.

We had cleared most of the food-shops close to us, and I had decided to extend our range a little. From my recollections of the neighbourhood I reckoned we ought to find another shopping street above half a mile to the north, so I led my party that way. We found the shops there, all right, but something else, too.

As we turned the corner and came into view of them, I stopped. In front of a chain-store grocery a party of men were trundling out cases and loading them on to a lorry. Save for the difference in the vehicle, I might have been watching my own party at work. I halted my group of twenty or so, wondering what line we should take. My inclination was to withdraw and avoid possible trouble by finding a clear field elsewhere; there was no sense in coming into conflict when there was plenty scattered in various stores for those who were organized enough to take it. But it did not fall to me to make the decision. Even while I hesitated a red-headed young man strode confidently out of

the shop door. There was no doubt that he was able to see—
or, a moment later, that he had seen us.

He did not share my indecision. He reached swiftly for
his pocket. The next moment a bullet hit the wall beside me
with a smack.

There was a brief tableau. His men and mine turning their
sightless eyes towards one another in an effort to understand what was going on. Then he fired again. I supposed
he had aimed at me, but the bullet found the man on my left.
He gave a grunt as though he was surprised, and folded up
with a kind of sigh. I dodged back round the corner,
dragging the other watchdog with me.

'Quick,' I said. 'Give me the key to these cuffs. I can't do
a thing, like this.'

He didn't do anything except give a knowing grin. He
was a one-idea man.

'Huh,' he said. 'Come orf it. You don't fool me.'

'Oh, for God's sake, you damned clown——' I said,
pulling on the chain to drag the body of watchdog number
one nearer so that we could get better cover.

The goon started to argue. Heaven knows what subtleties
his dim wits were crediting me with. There was enough
slack on the chain now for me to raise my arms. I did, and
hammered both fists at his head so that it went back against
the wall with a crack. That disposed of his argument. I
found the key in his side pocket.

'Listen,' I told the rest. 'Turn round, all of you, and keep
going straight ahead. Don't separate, or you'll have had it.
Get moving now.'

I got one wristlet open, ridded myself of the chain, and
scrambled over the wall into somebody's garden. I crouched
there while I got rid of the other cuff. Then I moved across
to peer cautiously over the far angle of the wall. The young
man with the pistol had not come rushing after us as I had

half-expected. He was still with his party, giving them an instruction. And now I came to think of it, why should he hurry? Since we had not fired back at him he could reckon we were unarmed, and we wouldn't be able to get away fast.

When he'd finished his directions he walked out confidently into the road to a point where he had a view of my retreating group, and then began to follow them. At the corner he stopped to look at the two prone watchdogs. Probably the chain suggested to him that one of them had been the eyes of our gang, for he put the pistol back in his pocket and began to follow the rest in a leisurely fashion.

That wasn't what I had expected, and it took me a minute to see his scheme. Then it came to me that his most profitable course would be to follow them to our headquarters, and see what pickings he could hijack there. He was, I had to admit, either much quicker than I at spotting chances, or had previously given more thought to the possibilities that might arise than I had. I was glad that I had told my lot to keep straight on. Most likely they'd get tired of it after a bit, but I reckoned they'd none of them be able to find the way back to the hotel and so lead him to it. As long as they kept together, I'd be able to collect them all later on without much difficulty. The immediate question was what to do about a man who carried a pistol, and didn't mind using it.

In some parts of the world one might go into the first house in sight, and pick up a convenient firearm. Hampstead was not like that; it was a highly respectable suburb, unfortunately. There might possibly be a sporting gun to be found somewhere, but I would have to hunt for it. The only thing I could think of was to keep him in sight and hope that some opportunity would offer a chance to deal with him. I broke a branch off a tree, scrambled back over the wall, and began to tap my way along the kerb, looking, I hoped, indistinguishable from the hundreds of blind men one had seen wandering the streets in the same way.

The road ran straight for some distance. The red-headed young man was perhaps fifty yards ahead of me, and my party another fifty ahead of him. We continued like that for something over half a mile. To my relief, none of the front party showed any tendency to turn into the road which led to our base. I was beginning to wonder how long it would be before they decided that they had gone far enough, when an unexpected diversion occurred. One man who had been lagging behind the rest finally stopped. He dropped his stick, and doubled up with his arms over his belly. Then he sagged to the ground and lay there, rolling with pain. The others did not stop for him. They must have heard his moans but probably they had no idea he was one of themselves.

The young man looked towards him, and hesitated. He altered his course, and bore across towards the contorted figure. He stopped a few feet away from him, and stood gazing down. For perhaps a quarter of a minute he regarded him carefully. Then slowly, but quite deliberately, he pulled his pistol out of his pocket, and shot him through the head.

The party ahead stopped at the sound of the shot. So did I. The young man made no attempt to catch up with them— in fact, he seemed suddenly to lose interest in them altogether. He turned round, and came walking back down the middle of the road. I remembered to play my part, and began to tap my way forward again. He paid me no attention as he passed, but I was able to see his face: it was worried, and there was a grim set to his jaw. . . . I kept going as I was until he was a decent distance behind me, then I hurried on to the rest. Brought up short by the sound of the shot, they were arguing whether to go on further or not.

I broke that off by telling them that now I was no longer encumbered with my two *i.q.*-minus watchdogs we would be ordering things differently. I was going to get a lorry, and I would be back in ten minutes or so to run them back to the billet in it.

The finding of another organized party at work produced a new anxiety, but we found the place intact. The only news they had for me there was that two more men and a woman had been taken with severe belly pains and removed to the other house.

We made what preparations we could for defence against any marauders arriving while I was away. Then I picked a new party, and we set off in the lorry, this time in a different direction.

I recalled that in former days when I had come up to Hampstead Heath it had often been by way of a bus terminus where a number of small shops and stores clustered. With the aid of the street-plan I found the place again easily enough—not only found it, but discovered it to be marvellously intact. Save for three or four broken windows, the area looked simply as if it had been closed up for a week-end.

But there were differences. For one thing, no such silence had ever before hung over the locality, weekday or Sunday. And there were several bodies lying in the street. By this time one was becoming accustomed enough to that to pay them little attention. I had, in fact, wondered that there were not more to be seen, and had come to the conclusion that most people sought some kind of shelter either out of fear, or later when they became weak. It was one of the reasons that one felt a disinclination to enter any dwelling-house.

I stopped the lorry in front of a provision store and listened for a few seconds. The silence came down on us like a blanket. There was no sound of tapping sticks, not a wanderer in sight. Nothing moved.

'Okay,' I said. 'Pile out, chaps.'

The locked door of the shop gave way easily. Inside there was a neat, unspoiled array of tubs of butter, cheeses, sides of bacon, cases of sugar, and all the rest of it. I got the others busy. They had developed tricks of working by now, and were more sure of their handling. I was able to leave them to get on with it for a bit while I examined the back store-room and then the cellar.

It was while I was below, investigating the nature of the cases down there that I heard a sound of shouts somewhere outside. Close upon it came a thunder of trampling boots on the floor above me. One man came down through the trap-door, and pitched on his head. He did not move or make another sound. I jumped to it that there must be a battle with a rival gang in progress up there. I stepped across the fallen man, and climbed the ladder-like stair cautiously, holding up one arm to protect my head.

The first view was of numerous scuffling boots, unpleasantly close, and backing towards the trap. I nipped up quickly and got clear before they were on me. I was up just in time to see the plate-glass window in the front give way. Three men from outside fell in with it. A long green lash whipped after them, striking one as he lay. The other two scrambled among the wreckage of the display, and came stumbling further into the shop. They pressed back against the rest, and two more men fell through the open trap-door.

It did not need more than a glimpse of that lash to tell what had happened. During the work of the past few days I had all but forgotten the triffids. By standing on a box I could see over the heads of the men. There were three triffids in my field of view: one out in the road, and two

closer, on the pavement. Four men lay on the ground out
there, not moving. I understood then why these shops had
been untouched; and why there had been no one to be seen
in the neighbourhood of the Heath. At the same time I
cursed myself for not having looked at the bodies in the
road more closely. One glimpse of a sting mark would have
been enough warning.

'Hold it,' I shouted. 'Stand where you are.'

I jumped down from the box, pushed away the men who
were standing on the folded back lid of the trap, and got it
closed.

'There's a door back here,' I told them. 'Take it easy
now.'

The first two took it easy. Then a triffid sent its sting
whistling into the room through the broken window. One
man gave a scream as he fell. The rest came on in panic, and
swept me before them. There was a jam in the doorway.
Behind us stings swished twice again before we were
clear.

In the back room I looked round panting. There were
seven of us there.

'Hold it,' I said again. 'We're all right in here.'

I went back to the door. The rear part of the shop was
out of the triffids' range—as long as they stayed outside. I
was able to reach the trap-door in safety, and raise it. The
two men who had fallen down there since I left re-emerged.
One nursed a broken arm; the other was merely bruised,
and cursing.

Behind the back room lay a small yard, and across that a
door in an eight-foot brick wall. I had grown cautious.
Instead of going straight to the door I climbed on the roof
of an outhouse to prospect. The door, I could see, gave into
a narrow alley running the full length of the block. It was
empty. But beyond the wall on the far side which seemed to

terminate the gardens of a row of private houses, I could make out the tops of two triffids motionless among the bushes. There might well be more. The wall on that side was lower, and their height would enable them to strike right across the alley with their stings. I explained to the others.

'Bloody unnatural brutes,' said one. 'I always did hate them bastards.'

I investigated further. The building next but one to the north side turned out to be a car-hire service with three of its cars on the premises. It was an awkward job getting the party over the two intervening walls, particularly the man with the broken arm, but we managed it. Somehow, too, I got them all packed into a large Daimler. When we were all set I opened the outer doors of the place, and ran back to the car.

The triffids weren't slow to be interested. That uncanny sensitiveness to sounds told them something was happening. As we drove out, a couple of them were already lurching towards the entrance. Their stings whipped out at us, and slapped harmlessly against the closed windows. I swung hard round, bumping one, and toppling it over. Then we were away up the road, making for a healthier neighbourhood.

The evening that followed was the worst I had spent since the calamity occurred. Freed of the two watchdogs, I took over a small room where I could be alone. I put six lighted candles in a row on the mantelshelf, and sat a long while in an armchair, trying to think things out. We had come back to find that one of the men who had been taken sick the night before was dead; the other was obviously dying—and there were four new cases. By the time our evening meal was over, there were two more still. What the complaint was I had no idea. With the lack of service and the way things were going in general, it might have been a number of things. I thought of typhoid, but I'd a hazy idea that the incubation period ruled that out—not that it would have made much difference if I had known. All I did know about it was that it was something nasty enough to make that red-haired young man use his pistol, and change his mind about following my party.

It began to look to me as if I had been doing my group a questionable service from the first. I had succeeded in keeping them alive, placed between a rival gang on one side, and triffids encroaching from the Heath on the other. Now there was this sickness, too. And, when all was said and done, I had achieved only the postponement of starvation for a little while.

As things were now, I did not see my way.

And then there was Josella on my mind. The same sorts of things, maybe worse, were as likely to be happening in her district. . . .

I found myself thinking of Michael Beadley and his lot again. I had known then that they were logical, now I began to think that perhaps they had a truer humanity, too. They had seen that it was hopeless to try to save any but a very few. To give an empty hope to the rest was little better than cruelty.

Besides, there were ourselves. If there were purpose in anything at all, what had we been preserved for? Not simply to waste ourselves on a forlorn task, surely . . .?

I decided that to-morrow I would go in search of Josella, and we would settle it together. . . .

The latch of the door moved with a click. The door itself opened slowly.

'Who's that?' I said.

'Oh, it *is* you,' said a girl's voice.

F

She came in, closing the door behind her.

'What do you want?' I asked.

She was tall and slim. Under twenty I guessed. Her hair waved slightly. Chestnut-coloured, it was. She was quiet, but one had to notice her—it was the texture of her as well as the line. She had placed my position by my movement and voice. Her gold-brown eyes were looking just over my left shoulder, otherwise I'd have been sure she was studying me.

She did not answer at once. It was an uncertainty which did not seem to suit the rest of her. I went on waiting for her to speak. A lump got into my throat somehow. You see, she was young, and she was beautiful. There should have been all life, maybe a wonderful life before her. . . . And isn't there something a little sad about youth and beauty in any circumstances . . .?

'You're going to go away from here?' she said. It was half question, half statement, in a quiet voice, a little unsteadily.

'I've never said that,' I countered.

'No,' she admitted, 'but that's what the others are saying —and they're right, aren't they?'

I did not say anything to that. She went on:

'You can't. You can't leave them like this. They need you.'

'I'm doing no good here,' I told her. 'All the hopes are false.'

'But suppose they turned out not to be false?'

'They can't—not now. We'd have known by this time.'

'But if they did, after all—and you had simply walked out——?'

'Do you think I haven't thought of that? I'm not doing any good, I tell you. I've been like the drugs they inject to keep the patient going a little longer—no curative value; just putting it off.'

She did not reply for some seconds. Then she said, unsteadily:

'Life is very precious—even like this.' Her control almost cracked.

I could not say anything. She recovered herself.

'You can keep us going. There's always a chance—just a chance that something may happen, even now.'

I had already said what I thought about that. I did not repeat it.

'It's so difficult,' she said, as though to herself. 'If I could only *see* you. . . . But then, of course, if I could . . . Are you young? You sound young.'

'I'm under thirty,' I told her. 'And very ordinary.'

'I'm eighteen. It was my birthday—the day the comet came.'

I could not think of anything to say to that that would not seem cruel. The pause drew out. I saw that she was clenching her hands together. Then she dropped them to her sides, the knuckles quite white. She made as if to speak, but did not.'

'What is it?' I asked. 'What can I do except prolong this a little?'

She bit her lip, then:

'They—they said perhaps you were lonely,' she said. 'I thought perhaps if'—her voice faltered, and her knuckles went a little whiter still—'perhaps if you had somebody . . . I mean, somebody here . . . you—you might not want to leave us. Perhaps you'd stay with us?'

'Oh, God,' I said, softly.

I looked at her, standing quite straight, her lips trembling slightly. There should have been suitors clamouring for her lightest smile. She should have been happy and uncaring for a while—then happy in caring. Life should have been enchanting to her, and love very sweet. . . .

'You'd be kind to me, wouldn't you?' she said. 'You see I haven't——'

'Stop it! Stop it!' I told her. 'You mustn't say these things to me. Please go away now.'

But she did not go. She stood staring at me from eyes that could not see me.

'Go away!' I repeated.

I could not stand the reproach of her. She was not simply herself—she was thousands upon thousands of young lives destroyed. . . .

She came closer.

'Why, I believe you're crying!' she said.

'Go away. For God's sake, go away!' I told her.

She hesitated, then she turned and felt her way back to the door. As she went out:

'You can tell them I'll be staying,' I said.

The first thing I was aware of the next morning was the smell. There had been whiffs of it here and there before, but luckily the weather had been cool. Now I found that I had slept late into what was already a warmer day. I'm not going into details about that smell, those who knew it will never forget it, for the rest it is indescribable. It rose from every city and town for weeks, and travelled on every wind that blew. When I woke to it that morning it convinced me beyond doubt that the end had come. Death is just the shocking end of animation: it is dissolution that is final.

I lay for some minutes thinking. The only thing to do now would be to load my party into lorries and take them in relays into the country. And all the supplies we had collected? They would have to be loaded and taken, too—and

I the only one able to drive. . . . It would take days—if we
had days. . . .

Upon that, I wondered what was happening in the building now. The place was oddly quiet. When I listened I could
hear a voice groaning in another room, beyond that nothing.
I got out of bed and hurried into my clothes with a feeling
of alarm. Out on the landing, I listened again. There was no
sound of feet about the house. I had a sudden nasty feeling
as if history were repeating itself and I were back in the
hospital again.

'Hey! Anybody here?' I called.

Several voices answered. I opened a nearby door. There
was a man in there. He looked very bad, and he was
delirious. There was nothing I could do. I closed the door
again.

My footsteps sounded loud on the wooden stairs. On the
next floor a woman's voice called: 'Bill—Bill!'

She was in bed in a small room there, the girl who had
come to see me the night before. She turned her head as I
came in. I saw that she had it, too.

'Don't come near,' she said. 'It *is* you, Bill?'

'I thought it must be. You can still walk: they have to
creep. I'm glad, Bill. I told them you'd not go like that—but
they said you had. Now they've all gone, all of them that
could.'

'I was asleep,' I said. 'What happened?'

'More and more of us like this. They were frightened.'

I said helplessly: 'What can I do for you? Is there anything I can get you?'

Her face contorted, she clutched her arms round her, and
writhed. The spasm passed, and left her with sweat trickling
down her forehead.

'Please, Bill. I'm not very brave. Could you get me
something to—to finish it?'

'Yes,' I said. 'I can do that for you.'

I was back from the chemist's in ten minutes. I gave her a glass of water, and put the stuff in her other hand.

She held it there a little. Then:

'So futile—and it might all have been so different,' she said. 'Good-bye, Bill—and thank you for trying.'

I looked down at her lying there. There was a thing that made it still more futile—I wondered how many would have said, 'Take me with you,' where she had said, 'Stay with us.'

And I never even knew her name.

9. Evacuation

IT was the memory of the red-headed young man who had fired on us that conditioned my choice of a route to Westminster.

Since I was sixteen my interest in weapons has decreased, but in an environment reverting to savagery it seemed that one must be prepared to behave more or less as a savage, or possibly cease to behave at all before long. In St. James's Street there used to be several shops which would sell you any form of lethalness from a rook-rifle to an elephant-gun with the greatest urbanity.

I left there with a mixed feeling of support and banditry. Once more I had a useful hunting-knife. There was a pistol with the precise workmanship of a scientific instrument in my pocket. On the seat beside me rested a loaded twelve-bore and boxes of cartridges. I had chosen a shot-gun in preference to a rifle—the bang is no less convincing, and it decapitates a triffid with a neatness which a bullet seldom achieves. And there were triffids to be seen right in London now. They still appeared to avoid the streets when they could, but I had noticed several lumbering across Hyde Park, and there were others in the Green Park. Very likely they were ornamental, safely docked specimens—on the other hand, maybe they weren't.

167

And so I came to Westminster.

The deadness, the finish of it all, was italicized there. The usual scatter of abandoned vehicles lay about the streets. Very few people were in sight. I saw only three who were moving. Two were tapping their way down the gutters of Whitehall, the third was in Parliament Square. He was sitting close to Lincoln's statue, and clutching to him his dearest possession—a side of bacon from which he was hacking a ragged slice with a blunt knife.

Above it all rose the Houses of Parliament, with the hands of the clock stopped at three minutes past six. It was difficult to believe that all that meant nothing any more, that now it was just a pretentious confection in uncertain stone which could decay in peace. Let it shower its crumbling pinnacles on to the terrace as it would—there would be no more indignant members complaining of the risk to their valuable lives. Into those halls which had in their day set world echoes to good intentions and sad expediencies the roofs could in due course fall; there would be none to stop them, and none to care. Alongside, the Thames flowed imperturbably on. So it would flow until the day the Embankments crumbled and the water spread out and Westminster became once more an island in a marsh.

Marvellously clear-fretted in the unsmoked air, the Abbey rose, silver-grey. It stood detached by the serenity of age from the ephemeral growths around it. It was solid on a foundation of centuries, destined, perhaps, for centuries yet to preserve within it the monuments to those whose work was now all destroyed.

I did not loiter there. In years to come I expect some will go to look at the old Abbey with romantic melancholy. But romance of that kind is an alloy of tragedy with retrospect. I was too close.

Moreover, I was beginning to experience something new

—the fear of being alone. I had not been alone since I walked from the hospital along Piccadilly, and then there had been bewildering novelty in all I saw. Now, for the first time I began to feel the horror that real loneliness holds for a species that is by nature gregarious. I felt naked, exposed to all the fears that prowled. . . .

I made myself drive on up Victoria Street. The sound of the car itself alarmed me with its echoes. My impulse was to leave it and sneak silently on foot, seeking safety in cunning, like a beast in the jungle. It needed all my will power to keep myself steady and hold to my plan. For I knew what I should have done had I chanced to be allocated to this district—I should have sought supplies in its biggest department-store.

Somebody had stripped the provision department of the Army and Navy Stores, all right, but there was no one there now.

I came out by a side door. A cat on the pavement was engaged in sniffing at something which might have been a bundle of rags, but was not. I clapped my hands at it. It glared at me, and then slunk off.

A man came round a corner. He had a gloating expression on his face, and was perseveringly rolling a large cheese along the middle of the road. When he heard my step he halted his cheese, and sat on it, brandishing his stick fiercely. I went back to my car in the main street.

The probability was that Josella, too, would have chosen a hotel as a convenient headquarters. I remembered that there were several around Victoria Station, so I drove on there. It turned out that there were vastly more of them than I had thought. After I had looked into a score or more without finding any evidence of organized squatting, it began to seem pretty hopeless.

I looked for someone to ask. There seemed a chance that

anyone still alive here might owe it to her. I had seen only half a dozen capable of moving since I arrived in the district. Now there seemed to be none. But at last, near the corner of Buckingham Palace Road, I came across an old woman sitting huddled on a doorstep.

She was tearing at a tin, with broken finger-nails, and alternately cursing and whimpering over it. I went to a small shop nearby and found half a dozen tins of beans over-looked on a high shelf, I discovered a tin-opener, too, and went back to her. She was still futilely scrabbling away at her tin.

'You'd better throw that away. It's coffee,' I told her.

I put the opener into her hand, and gave her a tin of beans.

'Listen to me,' I said. 'Do you know anything of a girl round here—a girl that can see? She'd be in charge of a party, most likely.'

I was not very hopeful, but something must have helped the old woman to keep going longer than most. It seemed almost too good to be true when she nodded.

'Yes,' she said, as she started the opener.

'You do! Where is she?' I demanded. Somehow it never occurred to me that it could be anyone but Josella.

But she shook her head.

'I don't know. I was with her lot for a bit, but I lost 'em. An old woman like me can't keep up with the young ones, so I lost 'em. They'd not wait for a poor old woman, and I couldn't never find 'em again.'

She went on cutting intently round the tin.

'Where is she living?' I asked.

'We was all in a 'otel. Dunno where it is, or I'd've found 'em again.'

'Don't you know the name of the hotel?'

'Not me. 'T'ain't no good knowing the names of places

when you can't see to read 'em, nor nobody else can't, neither.'

'But you must remember something about it.'

'No, I don't.'

She lifted the can, and sniffed cautiously at the contents.

'Look here,' I said, coldly. 'You want to keep those tins, don't you?'

She made a movement with one arm to gather them all to her.

'Well, then, you'd better tell me all you can about that hotel,' I went on. 'You must know, for instance, whether it was large or small.'

She considered, one arm still protectively about the tins.

'Downstairs it sounded sort of hollow—like it might be biggish. Likely it was smart, too—what I mean, it 'ad them quiet carpets, an' good beds, an' good sheets.'

'Nothing else about it?'

'No, not as I—— Yes, there was, though. It 'ad two small steps outside, an' you went in through one of them round-and-round doors.'

'That's better,' I said. 'You're quite sure of that? If I can't find it, I *can* find you again, you know.'

' 'S Gawd's truth, mister. Two small steps, an' a round-and-round door.'

She rummaged in a battered bag beside her, brought out a dirty spoon, and began to taste the beans as if they were one of the jams of paradise.

There were, I found, still more hotels round there than I had thought, and a surprising number of them had round-and-round doors. But I kept on. There was no mistaking it when I did find it. The traces and the smell were all too familiar.

'Anybody here?' I called, in the echoing lounge.

I was about to go further in when a groan came from one

corner. Over in a semi-dark recess a man was lying on a
settee. Even in the dimness it was possible to see that he
was far gone. I did not go too close. His eyes opened. For a
moment I thought that he could see.

'You there?' he said.

'Yes, I want to——'

'Water,' he said. 'Fer Christ's sake gimme some
water——'

I went across to the dining-room, and found the service-
room beyond. The taps were dry. I squirted a couple of
syphons into a big jug, and took it back with a cup. I put
them down where he could reach them.

'Thanks, mate,' he said. 'I can manage. You keep clear
o' me.'

He dipped the cup into the jug, and then drained it.

'Gawd,' he said. 'Did I need that!' And he repeated the
action. 'Wotcher doin', mate? 'T'ain't 'ealthy round 'ere,
you know.'

'I'm looking for a girl—a girl who can see. Her name's
Josella. Is she here?'

'She *was* here. But you're too late. chum.'

A sudden suspicion struck me like a physical stab.

'You—you don't mean——?'

'No. Ease orf, mate. She ain't got what I got. No, she's
just gone—same as all the rest what could.'

'Where did she go, do you know?'

'Can't tell you that, mate.'

'I see,' I said, heavily.

'You'd best be goin', too, chum. 'Ang around 'ere long,
an' you'll be stayin' for keeps, like me.'

He was right. I stood looking down at him.

'Anything else I can get you?'

'No. This'll last me. I reckon it won't be much longer I'll
need anything.' He paused. Then he added: ' 'Bye, mate,

'n' thanks a lot. An' if you do find 'er, look after 'er proper—
she's a good girl.'

While I was making a meal off tinned ham and bottled
beer a little later, it occurred to me that I had not asked the
man when Josella had left, but I decided that in his state he
would be unlikely to have any clear idea of time.

The one place I could think of to go to was the University
Building. I reckoned Josella would think the same—and
there was a hope that some others of our dispersed party
might have drifted back there in an effort to reunite. It was
not a very strong hope, for commonsense should have caused
them to leave the town days ago.

Two flags still hung above the tower, limp in the warm air
of the early evening. Of the two dozen or so lorries that had
been accumulated in the forecourt, four still stood there,
apparently untouched. I parked the car beside them, and
went into the building. My footsteps clattered in the silence.

'Hullo! Hullo, there!' I called. 'Is there anyone here?'

My voice echoed away down corridors and up wells,
diminishing to the parody of a whisper and then to silence.
I went to the doors of the other wing and called again. Once
more the echoes died away unbroken, settling softly as dust.
Only then as I turned back did I notice that an inscription
had been chalked on the wall inside the outer door. In large
letters it gave simply an address:

TYNSHAM MANOR
TYNSHAM
Nr. DEVIZES
WILTS.

That was something, at least.

I looked at it, and thought. In another hour or less it
would be dusk. Devizes I guessed at a hundred miles distant,
probably more. I went outside again and examined the

lorries. One of them was the last that I had driven in—the one in which I had stowed my despised anti-triffid gear. I recalled that the rest of its load was a useful assortment of food and supplies. It would be much better to arrive with that, than empty-handed in a car. Nevertheless, if there were no urgent reason for it, I did not fancy driving anything, much less a large, heavily-loaded lorry, by night along roads which might reasonably be expected to produce a number of hazards. If I were to pile it up, and the odds were that I should, I would lose a lot more time in finding another and transferring the load than I would by spending the night here. An early start in the morning offered much better prospects. I moved my boxes of cartridges from the car to the cab of the lorry in readiness. The gun I kept with me.

I found the room from which I had rushed to the fake fire-alarm, exactly as I had left it; my clothes on a chair, even the cigarette-case and lighter where I had placed them beside my improvised bed.

It was still too early to think of sleep. I lit a cigarette, put the case in my pocket, and decided to go out.

Before I went into the Russell Square garden I looked it over carefully. I had already begun to be suspicious of open spaces. Sure enough I spotted one triffid. It was in the northwest corner, standing perfectly still, but considerably taller than the bushes that surrounded it. I went closer, and blew the top of it to bits with a single shot. The noise in the silent Square could scarcely have been more alarming if I had let off a howitzer. When I was sure that there were no others lurking I went into the garden and sat, with my back against a tree.

I stayed there perhaps twenty minutes. The sun was low, and half the Square was thrown into shadow. Soon I would have to go in. While there was light I could sustain myself; in the dark, things could steal quietly upon me. Already I was on my way back to the primitive. Before long, perhaps, I should be spending the hours of darkness in fear as my remote ancestors must have done, watching, ever distrustfully, the night outside their cave. I delayed to take one more look around the Square as if it were a page of history I would learn before it was turned. And as I stood there, I heard the gritting of footsteps on the road—a slight sound, but as loud in the silence as a grinding millstone.

I turned, with my gun ready. Crusoe was no more startled at the sight of a footprint than I at the sound of a footfall, for it had not the hesitancy of a blind man's. I caught a glimpse in the dim light of the moving figure. As it left the road and entered the garden I saw that it was a man. Evidently he had seen me before I heard him, for he was coming straight towards me.

'You don't need to shoot,' he said, holding empty hands wide apart.

I did not know him until he came within a few yards. Simultaneously he recognized me.

'Oh, it's you, is it?' he said.

I kept the gun raised.

'Hullo, Coker. What are you after? Wanting me to go on another of your little parties?' I asked him.

'No. You can put that thing down. Makes too much noise, anyway. That's how I found you. No,' he repeated, 'I've had enough. I'm getting to hell out of here.'

'So am I,' I said, and lowered the gun.

'What happened to your bunch?' he asked.

I told him. He nodded.

'Same with mine. Same with the rest, I expect. Still, we tried . . .'

'The wrong way,' I said.

He nodded again.

'Yes,' he admitted. 'I reckon your lot did have the right

idea from the start—only it didn't *look* right, and it didn't sound right a week ago.'

'Six days ago,' I corrected him.

'A week,' said he.

'No, I'm sure—oh, well, what the hell's it matter, anyway?' I said. 'In the circumstances,' I went on, 'what do you say to declaring an amnesty, and starting over again?'

He agreed.

'I'd got it wrong,' he repeated. 'I thought I was the one who was taking it seriously—but I wasn't taking it seriously enough. I couldn't believe that it would last, or that some kind of help wouldn't show up. But now look at it! And it must be like this everywhere. Europe, Asia, America—think of America smitten like this! But they must be. If they weren't, they'd have been over here, helping out and getting the place straight—that's the way it'd take them. No, I reckon your lot understood it better from the start.'

We ruminated for some moments, then I asked:

'This disease, plague—what do you reckon it is?'

'Search me, chum. I thought it must be typhoid, but someone said typhoid takes longer to develop—so I'd not know. I don't know why I've not caught it myself—except that I've been able to keep away from those that have, and to see that what I was eating was clean. I've been keeping to tins I've opened myself, and I've drunk only bottled beer. Anyway, though I've been lucky so far, I don't fancy hanging around here much longer. Where do *you* go now?'

I told him of the address chalked on the wall. He had not yet seen it. He had been on his way to the University Building when the sound of my shot had caused him to scout round with some caution.

'It——' I began, and then stopped abruptly. From one of the streets west of us came the sound of a car starting. It ran up its gears quickly, and then diminished into the distance.

'Well, at least there's somebody else left,' said Coker. '*And* whoever wrote up that address. Have you any idea who that would be?'

I shrugged my shoulders. It was a justifiable assumption that it was a returned member of the group that Coker had raided—or possibly some sighted person that his party had failed to catch. There was no telling how long it had been there. He thought it over.

'It'll be better if there's two of us. I'll tag along with you and see what's doing. Okay?'

'Okay,' I agreed. 'I'm for turning in now, and an early start to-morrow.'

He was still asleep when I awoke. I dressed myself much more comfortably in the ski-suit and heavy shoes than in the garments I had been wearing since his party had provided them for me. By the time I returned with a bag of assorted packets and tins, he was up and dressed, too. Over breakfast we decided to improve our welcome at Tynsham by taking a loaded lorry each rather than travel together in one.

'And see that the cab window closes,' I suggested. 'There are quite a lot of triffid nurseries around London, particularly to the west.'

'Uh-huh. I've seen a few of the ugly brutes about,' he said, offhandedly.

'I've seen them about—and in action,' I told him.

At the first garage we came to we broke open a pump and filled up. Then, sounding in the silent streets like a convoy of tanks, we set off westwards with my three-tonner in the lead.

The going was wearisome. Every few dozen yards one had to weave round some derelict vehicle. Occasionally two or three together would block the road entirely so that it was necessary to go dead slow and nudge one of them out of the way. Very few of them were wrecked. The blindness seemed to have come upon the drivers swiftly, but not too suddenly for them to keep control. Usually they had been able to draw in to the side of the road before they stopped. Had the catastrophe occurred by day, the main roads would have been quite impassable, and to work our way clear from the centre by side-streets might have taken days—spent mostly in reversing before impenetrable thickets of vehicles and trying to find another way round. As it was I found that our over-all progress was less slow than it seemed in detail, and when, after a few miles I noticed an overturned car beside the road I realized that we were by this time on a route which others had followed and partially cleared ahead of us.

On the further outskirts of Staines we could begin to feel that London was behind us at last. I stopped, and went back to Coker. As he switched off, the silence closed, thick and unnatural, with only the click of cooling metal to break it. I realized suddenly that I had not seen a single living creature other than a few sparrows since we had started. Coker climbed out of his cab. He stood in the middle of the road, listening and looking around him.

> '*And yonder all before us lie*
> *Deserts of vast eternity . . .*'

he murmured.

I looked hard at him. His grave, reflective expression turned suddenly to a grin.

'Or do you prefer Shelley?' he asked:

> '*My name is Ozymandias, king of kings,*
> *Look on my works, ye mighty, and despair!*

Come on, let's find some food.'

'Coker,' I said, as we completed the meal sitting on a store counter and spreading marmalade on biscuits, 'you beat me. What are you? The first time I meet you I find you ranting—if you will forgive the appropriate word—in a kind of dockside lingo. Now you quote Marvell to me. It doesn't make sense.'

He grinned. 'It never did to me, either,' he said. 'It comes of being a hybrid—you never really know what you are. My mother never really knew what I was, either—at least, she never could prove it, and she always held it against me that on account of that she could not get an allowance for me. It made me kind of sour about things when I was a kid; and when I left school I used to go to meetings—more or less any kind of meetings as long as they were protesting against something. And that led to me getting mixed up with the lot that used to come to them. I suppose they found me kind of amusing. Anyway, they used to take me along to arty-political sorts of parties. After a bit I got tired of being amusing and seeing them give a kind of double laugh, half with me and half at me, whenever I said what I thought. I reckoned I needed some of the background knowledge they had, and then I'd be able to laugh at them a bit, maybe, so I started going to evening classes, and I practised talking the way they did, for use when necessary. There's a whole lot of people don't seem to understand that you have to talk to a man in his own language before he'll take you seriously. If you talk tough and quote Shelley they think you're cute, like a performing monkey or something, but they don't pay any attention to what you say. You have to talk the kind of lingo they're accustomed to taking seriously. And it works the other way, too. Half the political intelligentsia who talk to a working audience don't get the value of their stuff across—not so much because they're over their audience's heads, as because most of the chaps are listening to the voice and not to the words, so they knock a big discount off what they do hear because it's all a bit fancy, and not like ordinary normal talk. So I reckoned the thing to do was to make myself bilingual, and use the right one in the right place—and occasionally the wrong one in the wrong place, unexpectedly. Surprising how that jolts 'em. Wonderful thing, the English caste system. Since then I've made out quite nicely in the orating business. Not what you'd call a steady job, but full of interest and variety. Wilfred Coker. Meetings addressed. Subject no object. That's me.'

'How do you mean—subject no object?' I inquired.

'Well, I kind of supply the spoken word just like a printer supplies the printed word. He doesn't have to believe everything he prints.'

I left that for the moment. 'How's it happen you're not like the rest,' I asked. '*You* weren't in hospital, were you?'

'Me? No. It just so happened that I was addressing a meeting that was protesting over police partiality in a little matter of a strike. We began about six o'clock, and about half-past the police themselves arrived to break it up. I found a handy trapdoor, and went down into the cellar. They came down, too, to have a look, but they didn't find me where I had gone to earth in a pile of shavings. They went on tramping around up above for a bit, then it was quiet. But I stayed put. I wasn't walking out into any nice little trap. It was quite comfortable there, so I went to sleep. In the morning when I took a careful nose around, I found all this had happened.' He paused thoughtfully. 'Well, that racket's finished, it certainly doesn't look as if there's going to be much call for my particular gifts from now on,' he added.

I did not dispute it. We finished our meal. He slid himself off the counter.

'Come on. We'd better be shifting. "To-morrow to fresh fields and pastures new"—if you'd care for a really hackneyed quotation this time.'

'It's more than that, it's inaccurate,' I said. 'It's "woods," not "fields." '

He frowned, and thought.

'Well, — me, mate, so it is,' he admitted.

I began to feel the lightening of spirit that Coker was already showing. The sight of the open country gave one hope of a sort. It was true that the young green crops would never be harvested when they had ripened, nor the fruit from the trees gathered; that the countryside might never again look as trim and neat as it did that day, but for all that it would go on, after its own fashion. It was not like the towns, sterile, stopped for ever. It was a place one could work and tend, and still find a future. It made my existence of the previous week seem like that of a rat living on crumbs and ferreting in garbage heaps. As I looked out over the fields I felt my spirits expanding.

Places on our route, towns like Reading or Newbury, brought back the London mood for a while, but they were no more than dips in a graph of revival.

There is an inability to sustain the tragic mood, a phœnix quality of the mind. It may be helpful or harmful, it is just a part of the will to survive—yet, also, it has made it possible for us to engage in one weakening war after another. But it is a necessary part of our mechanism that we should be able to cry only for a time over even an ocean of spilt milk—the spectacular must soon become the commonplace if life is to be supportable. Under a blue sky where a few clouds sailed like celestial icebergs the cities became a less oppressive memory, and the sense of living freshened us again like a clean wind. It does not, perhaps, excuse, but it does at least explain why from time to time I was surprised to find myself singing as I drove.

At Hungerford we stopped for more food and fuel. The feeling of release continued to mount as we passed through miles of untouched country. It did not seem lonely yet, only sleeping and friendly. Even the sight of occasional little groups of triffids swaying across a field, or of others resting with their roots dug into the soil held no hostility to spoil my mood. They were, once again, the simple objects of my suspended professional interest.

Short of Devizes we pulled up once more to consult the map. A little further on we turned down a side-road to the right, and drove into the village of Tynsham.

10. Tynsham

THERE was little likelihood of anyone missing the Manor. Beyond the few cottages which constituted the village of Tynsham the high wall of an estate ran beside the road. We followed it until we came to massive wrought-iron gates. Behind them stood a young woman on whose face the sober seriousness of responsibility had suppressed all human expression. She was equipped with a shotgun which she clasped in inappropriate places. I signalled to Coker to stop, and called to her as I drew up. Her mouth moved, but not a word penetrated the clatter of the engine. I switched off.

'This is Tynsham Manor?' I asked.

She was not giving that or anything else away.

'Where are you from? And how many of you?' she countered.

I could have wished that she did not fiddle about with her gun in just the way she did. Briefly, and keeping an eye on her uneasy fingers, I explained who we were, why we came, roughly what we carried, and guaranteed that there were no more of us hidden in the trucks. I doubted whether she was taking it in. Her eyes were fixed on mine with a mournfully speculative expression more common in bloodhounds, but

183

not reassuring even there. My words did little to disperse that random suspicion which makes the highly conscientious so wearing. As she emerged to glance into the backs of the lorries and verify my statements, I hoped for her sake that she would not chance to encounter a party of whom her suspicions were justified. Admission that she was satisfied would have weakened her rôle of reliability, but she did eventually consent, still with reserve, to allow us in.

'Take the right fork,' she called up to me as I passed, and turned back at once to attend to the security of the gates. Beyond a short avenue of elms lay a park landscaped in the manner of the late eighteenth century and dotted with trees which had had space to expand into full magnificence. The house, when it came into view, was not a stately home in the architectural sense, but there was a lot of it. It rambled over a considerable ground area and through a variety of building styles as though none of its previous owners had been able to resist the temptation to leave his personal mark upon it. Each, while respecting the work of his forefathers, had apparently felt it incumbent upon him to express the spirit of his own age. A confident disregard of previous levels had resulted in a sturdy waywardness. It was inescapably a funny house, yet friendly, and reliable-looking.

The right fork led us to a wide courtyard where several vehicles stood already. Coach-houses and stables extended around it, seemingly over several acres. Coker drew up alongside me, and climbed down. There was no one in sight.

We made our way through the open rear door of the main building, and down a long corridor. At the end of it was a kitchen of baronial capacity where the warmth and smell of cooking lingered. From beyond a door on the far side came a murmur of voices and a clatter of plates, but we had to negotiate a further dark passage and another door before we reached them.

The place we entered had, I imagine, been the servants'
hall in the days when staffs were sufficiently large for the
term to be no misnomer. It was spacious enough to seat a
hundred or more at tables without crowding. The present
occupants, seated on benches at two long trestles, I guessed
to number between fifty and sixty, and it was clear at a
glance that they were blind. While they sat patiently a few
sighted persons were very busy. Over at a side-table three
girls were industriously carving chickens. I went up to one
of them.

'We've just come,' I said. 'What do we do?'

She paused, still clutching her fork, and pushed back a
lock of hair with the crook of her wrist.

'It'll help if one of you takes charge of the veg. and the
other helps with the plates,' she said.

I took command of two large tubs of potato and cabbage.
In the intervals of doling them out I looked over the
occupants of the hall. Josella was not amongst them—nor
could I see any of the more notable characters among the
group that had put forward its proposals at the University
Building—though I fancied I had seen the faces of some of
the women before.

The proportion of men was far higher than in the former
group, and they were curiously assorted. A few of them
might have been Londoners, or at least town-dwellers, but
the majority wore a countryman's working clothes. An
exception to either kind was a middle-aged clergyman, but
what every one of the men had in common was blindness.

The women were more diversified. Some were in town
clothes quite unsuited to their surroundings, others were
probably local. Among the latter group only one girl was
sighted, but the former group comprised half a dozen or so
who could see, and a number who, though blind, were not
clumsy.

Coker, too, had been taking stock of the place.

'Rum sort of set-up, this,' he remarked, *sotto voce* to me. 'Have you seen her yet?'

I shook my head, desolately aware that I had pinned more on the expectation of finding Josella there than I had admitted to myself.

'Funny thing,' he went on, 'there's practically none of the lot I took along with you—except that girl that's carrying up at the end there.'

'Has she recognized you?' I asked.

'I think so. I got a sort of dirty look from her.'

When the carrying and serving had been completed we took our own plates, and found places at the table. There was nothing to complain of in the cooking or the food, and living out of cold cans for a week sharpens the appreciation, anyway. At the end of the meal there was a knocking on the table. The clergyman rose, he waited for silence before he spoke:

'My friends, it is fitting that at the end of another day we should renew our thanks to God for His great mercy in preserving us in the midst of such disaster. I will ask you all to pray that He may look with compassion upon those who still wander alone in darkness, and that it may please Him to guide their feet hither that we may succour them. Let us all beseech Him that we may survive the trials and tribulations that lie ahead in order that in His time and with His aid we may succeed in playing our part in the rebuilding of a better world to His greater glory.'

He bowed his head.

'Almighty and most merciful God . . .'

After the 'amen' he led a hymn. When that was finished the gathering sorted itself out into parties, each keeping touch with his neighbour, and four of the sighted girls led them out.

I lit a cigarette. Coker took one from me absentmindedly, without making any comment. A girl came across to us.

'Will you help to clear up?' she asked. 'Miss Durrant will be back soon, I expect.'

'Miss Durrant?' I repeated.

'She does the organizing,' she explained. 'You'll be able to fix things up with her.'

It was an hour later and almost dark when we heard that Miss Durrant had returned. We found her in a small, study-like room lit only by two candles on the desk. I recognized her at once as the dark, thin-lipped woman who had spoken for the opposition at the meeting. For the moment, all her attention was concentrated on Coker. Her expression was no more amiable than upon the former occasion.

'I am told,' she said coldly, regarding Coker as though he were some kind of silt, 'I am told that you are the man who organized the raid on the University Building?'

Coker agreed, and waited.

'Then I may as well tell you, once and for all, that in our community here we have no use for brutal methods, and no intention of tolerating them.'

Coker smiled slightly. He answered her in his best middle-class speech:

'It is a matter of viewpoint. Who is to judge who were the more brutal?—those who saw an immediate responsibility and stayed, or those who saw a further responsibility and cleared out?'

She continued to look hard at him. Her expression remained unchanged, but she was evidently forming a different judgment of the type of man she had to deal with. Neither his reply nor its manner had been quite what she had expected. She shelved that aspect for a time, and turned to me.

'Were you in that, too?' she asked.

I explained my somewhat negative part in the affair, and put my own question:

'What happened to Michael Beadley, the Colonel, and the rest?'

It was not well received.

'They have gone elsewhere,' she said, sharply. 'This is a clean, decent community with standards—Christian standards—and we intend to uphold them. We have no place here for people of loose views. Decadence, immorality and lack of faith were responsible for most of the world's ills. It is the duty of those of us who have been spared to see that we build a society where that does not happen again. The cynical and the clever-clever will find they are not wanted here, no matter what brilliant theories they may put forward to disguise their licentiousness and their materialism. We are a Christian community, and we intend to remain so.' She looked at me challengingly.

'So you split, did you?' I said. 'Where did they go?'

She replied, stonily:

'They moved on, and we stayed here. That is what matters. So long as they keep their influence away from here they may work out their own damnation as they please. And since they choose to consider themselves superior to both the laws of God and civilized custom, I have no doubt that they will.'

She ended this declaration with a snap of the jaw which suggested that I should be wasting my time if I tried to question further, and turned back to Coker.

'What can you do?' she inquired.

'A number of things,' he said calmly. 'I suggest that I make myself generally useful until I see where I am needed most.'

She hesitated, a little taken aback. It had clearly been her intention to make the decision and issue the instruction, but she changed her mind.

'All right. Look round, and come and talk it over to-morrow evening,' she said.

But Coker was not to be dismissed quite so easily. He wanted particulars of the size of the estate, the number of persons at present in the house, the proportion of sighted to blind, along with a number of other matters, and he got them.

Before we left, I put in a question about Josella. Miss Durrant frowned.

'I seem to know that name. Now where——? Oh, did she stand in the Conservative interest in the last election?'

'I don't think so. She—er—she did write a book once,' I admitted.

'She——' she began. Then I saw recollection dawn. 'Oh, oh that——! Well, really, Mr. Masen, I can scarcely think she would be the sort of person to care for the kind of community we are building here.'

In the corridor outside Coker turned to me. There was just enough of the twilight left for me to see his grin.

'A somewhat oppressive orthodoxy around these parts,' he remarked. The grin disappeared as he added: 'Rum type, you know. Pride and prejudice. She's wanting help. She knows she needs it badly, but nothing's going to make her admit it.'

He paused opposite an open door. It was almost too dark now to make out anything in the room, but when we had passed it before, there had been enough light to reveal it as a men's dormitory.

'I'm going in to have a word with these chaps. See you later.'

I watched him stroll into the room and greet it collectively with a cheerful 'Wotcher, mates! 'Ow's it going?' and then made my own way back to the dining-hall.

The only light there came from three candles set close together on one table. Close beside them a girl peered exasperatedly at some mending.

'Hullo,' she said. 'Awful, isn't it? How on earth did they manage to do anything after dark in the old days?'

'Not such old days, either,' I told her. 'This is the future as well as the past—provided there's somebody to show us how to make candles.'

'I suppose so.' She raised her head, and regarded me. 'You came from London to-day?'

'Yes,' I admitted.

'It's bad there now?'

'It's finished,' I said.

'You must have seen some horrible sights there?' she suggested.

'I did,' I said, briefly. 'How long have you been here?'

She gave me the general picture of things without more encouragement.

Coker's raid on the University Building had netted all but half a dozen of the sighted. She and Miss Durrant had been two of those overlooked. During the following day Miss Durrant had taken somewhat ineffective charge. There had been no question of their leaving right away, since only one among them had ever attempted to drive a lorry. During that day and most of the next they had been in almost the same relationship to their party as I was to mine away in Hampstead. But during the later part of the second day, Michael Beadley and two others returned, and during the night a few more had straggled back. By noon the day after that they had drivers for a dozen vehicles. They had decided that it was more prudent to leave forthwith than to wait on the chance that others would come.

Tynsham Manor had been chosen as a tentative destination for little better reason than that it was known to the Colonel as a place which could offer the compact seclusion which was one of the qualities they sought.

It had been an ill-assorted party, with its leaders well aware of the fact. The day after their arrival there had been a meeting, smaller, but otherwise not unsimilar to that held earlier in the University Building. Michael and his section had announced that there was much to be done, and that it was not their intention to waste their energies in pacifying a group which was shot through with petty prejudice and squabbles. The whole business was too big for that, and time too pressing. Florence Durrant agreed. What had happened to the world was warning enough. How anyone could be so blindly ungrateful for the miracle that had preserved them as even to contemplate the perpetuation of the subversive theories which had been undermining the Christian faith for a century, she was unable to understand. For her part, she had no wish to live in a community where one section would be continually striving to pervert the simple faith of those who were not ashamed to show their gratitude to God by keeping His laws. She was no less able to see that the situation was serious. The proper course was to pay full heed to the warning God had given, and turn at once to His teaching.

The division of parties, though clear, left them very uneven. Miss Durrant had found her supporters to consist of five sighted girls, a dozen or so blind girls, a few middle-aged men and women, also blind, and no sighted males whatever. In the circumstances there could be no doubt whatever that the section which would have to move must be Michael Beadley's. With the lorries still loaded, there was little to delay them, and in the early afternoon they had driven away, leaving Miss Durrant and her followers to sink or swim by their principles.

Not until then had there been an opportunity to survey the potentialities of the Manor and its neighbourhood. The main part of the house had been closed, but in the servants' quarters they found traces of recent occupation. Investigation of the kitchen garden later gave a pretty clear picture of what had happened to those who had been looking after the place. The bodies of a man, a woman, and a girl lay close together there in a scatter of spilled fruit. Nearby a couple of triffids waited patiently with their roots dug in. Close to the model farm at the far end of the estate was a similar state of affairs. Whether the triffids had found their way into the park through some open gate, or some undocked specimens already there had broken free, was not clear, but they were a menace to be dealt with quickly before they could do more damage. Miss Durrant had sent off one sighted girl to make a circuit of the wall, closing every door or gate, and herself had broken into the gunroom. Despite inexperience, she and another young woman had succeeded in blowing the top off every triffid they could find, to the number of twenty-six. No more had been seen within the enclosure, and it was hoped that no more existed there.

The following day's investigation of the village had shown triffids about in considerable numbers. The surviving inhabitants were either those who had shut themselves into their houses to exist for as long as they could on what stores they had there, or those who had been lucky enough to encounter no triffids when they made brief foraging sorties. All who could be found had been collected and brought back to the Manor. They were healthy, and most of them were strong, but for the present at any rate, they were more of a burden than a help, for there was not one of them that could see.

Four more young woman had arrived in the course of the day. Two had come driving a loaded lorry by turns, and bringing a blind girl with them. The other had been alone in a car. After a brief look round she had announced that she found the set-up lacking in appeal, and driven on. Of the several who continued to arrive over the next few days only two had stayed. All but two of the arrivals had been women. Most of the men, it seemed, had been more forthright and ruthless in extricating themselves from Coker's group formations, and most of them had returned in time to join the original party.

Of Josella the girl could tell me nothing. Clearly she had never heard the name before, and my attempts at description roused no recollections.

While we were still talking, the electric lights in the room suddenly went on. The girl looked up at them with the awed expression of one receiving a revelation. She blew out the candles, and as she went on with her mending she looked up at the bulbs occasionally as if to make certain they were still there.

A few minutes later Coker strolled in.

'That was you, I suppose?' I said, nodding at the lights.

'Yes,' he admitted. 'They've got their own plant here. We might as well use up the petrol as let it evaporate.'

'Do you mean to say we could have had lights all the time we've been here?' asked the girl.

'If you had just taken the trouble to start the engine,' Coker said, looking at her. 'If you wanted light, why didn't you try to start it?'

'I didn't know it was there, besides, I don't know anything about engines or electricity.'

Coker went on looking at her, thoughtfully.

G

'So you just went on sitting in the dark,' he remarked. 'And how long do you think you are likely to survive if you just go on sitting in the dark when things need doing?'

She was stung by his tone.

'It's not my fault if I'm not any good at things like that.'

'I'll differ there,' Coker told her. 'It's not only your fault—it's a self-created fault. Moreover, it's an affectation to consider yourself too spiritual to understand anything mechanical. It is a petty, and a very silly form of vanity. Everyone starts by knowing nothing about anything, but God gives him—and even her—brains to find out with. Failure to use them is not a virtue to be praised: even in women it is a gap to be deplored.'

She looked understandably annoyed. Coker himself had been looking annoyed from the time he came in. She said:

'That's all very well, but different people's minds work on different lines. Men understand how machines and electricity work. Women just aren't much interested in that kind of thing as a rule.'

'Don't hand me a mess of myth and affectation; I'm not taking it,' said Coker. 'You know perfectly well that women can and do—or rather did—handle the most complicated and delicate machines when they took the trouble to understand them. What generally happens is that they're too lazy to take the trouble unless they have to. Why should they bother when the tradition of appealing helplessness can be rationalized as a womanly virtue—and the job just shoved off on to somebody else? Ordinarily it's a pose that it's not worth anyone's while to debunk. In fact, it has been fostered. Men have played up to it by stoutly repairing the poor darling's vacuum cleaner, and capably replacing the blown fuse. The whole charade has been acceptable to both parties. Tough practicality complements spiritual delicacy and charming dependence—and *he* is the mug who gets *his* hands dirty.

He lunged on, well started now:

'Hitherto we have been able to afford to amuse ourselves with that kind of mental laziness and parasitism. In spite of generations of talk about the equality of the sexes there has been much too great a vested interest in dependence for women to dream of dropping it. They have made a minimum of necessary modifications to changing conditions, but they have always been minimum—and grudged, at that.' He paused. 'You doubt that? Well, consider the fact that both the pert chit and the intellectual woman worked the higher-sensibility gag in their different ways—but when a war came and brought with it a social obligation and sanction both could be trained into competent engineers.'

'They weren't *good* engineers,' she remarked. 'Everybody says that.'

'Ah, the defensive mechanism in action. Let me point out that it was in nearly everybody's interest to say so. All the same,' he admitted, 'to some extent that was true. And why? Because nearly all of them not only had to learn hurriedly and without proper groundwork, but they had also to *unlearn* the habits carefully fostered for years of thinking such interests alien to them, and too gross for their delicate natures.'

'I don't see why you have to come and pitch on me with all this,' she said. 'I'm not the only one who didn't start the wretched engine.'

Coker grinned.

'You're quite right. It's unfair. It was simply finding the engine there ready to work and nobody doing a thing about it that started me off. Dumb futility gets me that way.'

'Then I think you might have said all that to Miss Durrant instead of to me.'

'Don't worry, I shall. But it isn't just her affair. It's yours —and everyone else's. I *mean* that, you know. Times have changed rather radically. You can't any longer say: "Oh, dear, I don't understand this kind of thing," and leave it to someone else to do for you. Nobody is going to be muddle-headed enough to confuse ignorance with innocence now— it's too important. Nor is ignorance going to be cute or funny any more. It is going to be dangerous, very dangerous. Unless all of us get around as soon as we can to under-standing a lot of things in which we had no previous interest, neither we nor those who depend on us are going to get through this lot.'

'I don't see why you need to pour all your contempt for women on to me—just because of one dirty old engine,' she said, peevishly.

Coker raised his eyes.

'Great God! And here have I been explaining that women have *all* the capacities if they only take the trouble to use them.'

'You said we were parasites. That wasn't at all a nice thing to say.'

'I'm not trying to say nice things. And what I did say was that in the world that has vanished women had a vested interest in acting the part of parasites.'

'And all that just because I don't happen to know any-thing about a smelly, noisy engine.'

'Hell!' said Coker. 'Just drop that engine a minute, will you.'

'Then why——?'

'The engine just happened to be a symbol. The point is, we'll all have to learn not simply what we like, but as much as we can about running a community and supporting it. The men can't just fill in a voting paper and hand the job to someone else. And it will no longer be considered that a woman has fulfilled all her social obligations when she has prevailed upon some man to support her and provide her with a niche where she can irresponsibly produce babies for somebody else to educate.'

'Well, I don't see what that has to do with engines. . . .'

'Listen,' said Coker, patiently. 'If you have a baby, do you want him to grow up to be a savage, or a civilized man?'

'A civilized man, of course.'

'Well, then, you have to see to it that he has civilized surroundings to do it in. The standards he'll learn, he'll learn from us. We've all got to understand as much as we can, and live as intelligently as we can in order to give him the most we can. It's going to mean hard work and more thinking for all of us. Changed conditions must mean changed outlooks.'

The girl gathered up her mending. She regarded Coker critically for a few moments.

'With views like yours I should think you'd find Mr. Beadley's party more congenial,' she said. 'Here we have no intention of changing our outlook—or of giving up our principles. That's why we separated from the other party. So if the ways of decent respectable people are not good enough for you, I should think you'd better go somewhere else.' And with a sound very like a sniff, she walked away.

Coker watched her leave. When the door closed he expressed his feelings with a fish-porter's fluency. I laughed.

'What did you expect?' I said. 'You prance in and address the girl as if she were a public meeting of delinquents—and responsible for the whole western social system, as well. And then you're surprised when she's huffed.'

'You'd expect her to see reason,' he muttered.

'I don't see why. Most of us don't—we see habit. She'll oppose any modification, reasonable or not, that conflicts with her previously trained feelings of what is right and polite—and be quite honestly convinced that she's showing steadfast strength of character. You're in too much of a hurry. Show a man the Elysian Fields when he's just lost his home, and he'll think mighty little of them: leave him there a bit, and he'll begin to think home was like them, only cosier. She'll adapt in time as she has to—and continue to deny with conviction that she's done so.'

'In other words, just improvise as necessary. Don't try to plan anything. That won't take us far.'

'That's where leadership comes in. The leader does the planning, but he's wise enough not to say so. As the changes become necessary, he slips them in as a concession—temporary, of course—to circumstances, but if he's good, he's slipping in the right bits for the ultimate shape. There are always overwhelming objections to any plan, but concessions have to be made to emergencies.'

'Sounds Machiavellian to me. I like to see what I'm aiming at, and go straight for it.'

'Most people don't, even though they'd protest that they do. They prefer to be coaxed or wheedled, or even driven. That way they never make a mistake: if there is one it's always due to something or somebody else. This going headlong for things is a mechanistic view, and people in general aren't machines. They have minds of their own—mostly peasant minds, at their easiest when they are in the familiar furrow.'

'It doesn't sound as if you'd bet much on Beadley's chance of making a go of it. He's all plan.'

'He'll have his troubles. But his party did choose. This lot is negative,' I pointed out. 'It is simply here on account of its resistance to any kind of plan.' I paused. Then I added: 'That girl was right about one thing, you know. You would be better off with his lot. Her reaction is a sample of what you'd get all round if you were to try to handle this lot your way. You can't drive a flock of sheep to market in a dead straight line, but there are ways of getting 'em there.'

'You're being unusually cynical, as well as metaphorical this evening,' Coker observed.

I objected to that.

'It isn't cynical to have noticed how a shepherd handles his sheep.'

'To regard human beings as sheep might be thought so by some.'

'But less cynical and much more rewarding than regarding them as a lot of chassis fitted for remote thought control.'

'H'm,' said Coker, 'I'll have to consider the implications of that.'

11. . . . And Further On

M Y next morning was desultory. I looked around, I
lent a hand here and there, and asked a lot of
questions.

It had been a wretched night. Until I lay down, I had not
fully realized the extent to which I had counted on finding
Josella at Tynsham. Weary though I was after the day's
journey, I could not sleep; I lay awake in the darkness
feeling stranded and planless. So confidently had I assumed
that she and the Beadley party would be there that there
had been no reason to consider any scheme beyond joining
them. It now came home to me for the first time that even
if I did succeed in catching up with them I still might not
find her. As she had only left the Westminster district a short
time before I arrived there in search of her, she must in any
case have been well behind the main party. Obviously the
thing to do was to make detailed inquiries regarding everyone who had arrived at Tynsham during the previous two
days.

For the present I must assume that she had come this way.
It was my only lead. And that meant assuming also that she
had gone back to the University and had found the chalked
address—whereas, it was quite on the cards that she had not

gone there at all, but, sickened by the whole thing, have taken the quickest route out of the reeking place that London had become.

The thing I had to fight hardest against admitting was that she might have caught the disease, whatever it was, that had dissolved both our groups. I would not consider the possibility of that until I had to.

In the sleepless clarity of the small hours I made one discovery—it was that my desire to join the Beadley party was very secondary indeed to my wish to find Josella. If, when I did find them, she was not with them . . . well, the next move would have to wait upon the moment, but it would not be resignation. . . .

Coker's bed was already empty when I awoke, and I decided to devote my morning chiefly to inquiries. One of the troubles was that it did not seem to have occurred to anyone to take note of the names of those who had found Tynsham uninviting, and had passed on. Josella's name meant nothing to anyone save those few who recollected it with disapproval. My description of her raised no memories that would stand detailed examination. Certainly there had been no girl in a navy-blue ski-suit—that I established, but then, I could by no means be certain that she would still be dressed that way. My inquiries ended by making everyone very tired of me and increasing my frustration. There was a faint possibility that a girl who had come and gone a day before our arrival might have been she, but I could not feel it likely that Josella could have left so slight an impression on anyone's mind—even allowing for prejudice. . . .

Coker reappeared again at the midday meal. He had been engaged on an extensive survey of the premises. He had taken a tally of the livestock and the number of blind among it. Inspected the farm equipment and machinery. Found out about the source of pure water supplies. Looked into the stores of feed, both human and stock. Discovered how many of the blind girls had been afflicted before the catastrophe, and arranged classes of the others for them to train as best they could.

He had found most of the men plunged in gloom by a well-meant assurance from the vicar that there would be plenty of useful things for them to do such as—er—basket-making, and—er—weaving, and he had done his best to dispel it with more hopeful prospects. Encountering Miss Durrant, he had told her that unless it could somehow be contrived that the blind women should take part of the work off the shoulders of the sighted the whole thing would break down within ten days, and also, that if the vicar's prayer for more blind people to join them should happen to be granted the place would become entirely unworkable. He was embarking upon further observations, including the necessity for starting immediately to build up food reserves, and to begin the construction of devices which would enable blind men to do useful work, when she cut him short. He could see that she was a great deal more worried than she would admit, but the determination which had led her to sever relations with the other party caused her to blaze back at him unthankfully. She ended by letting him know that on her information neither he nor his views were likely to harmonize with the community.

'The trouble about that woman is that she means to be boss,' he said. 'It's constitutional—quite apart from the lofty principles.'

'Slanderous,' I said. 'What you mean is that her principles are so impeccable that everything is her responsibility—and so it becomes her duty to guide others.'

'Much the same thing,' he said.

'But it sounds a lot better,' I pointed out.

He was thoughtful for a moment.

'She's going to run this place into one hell of a mess unless she gets right down to the job of organizing it pretty quickly. Have you looked the outfit over?'

I shook my head. I told him how my morning had been spent.

'You don't seem to have got much change for it. So what?' he said.

'I'm going on after the Michael Beadley crowd,' I told him.

'And if she's not with them?'

'At present I'm just hoping she is. She must be. Where else would she be?'

He started to say something, and stopped. Then he went on:

'I reckon I'll come along with you. It's likely that crowd won't be any more glad to see me than this one, considering everything—but I can live that down. I've watched one lot fall to bits, and I can see this one's going to do the same—more slowly and, maybe, more nastily. It's queer, isn't it? Decent intentions seem to be the most dangerous things around just now. It's a damned shame because this place *could* be managed, in spite of the proportion of blind. Everything it needs is lying about for the taking, and will be for a while yet. It's only organizing that's wanted.'

'And willingness to be organized,' I suggested.

'That, too,' he agreed. 'You know, the trouble is that in spite of all that's happened this thing hasn't got home to these people yet. They don't want to turn to—that'd be making it too final. At the back of their minds they're all camping out, hanging on, and waiting for something or other.'

'True—but scarcely surprising,' I admitted. 'It took plenty to convince us, and they've not seen what we have. And, somehow, it does seem less final and less—less immediate out here in the country.'

'Well, they've got to start realizing it soon if they're going to get through,' Coker said, looking round the hall again. 'There's no miracle coming to save them.'

'Give 'em time. They'll come to it, as we did. You're always in such a hurry. Time's no longer money, you know.'

'Money isn't important any longer, but time is. They ought to be thinking about the harvest, rigging a mill to grind flour, seeing about winter feed for the stock.'

I shook my head.

'It's not as urgent as all that, Coker. There must be huge stocks of flour in the towns, and, by the look of things, mighty few of us to use it. We can live on capital for a long while yet. Surely the immediate job is to teach the blind *how* to work before they really have to get down to it.'

'All the same, unless something is done, the sighted ones here are going to crack up. It only needs that to happen to one or two of them, and the place'll be in a proper mess."

I had to concede that.

Later in the afternoon I managed to find Miss Durrant. No one else seemed to know or care where Michael Beadley and his lot had gone, but I could not believe that they had not left behind some indications for those who might follow. Miss Durrant was not pleased. At first I thought she was going to refuse to tell me. It was not due solely to my implied preference for other company. The loss of even an uncongenial able-bodied man was serious in the circumstances. Nevertheless, she preferred not to show the weakness of asking me to stay. In the end she said curtly:

'They were intending to make for somewhere near

Beaminster in Dorset. I can tell you no more than
that.'

I went back and told Coker. He looked around him. Then
he shook his head, though with a touch of regret.

'Okay,' he said. 'We'll check out of this dump to-morrow.'

'Spoken like a pioneer,' I told him. '—At least, more like
a pioneer than an Englishman.'

Nine o'clock the next morning saw us already twelve miles
or so on our road, and travelling as before in our two lorries.
There had been a question whether we should not take a
handier vehicle and leave the trucks for the benefit of the
Tynsham people, but I was reluctant to abandon mine. I had
personally collected the contents, and knew what was in it.
Apart from the cases of anti-triffid gear which Michael
Beadley had so disapproved, I had given myself slightly
wider scope on the last load, and there was a selection of
things made with consideration of what might be difficult to
find outside a large town; such things as a small lighting set,
some pumps, cases of good tools. All these things would be
available later for the taking, but there was going to be an
interlude when it would be advisable to keep away from
towns of any size. The Tynsham people had the means to
fetch supplies from towns where there was no sign yet of the
disease. A couple of loads would not make a great deal of
difference to them either way, so, in the end, we went as we
had come.

The weather still held good. On the higher ground there
was still little taint in the fresh air, though most villages had
become unpleasant. Rarely we saw a still figure lying in a
field or by the roadside, but just as in London, the main
instinct seemed to have been to hide away in shelter of some
kind. Most of the villages showed empty streets, and the
countryside around them was as deserted as if the whole

human race and most of its animals had been spirited away. Until we came to Steeple Honey.

From our road we had a view of the whole of Steeple Honey as we descended the hill. It clustered at the further end of a stone bridge which arched across a small, sparkling river. It was a quiet little place centred round a sleepy-looking church, and stippled off at its edges with white-washed cottages. It did not look as if anything had occurred in a century or more to disturb the quiet life under its thatched roofs. But like other villages it was now without stir or smoke. And then, when we were half-way down the hill, a movement caught my eye.

On the left, at the far end of the bridge one house stood slightly aslant from the road so that it faced obliquely towards us. An inn sign hung from a bracket on its wall, and from the window immediately above that something white was being waved. As we came closer I could see the man who was leaning out and frantically flagging us with a towel. I judged that he must be blind, otherwise he would have come out into the road to intercept us. He was waving too vigorously for a sick man.

I signalled back to Coker, and pulled up as we cleared the bridge. The man at the window dropped his towel. He shouted something which I could not hear above the noise of the engines, and disappeared. We both switched off. It was so quiet that we could hear the clumping of the man's feet on the wooden stairs inside the house. The door opened, and he stepped out, holding both hands before him. Like lightning something whipped out of the hedge on his left, and struck him. He gave a single, high-pitched shout, and dropped where he stood.

I picked up my shotgun, and climbed out of the cab. I circled a little until I could make out the triffid skulking in the shadows of a bush. Then I blew the top off it.

Coker was out of his truck, too, and standing close beside me. He looked at the man on the ground, and then at the shorn triffid.

'It was—no, damn it, it can't have been *waiting* for him?' he said. 'It must just have happened. . . . It couldn't have *known* he'd come out of that door. . . . I mean, it *couldn't*—could it?'

'Or could it? It was a remarkably neat piece of work,' I said.

Coker turned uneasy eyes on me.

'Too damn' neat. You don't really believe . . .?'

'There's a kind of conspiracy not to believe things about triffids,' I said, and added: 'There might be more around here.'

We looked the adjacent cover over carefully, and drew blank.

'I could do with a drink,' suggested Coker.

But for the dust on the counter, the small bar of the inn looked normal. We poured a whisky each. Coker downed his in one. He turned a worried look on me.

'I didn't like that. Not at all, I didn't. You ought to know a lot more about these bloody things than most people, Bill. It wasn't—I mean, it must just have *happened* to be there, mustn't it?'

'I think——' I began. Then I stopped, listening to the staccato drumming outside. I walked over and opened the window. I let the already trimmed triffid have the other barrel, too; this time just above the bole. The drumming stopped.

'The trouble about triffids,' I said, as we poured another drink, 'is chiefly the things we don't know about them.' I told him one or two of Walter's theories. He stared.

'You don't seriously suggest that they're "talking" when they make that rattling noise?'

'I've never made up my mind,' I admitted. 'I'll go so far as to say I'm sure it's a signal of some sort. But Walter considered it to be real "talk"—and he did know more about them than anyone else that I know.'

I ejected the two spent cartridge cases, and reloaded.

'And he actually mentioned their advantage over a blind man?'

'A number of years ago, that was,' I pointed out.

'Still—it's a funny coincidence.'

'Impulsive as ever,' I said. 'Pretty nearly any stroke of fate can be made to look like a funny coincidence if you try hard enough and wait long enough.'

We drank up, and turned to go. Coker glanced out of the window. Then he caught my arm, and pointed. Two triffids had swayed round the corner, and were making for the hedge which had been the hiding-place of the first. I waited until they paused, and then decapitated both of them. We left by the window, which was out of range of any triffid cover, and looked about us carefully as we approached the lorries.

'Another coincidence? Or were they coming to see what had happened to their pal?' asked Coker.

We cleared the village, running on along small, cross-country roads. There seemed to me to be more triffids about now than we had seen on our previous journey—or was it that I had been made more conscious of them? It might have been that in travelling hitherto chiefly by main roads we had encountered fewer. I knew from experience that they tended to avoid a hard surface, and thought that it perhaps caused them some discomfort in their limb-like roots. Now I began to be convinced that we *were* seeing more of them, and I started to get an idea that they were not entirely indifferent to us—though it was not possible to be sure whether those that we saw approaching across fields from time to time just happened to be coming in our direction.

A more decisive incident occurred when one slashed at me from the hedgerow as I passed. Luckily it was inexpert in its aim at a moving vehicle. It let fly a moment too soon, and left its print in little dots of poison across the windscreen. I was past before it could strike again. But thenceforward, in spite of the warmth I drove with the nearside window closed.

During the past week or more I had given thought to the triffids only when I encountered them. Those I had seen at Josella's home had worried me as had the others that had attacked our group near Hampstead Heath, but most of the time there had been more immediate things to worry about. But, looking back now over our trip, the state of things at Tynsham before Miss Durrant had taken steps to clear it up with shotguns, and the condition of the villages we had passed through, I began to wonder just how big a part the triffids might have been playing in the disappearance of the inhabitants.

In the next village I drove slowly, and looked carefully. In several of the front gardens I could see bodies lying as they had evidently lain for some days—and almost always there was a triffid discernible close by. It looked as if the triffids only ambushed in places where there was soft earth for them to dig their roots into while they waited. One seldom saw a body, and never a triffid in those parts where the house-doors opened straight into the street.

At a guess I would say that what had happened in most of the villages was that the inhabitants emerging for food moved in comparative safety while they were in paved areas, but the moment they left them, or even passed close to a garden wall or fence, they stood in danger of the stings slashing out at them. Some would cry out as they were struck, and when they did not come back those who remained would grow more afraid. Now and then another would be driven out by hunger. A few might be lucky enough to get back, but most would lose themselves and wander on until they dropped, or came within range of a triffid. Those who were left might, perhaps, guess what was happening. Where there was a garden they might have heard the swish of the sting, and known that they faced the alternatives of starvation in the house or the same fate that had overtaken the others who had left it. Many would remain there, living on what food they had while they waited for help that was never going to come. Something like that must have been the predicament of the man in the inn at Steeple Honey.

The likelihood that in the other villages we were passing through there might still be houses in which isolated groups had managed to keep going was not a pleasant thought. It raised again the same kind of question that we had faced in London—the feeling that one should, by all civilized standards, try to find them and do something for them; and the frustrating knowledge of the frittering decline which would overtake any such attempt as it had before.

The same old question. What could one do, with the best will in the world, but prolong the anguish? Placate one's conscience for a while again, just to see the result of the effort wasted once more.

It was not, I had to tell myself firmly, any good at all going into an earthquake area while the buildings were still falling—the rescue and the salvage had to be done when the tremors had stopped. But reason did not make it easy. The old Doctor had been only too right when he stressed the difficulties of mental adaptation. . . .

The triffids were a complication on an unexpected scale. There were, of course, very many nurseries besides our own company's plantations. They raised them for us, for private buyers, or for sale to a number of lesser trades where their derivatives were used, and the majority of them were, for climatic reasons situated in the south. Nevertheless, if what we had already seen was a fair sample of the way they had broken loose and distributed themselves they must have been far more numerous than I had supposed. The prospect of more of them reaching maturity every day and of the docked specimens steadily regrowing their stings was far from reassuring. . . .

With only two more stops, one for food and the other for fuel, we made good time, and ran into Beaminster about half-past four in the afternoon. We had come right into the centre of the town without having seen a sign to suggest the presence of the Beadley party.

At first glimpse the place was as void of life as any other we had seen that day. The main shopping street when we entered it was bare and empty save for a couple of lorries drawn up on one side. I had led the way down it for perhaps twenty yards when a man stepped out from behind one of the lorries, and levelled a rifle. He fired deliberately over my head, and then lowered his aim.

12. Dead End

THAT'S the kind of warning I don't debate about. I pulled up.

The man was large and fair-haired. He handled his rifle with familiarity. Without taking it out of the aim, he jerked his head twice sideways. I accepted that as a sign to climb down. When I had done so, I displayed my empty hands. Another man, accompanied by a girl, emerged from behind the stationary lorry as I approached it. Coker's voice called from behind me:

'Better put up that rifle, chum. You're all in the open.'

The fair man's eyes left mine to search for Coker. I could have jumped him then if I'd wanted to, but I said:

'He's right. Anyway, we're peaceful.'

The man lowered his rifle, not quite convinced. Coker emerged from the cover of my lorry which had hidden his exit from his own.

'What's the big idea? Dog eat dog?' he inquired.

'Only two of you?' the second man asked.

Coker looked at him.

'What would you be expecting? A convention? Yes, just two of us.'

The trio visibly relaxed. The fair man explained:

'We thought you might be a gang from a city. We've been expecting them here raiding for food.'

'Oh,' said Coker. 'From which we assume that you've not taken a look at any city lately. If that's your only worry, you might as well forget it. What gangs there are, are more likely to be working the other way round—at present. In fact, doing—if I may say so—just what you are.'

'You don't think they'll come?'

'I'm darned sure they won't.' He regarded the three. 'Do you belong to Beadley's lot?' he asked.

The response was convincingly blank.

'Pity,' said Coker. 'That'd have been our first real stroke of luck in quite a time.'

'What is or are Beadley's lot?' inquired the fair man.

I was feeling wilted and dry after some hours in the driving cab with the sun on it. I suggested that we might remove discussion from the middle of the street to some more congenial spot. We passed round their vans through a familiar litter of cases of biscuits, chests of tea, sides of bacon, sacks of sugar, blocks of salt, and all the rest of it to a small bar-parlour next door. Over pint pots Coker and I gave them a short résumé of what we'd done and what we knew. Then it was their turn.

They were, it seemed, the more active half of a party of six—the other two women and a man being stationed at the house they had taken over for a base.

Around the noon of Tuesday, May 7th, the fair-haired man and the girl with him had been travelling westwards in his car. They had been on their way to spend a two weeks holiday in Cornwall, and making pretty good time until a double-decker bus emerged from a turning somewhere near Crewkerne. The car had made contact with it in a decisive way, and the last thing the fair-haired young man remembered was a horrified glimpse of the bus looking as tall as a cliff, and heeling over right above them.

He had wakened up in bed to find, much as I had, a mysterious silence all about him. Apart from soreness, a few cuts, and a thumping head, there didn't appear to be a lot wrong with him. When, as he said, nobody kept on coming, he had investigated the place, and found it to be a small cottage-hospital. In one ward he had found the girl and two other women, one of whom was conscious, but incapacitated by a leg and an arm in plaster. In another were two men— one of them his present companion, the other suffering from a broken leg, also in plaster. Altogether there had been eleven people in the place, eight of whom were sighted. Of the blind, two were bedridden and seriously ill. Of the staff there was no sign at all. His experience had been, to begin with, more baffling than mine. They had stayed in the little hospital, doing what they could for the helpless, wondering what went on, and hoping that someone would show up to help. They had no idea what was wrong with the two blind patients nor how to treat them. They could do nothing but feed and try to ease them. Both had died the next day. One man disappeared, and no one had seen him go. Those who were there for injuries suffered when the bus had overturned were local people. Once they were sufficiently recovered, they set out to find relatives. The party had dwindled down to six, two of whom had broken limbs.

By now they had realized that the breakdown was big enough to mean that they must fend for themselves for a time at least, but they were still far from grasping its full extent. They decided to leave the hospital and find some more convenient place, for they imagined that many more sighted people would exist in the cities and that the disorganization would have brought mob rule. Daily they were expecting the arrival of these mobs when the food

stores in the towns should be finished, and had pictured
them moving like a locust army across the countryside.
Their chief concern, therefore, had been to gather supplies
in preparation for a siege.

With our assurances that that was the least likely thing
to happen, they looked at one another a little bleakly.

They were an oddly assorted trio. The fair-haired man
turned out to be a member of the Stock Exchange by the
name of Stephen Brennell. His companion was a good-
looking, well-built girl with an occasional superficial
petulance, but no real surprise over whatever life might
hand her next. She had led one of those fringe careers—
modelling dresses, selling them, putting in movie-extra work,
missing opportunities of going to Hollywood, hostessing for
obscure clubs, and helping out these activities by such other
means as offered themselves—the intended holiday in Cornwall being apparently one such. She had an utterly unshake-
able conviction that nothing serious could have happened to
America, and that it was only a matter of holding out for a
while until the Americans arrived to put everything in order.
She was quite the least troubled person I had encountered
since the catastrophe took place. Though just occasionally
she pined a little for the bright lights which she hoped the
Americans would hurry up and restore.

The third member, the dark young man, nursed a grudge.
He had worked hard and saved hard in order to start his
small radio store, and he had ambitions. 'Look at Ford,' he
told us, 'and look at Lord Nuffield—he started with a bike
shop no bigger than my radio store, and see where he got to!
That's the kind of thing I was going to do. And now look at
the damned mess things are in! It ain't fair!' Fate, as he saw
it, didn't want any more Fords or Nuffields—but he didn't
intend to take that lying down. This was only an interval
sent to try him—one day would see him back in his

radio store with his foot set firmly on the first rung to millionairedom.

The most disappointing thing about them was to find that they knew nothing of the Michael Beadley party. Indeed, the only group they had encountered was in a village just over the Devon border where a couple of men with shotguns had advised them not to come that way again. Those men, they said, were obviously local. Coker suggested that that meant a small group.

'If they had belonged to a large one they'd have shown less nervousness and more curiosity,' he maintained. 'But if the Beadley lot are round here, we ought to be able to find them somehow.' He put it to the fair man: 'Look here, suppose we come along with you? We can do our whack, and when we do find them it will make things easier for all of us.'

The three of them looked questioningly at one another, and then nodded.

'All right. Give us a hand with the loading, and we'll be getting along,' the man agreed.

By the look of Charcot Old House it had once been a fortified manor. Refortification was now under way. At some time in the past the encircling moat had been drained. Stephen, however, was of the opinion that he had successfully ruined the drainage system so that it would fill up again by degrees. It was his plan to blow up such parts as had been filled in, and thus complete the re-encirclement. Our news, suggesting that this might not be necessary, induced a slight wistfulness in him, and a look of disappointment. The stone walls of the house were thick. At least three of the windows in the front displayed machine guns, and he pointed out two more mounted on the roof. Inside the main door was stacked a small arsenal of mortars and bombs, and, as he proudly showed us, several flame-throwers.

'We found an arms depot,' he explained, 'and spent a day getting this lot together.'

As I looked over the stuff I realized for the first time that the catastrophe by its very thoroughness had been more merciful than the things that would have followed a slightly lesser disaster. Had ten or fifteen per cent. of the population remained unharmed it was very likely that little communities like this would indeed have found themselves fighting off starving gangs in order to preserve their own lives. As things were, however, Stephen had probably made his warlike preparations in vain. But there was one appliance that could be out to good use. I pointed to the flame-throwers.

'Those might be handy for triffids,' I said.

He grinned.

'You're right. Very effective. The one thing we've used them for. And incidentally the one thing I know that really makes a triffid beat it. You can go on firing at them until they're shot to bits, and they don't budge. I suppose they don't know where the destruction's coming from. But one warm lick from this, and they're plunging off fit to bust themselves.'

'Have you had a lot of trouble with them?' I asked.

It seemed that they had not. From time to time one, perhaps two or three would approach, and be scorched away. On their expeditions they had had several lucky escapes, but usually they were out of their vehicles only in built-up areas where there was little likelihood of prowling triffids.

That night after dark we all went up to the roof. It was too early for the moon. We looked out upon an utterly black landscape. Search it as we would, not one of us was able to discover the least pinpoint of a tell-tale light. Nor could any of the party recall ever having seen a trace of smoke by day. I was feeling depressed when we descended again to the lamplit living-room.

'There's only one thing for it, then,' Coker said. 'We'll have to divide the district up into areas, and search them.'

But he did not say it with conviction. I suspected that he was thinking it likely, as I was, that the Beadley party would continue to show a deliberate light by night, and some other sign—probably a smoke column—by day.

However, no one had any better suggestion to make, so we got down to the business of dividing the map up into sections, doing our best to contrive that each should include some high ground to give an extensive view beyond it.

The following day we went into the town in a lorry, and from there dispersed in smaller cars for the search.

That was, without a doubt, the most melancholy day I had spent since I had wandered about Westminster searching for traces of Josella there.

Just at first it wasn't too bad. There was the open road in the sunlight, the fresh green of early summer. There were signposts which pointed to 'Exeter and The West,' and other places as if they still pursued their habitual lives. There were sometimes, though rarely, birds to be seen. And there were wild flowers beside the lanes, looking as they had always looked.

But the other side of the picture was not so good. There were fields in which cattle lay dead or wandered blindly, and untended cows lowed in pain; where sheep in their easy discouragement had stood resignedly to die rather than pull themselves free from bramble or barbed wire, and other sheep grazed erratically, or starved with looks of reproach in their blind eyes.

Farms were becoming unpleasant places to pass closely.

For safety's sake I was giving myself only an inch of ventilation at the top of the window, but I closed even that whenever I saw a farm beside the road ahead.

Triffids were at large. Sometimes I saw them crossing fields or noticed them inactive against hedges. In more than one farmyard they had found the middens to their liking and enthroned themselves there while they waited for the dead stock to attain the right stage of putrescence. I saw them now with a disgust that they had never roused in me before. Horrible alien things which some of us had somehow created and which the rest of us in our careless greed had cultured all over the world. One could not even blame nature for them. Somehow they had been bred—just as we bred ourselves beautiful flowers, or grotesque parodies of dogs. . . . I began to loathe them now for more than their carrion-eating habits—they, more than anything else, seemed able to profit and flourish on our disaster. . . .

As the day went on, my sense of loneliness grew. On any hill or rise I stopped to examine the country as far as field-glasses would show me. Once I saw smoke and went to the source to find a small railway train burnt out on the line—I still do not know how that could be, for there was no one near it. Another time a flag upon a staff sent me hurrying to a house to find it silent—though not empty. Yet another time a white flutter of movement on a distant hillside caught my eye, but when I turned the glasses on it I found it to be half a dozen sheep milling in panic while a triffid struck continually and ineffectively across their woolly backs. Nowhere could I see a sign of living human beings.

When I stopped for food I did not linger longer than I needed. I ate it quickly, listening to a silence that was beginning to get on my nerves, and anxious to be on my way again with at least the sound of the car for company.

One began to fancy things. Once I saw an arm waving

from a window, but when I got there it was only a branch swaying in front of the window. I saw a man stop in the middle of a field and turn to watch me go by; but the glasses showed me that he couldn't have stopped or turned: he was a scarecrow. I heard voices calling to me, just discernible above the engine noise; I stopped, and switched off. There were no voices, nothing; but far, far away, the plaint of an unmilked cow.

It came to me that here and there, dotted about the country there must be men and women who were believing themselves to be utterly alone, sole survivors. I felt as sorry for them as for anyone else in the disaster.

During the afternoon, with lowered spirits and little hope, I kept doggedly on quartering my section of the map because I dared not risk failing to make my inner certainty sure. At last, however, I satisfied myself that if any sizeable party did exist in the area I had been allotted it was deliberately hiding. It had not been possible for me to cover every lane and by-road, but I was willing to swear that the sound of my by no means feeble horn had been heard in every acre of my sector. I finished up, and drove back to the place where we had parked the lorry, in the gloomiest mood I had yet known. I found that none of the others had shown up yet, so to pass the time, and because I needed it to keep out the spiritual cold, I turned into the nearby pub and poured myself a good brandy.

Stephen was the next. The expedition seemed to have affected him much as it had me, for he shook his head in answer to my questioning look, and made straight for the bottle I had opened. Ten minutes later the radio-ambitionist joined us. He brought with him a dishevelled, wild-eyed young man who appeared not to have washed or shaved for several weeks. This person had been on the road; it was, it seemed, his only profession. One evening, he could not say for certain of what day, he had found a fine comfortable barn in which to spend the night. Having done somewhat more than his usual quota of miles that day he had fallen asleep almost as soon as he lay down. The next morning he had awakened in a nightmare, and he still seemed a little uncertain whether it was the world or himself that was crazy. We reckoned he was, a little, anyway, but he still retained a clear knowledge of the use of beer.

Another half hour or so passed, and then Coker arrived. He was accompanied by an Alsatian puppy and an unbelievable old lady. She was dressed in what was obviously her best. Her cleanliness and precision were as notable as were the lack of them in our other recruit. She paused with a genteel hesitation on the threshold of the bar-parlour. Coker performed the introduction.

'This is Mrs. Forcett, sole proprietor of Forcett's Universal Stores, in a collection of about ten cottages, two pubs, and a church, known as Chippington Durney—and Mrs. Forcett can cook. Boy, can she cook!'

Mrs. Forcett acknowledged us with dignity, advanced with confidence, seated herself with circumspection, and consented to be pressed to a glass of port, followed by another glass of port.

In answer to our questions she confessed to sleeping with unusual soundness during the fatal evening and the night that followed. Into the precise cause of this she did not enter, and we did not inquire. She had continued to sleep, since nothing had occurred to awaken her, through half the following day. When she awoke she was feeling unwell, and so did not attempt to get up until mid-afternoon. It had seemed to her curious but providential that no one had required her in the shop. When she did get up and go to the door she had seen 'one of them horrid triffid things' standing in her garden, and a man lying on the path just outside her

gate—at least, she could see his legs. She had been about
to go out to him when she had seen the triffid stir, and she
had slammed the door to just in time. It had clearly been a
nasty moment for her, and the recollection of it agitated her
into pouring herself a third glass of port.

After that, she had settled down to wait until someone
should come to remove both the triffid and the man. They
seemed a strangely long time in coming, but she had been
able to live comfortably enough upon the contents of her
shop. She had still been waiting, she explained as she poured
herself a fourth glass of port with a nice absentmindedness,
when Coker, interested by the smoke from her fire, had shot
the top off the triffid, and investigated.

She had given Coker a meal, and he in return had given
her advice. It had not been easy to make her understand the
true state of things. In the end he had suggested that she
should take a look up the village, keeping a wary eye for
triffids, and that he would be back at five o'clock to see how
she felt about it. He had returned to find her dressed up, her
bag packed, and herself quite ready to leave.

Back in Charcott Old House that evening we gathered
again around the map. Coker started to mark out new areas
of search. We watched him without enthusiasm. It was
Stephen who said what all of us, including, I think, Coker
himself, were thinking:

'Look here, we've been over all the ground for a circle of
some fifteen miles between us. It's clear they aren't in the
immediate neighbourhood. Either your information is
wrong, or they decided not to stop here, and went on. In
my view it would be a waste of time to go on searching the
way we did to-day.'

Coker laid down the compasses he was using.

'Then what do you suggest?'

'Well, it seems to me we could cover a lot of the district

pretty quickly from the air, and well enough. You can bet your life that anyone who hears an aircraft engine is going to turn out and make a sign of some kind.'

Coker shook his head. 'Now, why didn't we think of that before. It ought to be a helicopter, of course—but where do we get one, and who's going to fly it?'

'Oh, I can make one of them things go all right,' said the radio man, confidently.

There was something in his tone.

'Have you ever flown one?' asked Coker.

'No,' admitted the radio man, 'but I reckon there'd not be a lot to it, once you got the knack.'

'H'm,' said Coker, looking at him with reserve.

Stephen recalled the locations of two R.A.F. stations not far away, and that there had been an air-taxi business operating from Yeovil.

In spite of our doubts the radio man was as good as his word. He seemed to have complete confidence that his instinct for mechanism would not let him down. After practising for half an hour he took the helicopter off, and flew it back to Charcott.

For four days the machine hovered around in widening circles. On two of them Coker observed, on the other two I replaced him. In all, we discovered ten little groups of people. None of them knew anything of the Beadley party, and none of them contained Josella. As we found each lot, we landed. Usually they were in twos and threes. The largest was seven. They would greet us in hopeful excitement, but soon, when they found that we represented only a group similar to their own, and were not the spearhead of a rescue party on the grand scale their interest would lapse. We could offer them little that they had not got already. Some of them became irrationally abusive and threatening in their disappointment, but most simply dropped back into despondency. As a rule they showed little wish to join up with other parties, and were inclined rather to lay hands on what they could, building themselves into refuges as comfortably as possible while they waited for the arrival of the Americans who were bound to find a way. There seemed to be a widespread and fixed idea about this. Our suggestions that any surviving Americans would be likely to have their hands more than full at home was received as so much wetblanketry. The Americans, they assured us, would never have allowed such a thing to happen in their country. Nevertheless, and in spite of this Micawber fixation on American fairy godmothers, we left each party with a map showing them the approximate positions of groups we had already discovered in case they should change their minds, and think about getting together for self-help.

As a task, the flights were far from enjoyable, but at least they were to be preferred to lonely scouting on the ground. However, at the end of the fruitless fourth day it was decided to abandon the search.

At least, that was what the rest of them decided. I did not feel the same way about it. My quest was personal, theirs was not. Whoever they found, now or eventually, would be strangers to them. I was searching for Beadley's party as a means, not an end in itself. If I should find them and discover that Josella was not with them, then I should go on searching. But I could not expect the rest to devote any more time to searching purely on my behalf.

Curiously I realized that in all this I had met no other person who was searching for someone else. Every one of them had been, save for the accident of Stephen and his girl friend, snapped clean away from friends or relatives to link him with the past, and was beginning a new life with people who were strangers. Only I, as far as I could see, had promptly formed a new link—and that so briefly that I had scarcely been aware how important it was to me at the time. . . .

Once the decision to abandon the search had been taken, Coker said:

'All right. Then that brings us to thinking about what we are going to do for ourselves.'

'Which means laying in stores against the winter, and just going on as we are. What else should we do?' asked Stephen.

'I've been thinking about that,' Coker told him. 'Maybe it'd be all right for a while—but what happens afterwards?'

'If we do run short of stocks, well, there's plenty more lying around,' said the radio man.

'The Americans will be here before Christmas,' said Stephen's girl friend.

'Listen,' Coker told her patiently. 'Just put the Americans in the jam-to-morrow-pie-in-the-sky department awhile, will you. Try to imagine a world in which there aren't any Americans—can you do that?'

The girl stared at him.

'But there must be,' she said.

Coker sighed sadly. He turned his attention to the radio man.

'There won't always be those stores. The way I see it, we've been given a flying start in a new kind of world. We're endowed with a capital of enough of everything to begin with, but that isn't going to last for ever. We couldn't eat up all the stuff that's there for the taking, not in generations —if it would keep. But it isn't going to keep. A lot of it is going to go bad pretty rapidly. And not only food. Every-thing is going, more slowly, but quite surely, to drop to pieces. If we want fresh stuff to eat next year we shall have to grow it ourselves, and it may seem a long way off now,

H

but there's going to come a time when we shall have to grow everything ourselves. There'll come a time, too, when all the tractors are worn out or rusted, and there's no more petrol to run them, anyway—when we'll come right down to nature and bless horses—if we've got 'em.

'This is a pause—just a heaven-sent pause—while we get over the first shock and start to collect ourselves, but it's no more than a pause. Later, we'll have to plough, still later we'll have to learn how to make plough-shares, later than that we'll have to learn how to smelt iron to make the shares. What we are on now is a road that will take us back and back and back until we can—*if* we can—make good all that we wear out. Not until then shall we be able to stop our-selves on the trail that's leading down to savagery. But once we can do that, then may we'll begin to crawl slowly up again.'

He looked round the circle to see if we were following him.

'We *can* do that—if we will. The most valuable part of our flying start is knowledge. That's the short cut to save us starting where our ancestors did. We've got it all there in the books if we take the trouble to find out about it.'

The rest were looking at Coker curiously. It was the first time they had heard him in one of his oratorical moods.

'Now,' he went on, 'from my reading of history, the thing you have to have to use knowledge is leisure. Where *everybody* has to work hard just to get a living and there is no leisure to think, knowledge stagnates, and people with it. The thinking has to be done largely by people who are not directly productive—by people who appear to be living almost entirely on the work of others, but are, in fact, a long-term investment. Learning grew up in the cities and in great institutions—it was the labour of the countryside that supported them. Do you agree with that?'

Stephen knitted his brows.

'More or less—but I don't see what you're getting at?'

'It's this—the economic size. A community of our present size cannot hope to do more than exist and decline. If we stay here as we are, just ten of us now, the end is, quite inevitably, a gradual and useless fade-out. If there are children we shall be able to spare only enough time from our labour to give them just a rudimentary education; one generation further, and we shall have savages or clods. To hold our own, to make any use at all of the knowledge in the libraries we must have the teacher, the doctor, and the leader, and we must be able to support them while they help us.'

'Well?' said Stephen, after a pause.

'I've been thinking of that place Bill and I saw at Tynsham. We've told you about it. The woman who is trying to run it wanted help, and she wanted it badly. She has about fifty or sixty people on her hands, and a dozen or so of them able to see. That way she can't do it. She knows she can't—but she wasn't going to admit it to us. She wasn't going to put herself in our debt by asking us to stay. But she'd be very glad if we were to go back there after all, and ask to be admitted.'

'Good Lord,' I said. 'You don't think she deliberately put us on the wrong track?'

'I don't know. I may be doing her an injustice, but it is an odd thing that we've not seen or heard a single sign of Beadley and Co., isn't it? Anyhow, whether she meant it or not, that's the way it works, because I've decided to go back there. If you want my reasons, here they are—the two main ones. First, unless that place is taken in hand it's going to crash, which would be a waste and a shame for all those people there. The other is that it is much better situated than this. It has a farm which should not take a lot of putting in order; it is practically self-contained, but could be extended if necessary. This place would cost a lot more labour to start and to work.

'More important, it is big enough to afford time for teaching—teaching both the present blind there, and the sighted children they'll have later on. I believe it can be done, and I'll do my best to do it—and if the haughty Miss Durrant can't take it, she can go jump in the river.

'Now the point is this. I *think* I could do it as it stands— but I *know* that if the lot of us were to go we could get the place reorganized and running in a few weeks. Then we'd be living in a community that's going to grow and make a damned good attempt to hold its own. The alternative is to stay in a small party which is going to decline and get more desperately lonely as time goes on. So, how about it?'

There was some debate and inquiry for details, but not much doubt. Those of us who had been out on the search had had a glimpse of the awful loneliness that might come. No one was attached to the present house. It had been chosen for its defensible qualities, and had little more to commend it. Most of them could feel the oppression of isolation growing round them already. The thought of wider and more varied company was in itself attractive. The end of an hour found the discussion dealing with questions of transport and details of the removal, and the decision to adopt Coker's suggestion had more or less made itself. Only Stephen's girl friend was doubtful.

'This place Tynsham—it's pretty much off the map?' she asked, uneasily.

'Don't you worry,' Coker reassured her. 'It's marked on all the best American maps.'

It was some time in the early hours of the following morning that I knew I was not going to Tynsham with the rest. Later, perhaps I would, but not yet. . . .

My first inclination had been to accompany them if only
for the purpose of choking the truth out of Miss Durrant
regarding the Beadley party's destination. But then I had to
make again the disturbing admission that I did not know
that Josella was with them—and, indeed, that all the information I had been able to collect so far suggested that
she was not. She had pretty certainly not passed through
Tynsham. But if she had not gone in search of them, then
where had she gone? It was scarcely likely that there had
been a second direction in the University Building, one that
I had missed. . . .

And then, as if it had been a flash of light, I recalled the
discussion we had had in our commandeered flat. I could
see her sitting there in her blue party frock, with the light
of the candles catching the diamonds as we talked. . . . 'What
about the Sussex Downs?—I know a lovely old farmhouse
on the north side . . .' And then I knew what I must do. . . .

I told Coker about it in the morning. He was sym-
pathetic, but obviously anxious not to raise my hopes too
much.

'Okay. You do as you think best,' he agreed. 'I hope—
well, anyway, you'll know where we are, and you can both
come on to Tynsham and help to put that woman through
the hoop until she sees sense.'

That morning the weather broke. The rain was falling in
sheets as I climbed once more into the familiar lorry. Yet I
was feeling elated and hopeful, it could have rained ten
times harder without depressing me or altering my plan.
Coker came out to see me off. I knew why he made a point
of it, for I was aware without his telling me that the
memory of his first rash plan and its consequences troubled
him. He stood beside the cab with his hair flattened
and the water trickling down his neck, and held up his
hand.

'Take it easy, Bill. There aren't any ambulances these days, and she'll prefer you to arrive all in one piece. Good luck—and my apologies for everything to the lady when you find her.'

The word was 'when,' but the tone was 'if.'

I wished them well at Tynsham. Then I let in the clutch and splashed away down the muddy drive.

13. Journey in Hope

THE morning was infected with minor mishaps. First it was water in the carburettor. Then I contrived to travel a dozen miles north under the impression I was going east, and before I had that fully rectified I was in trouble with the ignition system on a bleak upland road miles from anywhere. Either these delays or a natural reaction did a lot to spoil the hopeful mood in which I had started. By the time I had the trouble straightened out it was one o'clock, and the day had cleared up.

The sun came out. Everything looked bright and refreshed, but even that, and the fact that for the next twenty miles all went smoothly, did not shift the mood of depression that was closing over me again. Now I was really on my own I could not shut out the sense of loneliness. It came upon me again as it had on that day when we had split up to search for Michael Beadley—only with double the force. . . . Until then I had always thought of loneliness as something negative—and absence of company, and, of course, something temporary. . . . That day I had learned that it was much more. It was something which could press and oppress, could distort the ordinary, and play tricks with the mind. Something which lurked inimically all around, stretching the nerves and twanging them with alarms, never letting one forget that there was no one to help, no one to care. It showed one as an atom adrift in vastness, and it waited all the time its chance to frighten and frighten horribly—that was what loneliness was really trying to do; and that was what one must never let it do. . . .

To deprive a gregarious creature of companionship is to maim it, to outrage its nature. The prisoner and the cenobite are aware that the herd exists beyond their exile; they are an aspect of it. But when the herd no longer exists there is, for the herd creature, no longer entity. He is a part of no whole; a freak without a place. If he cannot hold on to his reason, then he is lost indeed; most utterly, most fearfully lost, so that he becomes no more than the twitch in the limb of a corpse.

It needed far more resistance now that it had before. Only the strength of my hope that I would find companionship at my journey's end kept me from turning back to find relief from the strain in the presence of Coker and the others.

The sights which I saw by the way had little or nothing to do with it. Horrible though some of them were, I was hardened to such things by now. The horror had left them just as the horror which broods over great battlefields fades into history. Nor did I any longer see these things as part of a vast, impressive tragedy. My struggle was all a personal conflict with the instincts of my kind. A continual defensive action, with no victory possible. I knew in my very heart that I would not be able to sustain myself for long alone.

To give myself occupation I drove faster than I should. In some small town with a forgotten name I rounded a corner and ran straight into a van which blocked the whole street. Luckily my own tough lorry suffered no more than scratches, but the two vehicles managed to hitch themselves together with diabolical ingenuity so that it was an awkward business singlehanded and in a confined space, to separate them. It was a problem which took me a full hour to solve, and did me good by turning my mind to practical matters.

After that I kept to a more cautious pace except for a few minutes soon after I entered the New Forest. The cause of that was a glimpse through the trees of a helicopter cruising at no great height. It was set to cross my course some way ahead. By ill luck the trees there grew close to the sides of the road, and must have hidden it almost completely from the air. I put on a spurt, but by the time I reached more open ground the machine was no more than a speck floating away in the distance to the north. Nevertheless, even the sight of it seemed to give me some support.

A few miles further on I ran through a small village which was disposed neatly about a triangular green. At first sight it was as charming in its mixture of thatched and red-tiled cottages with their flowering gardens as something out of a picture-book. But I did not look too closely into the gardens as I passed; too many of them showed the alien shape of a triffid towering incongruously among the flowers. I was almost clear of the place when a small figure bounded out of one of the last garden gates and came running up the road towards me, waving both arms. I pulled up, looked around for triffids in a way that was becoming instinctive, picked up my gun, and climbed down.

The child was dressed in a blue cotton frock, white socks, and sandals. She looked about nine or ten years old. A pretty little girl—I could see that even though her dark brown curls were now uncared for, and her face dirtied with smeared tears. She pulled at my sleeve.

'Please, please,' she said, urgently, 'please come and see what's happened to Tommy.'

I stood staring down at her. The awful loneliness of the day lifted. My mind seemed to break out of the case I had made for it. I wanted to pick her up and hold her to me. I could feel tears close behind my eyes. I held out my hand to her, and she took it. Together we walked back to the gate through which she had come.

'Tommy's there,' she said, pointing.

A little boy about four years of age lay on the diminutive patch of lawn between the flower-beds. It was quite obvious at a glance why he was there.

'The *thing* hit him,' she said. 'It hit him and he fell down. And it wanted to hit me when I tried to help him. Horrible *thing!*'

I looked up and saw the top of a triffid rising above the fence that bordered the garden.

'Put your hands over your ears. I'm going to make a bang,' I said.

She did so, and I blasted the top off the triffid.

'Horrible *thing!*' she repeated. 'Is it dead now?'

I was about to assure her that it was when it began to rattle the little sticks against its stem, just as the one at Steeple Honey had done. As then, I gave it the other barrel to shut it up.

'Yes,' I said. 'It's dead now.'

We walked across to the little boy. The scarlet slash of the sting was vivid on his pale cheek. It must have happened some hours before. She knelt beside him.

'It isn't any good,' I told her, gently.

She looked up, fresh tears in her eyes.

'Is Tommy dead, too?'

I squatted down beside her, and shook my head.

'I'm afraid he is.'

After a while she said:

'Poor Tommy! Will we bury him—like the puppies?'

'Yes,' I told her.

In all the overwhelming disaster that was the only grave

I dug—and it was a very small one. She gathered a little bunch of flowers, and laid them on top of it. Then we drove away.

Susan was her name. A long time ago, as it seemed to her, something had happened to her father and mother so that they could not see. Her father had gone out to try to get some help, and he had not come back. Her mother went out later, giving the children strict instructions not to leave the house. She had come back crying. The next day she went out again: this time she did not come back. The children had eaten what they could find, and then began to grow hungry. At last Susan was hungry enough to disobey instructions and seek help from Mrs. Walton at the shop. The shop itself was open, but Mrs. Walton was not there. No one came when Susan called, so she had decided to take some cakes and biscuits and sweets, and tell Mrs. Walton about it later.

She had seen some of the *things* about as she came back. One of them had struck at her, but it had misjudged her height, and the sting had passed over her head. It frightened her, and she ran the rest of the way home. After that. she had been very careful about the *things*, and on further expeditions had taught Tommy to be careful about them, too. But Tommy had been so little, he had not been able to see the one that was hiding in the next garden when he went out to play that morning. Susan had tried half a dozen times to get to him, but each time, however careful she was, she had seen the top of the triffid tremble and stir slightly. . . .

An hour or so later I decided it was time to stop for the night. I left her in the truck while I prospected a cottage or two until I found one that was fit, and then we set about getting a meal together. I did not know much of small girls, but this one seemed to be able to dispose of an astonishing quantity of the result; confessing while she did so that a diet consisting almost entirely of biscuits, cake, and sweets had proved less completely satisfying than she had expected. After we had cleaned her up a bit, and I, under instruction, had wielded her hairbrush, I began to feel rather pleased with the results. She, for her part, seemed able for a time to forget all that had happened in her pleasure at having someone to talk to.

I could understand that. I was feeling exactly the same way myself.

But not long after I had seen her to bed and come downstairs again I heard the sound of sobbing. I went back to her.

'It's all right, Susan,' I said. 'It's all right. It didn't really hurt poor Tommy, you know—it was so quick.' I sat down on the bed beside her, and took her hand. She stopped crying.

'It wasn't just Tommy,' she said. 'It was after Tommy—when there was nobody, nobody at all. I was so frightened...'

'I know,' I told her. 'I *do* know. I was frightened, too.'

She looked up at me.

'But you aren't frightened now?'

'No. And you aren't, either. So you see we'll just have to keep together to stop one another being frightened.'

'Yes,' she agreed, with serious consideration. 'I think that'll be all right...'

So we went on to discuss a number of things until she fell asleep.

'Where are we going?' Susan asked, as we started off again the following morning.

I said that we were looking for a lady.

'Where is she?' asked Susan.

I wasn't sure of that.

'When shall we find her?' asked Susan.

I was pretty unsatisfactory about that, too.

'Is she a pretty lady?' asked Susan.

'Yes,' I said, glad to be more definite, this time.

It seemed, for some reason, to give Susan satisfaction.

'Good,' she remarked, approvingly, and we passed to other subjects.

Because of her I tried to skirt the larger towns, but it was impossible to avoid many unpleasant sights in the country. After a while I gave up pretending that they did not exist. Susan regarded them with the same detached interest as she gave to the normal scenery. They did not alarm her, though they puzzled her, and prompted questions. Reflecting that the world in which she was going to grow up would have little use for the over-niceties and euphemisms that I had learnt as a child, I did my best to treat the various horrors and curiosities in the same objective fashion. That was really very good for me, too.

By midday the clouds had gathered, and the rain began once more. When, at five o'clock, we pulled up on the road just short of Pulborough it was still pouring hard.

'Where do we go now?' inquired Susan.

'That,' I acknowledged, 'is just the trouble. It's somewhere over there.' I waved my arm towards the misty line of the Downs, to the south.

I had been trying hard to recall just what else Josella had said of the place, but I could remember no more than that the house stood on the north side of the hills, and I had the impression that it faced across the low, marshy country that separated them from Pulborough. Now that I had come so far, it seemed a pretty vague instruction: the Downs stretched away for miles to the east and to the west.

'Maybe the first thing to do is to see if we can find any smoke across there,' I suggested.

'It's awfully difficult to see anything at all in the rain,' Susan said, practically, and quite rightly.

Half an hour later the rain obligingly held off for a while. We left the lorry and sat on a wall side by side. We studied the lower slopes of the hills carefully for some time, but neither Susan's sharp eyes nor my field-glasses could discover any trace of smoke or signs of activity. Then it started to rain again.

'I'm hungry,' said Susan.

Food was a matter of trifling interest to me just then. Now that I was so near, my anxiety to know whether my guess had been right overcame everything else. While Susan was still eating I took the lorry a little way up the hill behind us to get a more extensive view. In between showers, and in a worsening light we scanned the other side of the valley again without result. There was no life or movement in the whole valley save for a few cattle and sheep, and an occasional triffid lurching across the fields below.

An idea came to me, and I decided to go down to the village. I was reluctant to take Susan, for I knew the place would be unpleasant, but I could not leave her where she was. When we got there I found that the sights affected her less than they did me; children have a different convention of the fearful until they have been taught the proper things to be shocked at. The depression was all mine. Susan found more to interest than to disgust her. Any sombreness was quite offset by her delight in a scarlet silk mackintosh with which she equipped herself in spite of its being several sizes too large. My search, too, was rewarding. I returned to the lorry laden with a headlamp like a minor searchlight which we had found upon an illustrious-looking Rolls-Royce.

I rigged the thing up on a kind of pivot beside the cab window, and made it ready to plug in. When that was fixed there was nothing to do but wait for darkness, and hope that the rain would let up.

By the time it was fully dark the raindrops had become a mere spatter. I switched on, and sent a magnificent beam piercing the night. Slowly I turned the lamp from side to side, keeping its ray levelled towards the opposite hills, while I anxiously tried to watch the whole line of them simultaneously for an answering light. A dozen times or more I traversed it steadily, switching off for a few seconds at the end of each sweep while we sought the least flicker in the darkness. But each time the night over the hills remained pitchy black. Then the rain came on more heavily again. I set the beam full ahead, and sat waiting, listening to the drumming of the drops on the roof of the cab while Susan fell asleep leaning against my arm. An hour passed before the drumming dwindled to a patter, and ceased. Susan woke up as I started the beam raking across again. I had completed the sixth travel when she called out:

'Look, Bill! There it is! There's a light!'

She was pointing a few degrees left of our front. I switched off the lamp, and followed the line of her finger. It was difficult to be sure. If it were not a trick of our eyes, it was something as dim as a distant glow-worm. And even as we were looking at it, the rain came down on us again in sheets. By the time I had my glasses in my hand there was no view at all.

I hesitated to move. It might be that the light, if it had been a light, would not be visible from lower ground. Once more I trained our light forward, and settled down to wait with as much patience as I could manage. Almost another hour passed before the rain cleared again. The moment it did, I switched off our lamp.

'It is!' Susan cried, excitedly. 'Look! Look!'

It was. And bright enough now to banish any doubts, though the glasses showed me no details.

I switched on again, and gave the V-sign in Morse—it is the only Morse I know except S O S, so it had to do. While we watched the other light it blinked, and then began a series of deliberate longs and shorts which unfortunately meant nothing to me. I gave a couple more V's for good measure, drew the approximate line of the far light on our map, and switched on the driving lights.

'Is that the lady?' asked Susan.

'It's got to be,' I said. 'It's *got* to be.'

That was a poorish trip. To cross the low marshland it was necessary to take a road a little to the west of us and then work back to the east along the foot of the hills. Before we had gone more than a mile something cut off the sight of the light from us altogether, and to add to the difficulty of finding our way in the dark lanes the rain began again in earnest. With no one to care for the drainage sluices some fields were already flooded, and the water was over the road in places. I had to drive with a tedious care when all my urge was to put my foot flat down.

Once we reached the further side of the valley we were free of flood water, but we made little better speed for the lanes were full of primitive wanderings and improbable turns. I had to give the wheel all my attention while the child peered up at the hills beside us, watching for the reappearance of the light. We reached the point where the line on my map intersected with what appeared to be our present road without seeing a sign of it. I tried the next uphill turning. It took about half an hour to get back to the road again from the chalkpit into which it led us.

We ran on further along the lower road. Then Susan caught a glimmer between the branches to our right. The next turning was luckier. It took us back at a slant up the side of the hill until we were able to see a small, brilliantly lit square of window half a mile or more along the slope.

Even then, and with the map to help, it was not easy to find the lane that led to it. We lurched along, still climbing in low gear, but each time we caught sight of the window again it was a little closer. The lane had not been designed for ponderous lorries. In the narrower parts we had to push our way along it between bushes and brambles which scrabbled along the sides as though they were trying to pull us back.

But at last there was a lantern waving in the road ahead. It moved on, swinging to show us the turn through a gate. Then it was set stationary on the ground. I drove to within a yard or two of it, and stopped. As I opened the door a flashlight shone suddenly into my eyes. I had a glimpse of a figure behind it in a raincoat shining with wetness.

A slight break marred the intended calm of the voice that spoke.

'Hullo, Bill. You've been a long time.'

I jumped down.

'Oh, Bill. I can't—Oh, my dear, I've been hoping so much . . . Oh, Bill . . .' said Josella.

I had forgotten all about Susan until a voice came from above.

'You *are* getting wet, you silly. Why don't you kiss her indoors?' it asked.

14. Shirning

T HE sense with which I arrived at Shirning Farm—the one that told me that most of my troubles were now over—is interesting only in showing how wide of the mark a sense can be. The sweeping of Josella into my arms went off pretty well, but its corollary of carrying her away forthwith to join the others at Tynsham did not, for several reasons.

Ever since her possible location had occurred to me I had pictured her in, I must admit, a rather cinematic way, as battling bravely against all the forces of nature, etc., etc. In a fashion I suppose she was, but the set-up was a lot different from my imaginings. My simple plan of saying: 'Jump aboard. We're off to join Coker and his little gang,' had to go by the board. One might have known that things would not turn out so simply—on the other hand it is surprising how often the better thing is disguised as the worse. . . .

Not that I didn't from the start prefer Shirning to the thought of Tynsham—but to join a larger group was obviously a sounder move. But Shirning was charming. The word 'farm' had become a courtesy title for the place. It had been a farm until some twenty-five years before, and

242

it still looked like a farm, but in reality it had become a country house. Sussex and the neighbouring counties were well dotted with such houses and cottages which tired Londoners had found adaptable to their needs. Internally the house had been modernized and reconstructed to a point where it was doubtful whether its previous tenants would be able to recognize a single room. Outside it had become spick. The yards and sheds had a suburban rather than a rural tidiness and had for years known no form of animal life rougher than a few riding horses and ponies. The farmyard showed no utilitarian sights and gave forth no rustic smells; it had been laid over with close green turf like a bowling green. The fields across which the windows of the house gazed from beneath weathered red tiles had long been worked by the occupiers of other and more earthy farmhouses. But the sheds and barns remained in good condition.

It had been the ambition of Josella's friends, the present owners, to restore the place one day to work on a limited scale, and to this end they had continually refused tempting offers for it in the hope that at some time, and in some manner not clearly perceived, they would acquire enough money to start buying back the land rightfully belonging to it.

With its own well and its own power plant, the place had plenty to recommend it—but as I looked it over I understood Coker's wisdom in speaking of co-operative effort. I knew nothing of farming, but I could feel that if we had intended to stay there it would take a lot of work to feed six of us.

The other three had been there already when Josella had arrived. They were Dennis and Mary Brent, and Joyce Taylor. Dennis was the owner of the house. Joyce had been there on an indefinite visit, at first to keep Mary company, and then to keep the house running when Mary's expected baby should be born.

On the night of the green flashes—of the comet you would say if you were one who still believes in that comet—there had been two other guests, Joan and Ted Danton, spending a week's holiday there. All five of them had gone out into the garden to watch the display. In the morning all five awoke to a world that was perpetually dark. First they had tried to telephone, when they found that impossible they waited hopefully for the arrival of the daily help. She, too, failing them, Ted had volunteered to try to find out what had happened. Dennis would have accompanied him but for his wife's almost hysterical state. Ted, therefore, had set out alone. He did not come back. At some time late in the day, and without saying a word to anyone, Joan had slipped off, presumably to try to find her husband. She, too, disappeared completely.

Dennis had kept track of time by touching the hands of the clock. By late afternoon it was impossible to sit any longer doing nothing. He wanted to try to get down to the village. Both the women had objected to that. Because of Mary's state he had yielded, and Joyce determined to try. She went to the door, and began to feel her way with a stick outstretched before her. She was barely over the threshold when something fell with a swish across her left hand, burning like a hot wire. She jumped back with a cry, and collapsed in the hall where Dennis had found her. Luckily she was conscious, and able to moan of the pain in her hand. Dennis, feeling the raised weal had guessed it for what it was. In spite of their blindness, he and Mary had somehow contrived to apply hot fomentations, she heating the kettle while he put on a tourniquet and did his best to suck out the poison. After that they had had to carry her up to bed where she stayed for several days while the effect of the poison wore off.

Meanwhile Dennis had made tests, first at the front and then at the back of the house. With the door slightly open, he cautiously thrust out a broom at head level. Each time there was the whistle of a sting, and he felt the broom handle tremble slightly in his grip. At one of the garden windows the same thing happened: the others seemed to be clear. He would have tried to leave by one of them but for Mary's distress. She was sure that if there were triffids close round the house there must be others about, and would not let him take the risk.

Luckily they had food enough to last them some time, though it was difficult to prepare it; also Joyce, in spite of a high temperature, appeared to be holding her own against the triffid poison, so that the situation was less urgent than it might have been. Most of the next day Dennis devoted to contriving a kind of helmet for himself. He had wire net only of large mesh so that he had to construct it of several layers overlapped and tied together. It took him some time, but, equipped with this and a pair of heavy gauntlet gloves, he was able to start out for the village late in the day. A triffid had struck at him before he was three paces away from the house. He groped for it until he found it, and twisted its stem for it. A minute or two later another sting thudded across his helmet. He could not find that triffid to grapple with it, though it made half a dozen slashes before it gave up. He found his way to the toolshed, and thence across to the lane, encumbered now with three large balls of gardening twine which he paid out as he went to guide him back.

Several times in the lane more stings whipped at him. It took an immensely long time for him to cover the mile or so to the village, and, before he reached it, his supply of twine had given out. And all the time he had walked and stumbled through a silence so complete that it frightened him. Now and then he would stop and call, but no one answered. More than once he was afraid that he had lost his way, but when his feet discovered a better laid road surface he knew where he was, and was able to confirm it by locating a signpost. He groped his way further on.

After a seemingly vast distance he had become aware that his footsteps were sounding differently; they had a faint echo. Making to one side he found a footpath, and then a wall. A little further along he discovered a post-box let into the brickwork, and knew that he must be actually in the village at last. He called out once more. A voice, a woman's voice called back, but it was some distance ahead, and the words were indistinguishable. He called again, and began to move towards it. Its reply was suddenly cut off by a scream. After that there was silence again. Only then, and still half-incredulously, did he realize that the village was in no better plight than his own household. He sat down on the grassed verge of the path to think out what he should do.

By the feeling in the air he thought that night must have come. He must have been away fully four hours—and there was nothing to do but go back. All the same, there was no reason why he should go back empty-handed. . . . With his stick he rapped his way along the wall until it rang on one of the tinplate advertisements which adorned the village shop. Three times in the last fifty or sixty yards stings had slapped on his helmet. Another struck as he opened the gate, and he tripped over a body lying on the path. A man's body, quite cold.

He had the impression that there had been others in the shop before him. Nevertheless, he found a sizeable piece of bacon. He dropped it, along with packets of butter or margarine, biscuits and sugar into a sack, and added an assortment of tins which came from a shelf that, to the best of his recollection, was devoted to food—the sardine tins, at any rate, were unmistakable. Then he sought for, and found, a dozen or more balls of string, shouldered his sack, and set off for home.

He had missed his way once, and it had been hard to keep down panic while he retraced his steps and reorientated himself. But at last he knew that he was again in the familiar lane. By groping right across it he managed to locate the twine of his outward journey, and join it to the string. From there the rest of the journey back had been comparatively easy.

Twice more in the week that followed he had made the journey to the village shop again, and each time the triffids round the house and on the way had seemed more numerous. There had been nothing for the isolated trio to do but wait in hope. And then, like a miracle, Josella had arrived.

It was clear at once, then, that the notion of an immediate move to Tynsham was out. For one thing, Joyce Taylor was still in an extremely weak state—when I looked at her I was surprised that she was alive at all. Dennis's promptness had saved her life, but their inability to give her the proper restoratives or even suitable food during the following week had slowed down her recovery. It would be folly to try to move her a long distance for a week or two yet. And then, too, Mary's confinement was close enough to make the journey inadvisable for her, so that the only course seemed to be for us all to remain where we were until these crises should have passed.

Once more it became my task to scrounge and forage. This time I had to work on a more elaborate scale to include not merely food, but petrol for the lighting system, hens that were laying, two cows that had recently calved (and still survived though their ribs were sticking out), medical necessities for Mary, and a surprising list of sundries.

The area was more beset with triffids than any other I had yet seen. Almost every morning revealed one or two new ones lurking close to the house, and the first task of the day was to shoot the tops off them, until I had constructed a netting fence to keep them out of the garden. Even then they would come right up and loiter suggestively against it until something was done about them.

I opened some of the cases of gear, and taught young Susan how to use a triffid-gun. She quite rapidly became an expert at disarming the *things* as she continued to call them. It became her department to work daily vengeance on them.

From Josella I learnt what had happened to her after the fire alarm at the University Building.

She had been shipped off with her party much as I with mine, but her manner of dealing with the two women to whom she was attached had been summary. She had issued a flat ultimatum: either she became free of all restraints, in which case she would help them as far as she was able; or, if they continued to coerce her, there would be likely to come a time when they would find themselves drinking prussic acid or eating cyanide of potassium on her recommendation. They could take their choice. They had chosen sensibly.

There was little difference in what we had to tell one another about the days that had followed. When her group had in the end dissolved, she had reasoned much as I did. She took a car, and went up to Hampstead to look for me. She had not encountered any survivors from my group, nor run across that led by the quick-triggered, red-headed man. She had kept on there until almost sunset, and then decided

to make for the University Building. Not knowing what to
expect, she had cautiously stopped the car a couple of streets
away, and approached on foot. When she was still some
distance from the gates she heard a shot. Wondering what
that might indicate, she had taken cover in the garden that
had sheltered us before. From there she had observed Coker
also making a circumspect advance. Without knowing that
I had fired at the triffid in the Square, and that the sound of
the shot was the cause of Coker's caution, she suspected
some kind of trap. Determined not to fall into one a second
time, she had returned to the car. She had no idea where the
rest had gone—if they had gone at all. The only place of
refuge she could think of that would be known to anyone at
all was the one she had mentioned almost casually to me.
She had decided to make for it in the hope that I, if I were
still in existence, would remember, and try to find it.

'I curled up and slept in the back of the car once I was
clear of London,' she said. 'It was still quite early when I got
here the next morning. The sound of the car brought Dennis
to an upstairs window warning me to look out for triffids.
Then I saw that there were half a dozen or more of them
close around the house for all the world as if they were
waiting for someone to come out of it. Dennis and I shouted
back and forth. The triffids stirred and one of them began
to move towards me, so I nipped back into the car for safety.
When it kept on coming, I started up the car, and deliberately ran it down. But there were still the others, and I had
no kind of weapon but my knife. It was Dennis who solved
that difficulty.

' "If you have a can of petrol to spare, throw some of it
their way, and follow it up with a bit of burning rag," he
suggested. "That ought to shift 'em."

'It did. Since then I've been using a garden syringe. The
wonder is that I've not set the place on fire.'

With the aid of a cook-book Josella had managed to produce meals of a kind, and had set about putting the place more or less to rights. Working, learning and improvising had kept her too busy to worry about a future which lay beyond the next few weeks. She had seen no one else at all during those days, but, certain that there must be others somewhere, she had scanned the whole valley for signs of smoke by day or lights by night. She had seen no smoke, and in all the miles within her view there had not been a gleam of light until the evening I came.

In a way, the worst affected of the original trio was Dennis. Joyce was still weak and in a semi-invalid state. Mary held herself withdrawn and seemed capable of finding endless mental occupation and compensation in the contemplation of prospective motherhood. But Dennis was like an animal in a trap. He did not curse in the futile way I had heard so many others do, he resented it with a vicious bitterness as if it had forced him into a cage where he did not intend to stay. Already, before I arrived, he had prevailed upon Josella to find the Braille system in the encyclopædia and make an indented copy of the alphabet for him to learn. He spent dogged hours each day making notes in it, and attempting to read them back. Most of the rest of the time he fretted over his own uselessness, though he scarcely mentioned it. He would keep on trying to do this or that with a grim persistence that was painful to watch, and it required all my self-control to stop me offering him help—one experience of the bitterness which unasked help could arouse in him was quite enough. I began to be astonished at the things he was painfully teaching himself to do, though still the most impressive to me was his construction of an efficient mesh helmet on only the second day of his blindness.

It took him out of himself to accompany me on some of

my foraging expeditions, and it pleased him that he could be useful in helping to move the heavier cases. He was anxious for books in Braille, but these, we decided, would have to wait until there was less risk of contamination in towns large enough to be likely sources.

The days began to pass quickly, certainly for the three of us who could see. Josella was kept busy, mostly in the house, and Susan was learning to help her. There were plenty of jobs, too, waiting to be done by me. Joyce recovered sufficiently to make a shaky first appearance, and then began to pick up more rapidly. Soon after that Mary's pains began.

That was a bad night for everyone. Worst, perhaps, for Dennis in knowing that everything depended on the care of two willing, but inexperienced girls. His self-control aroused my helpless admiration.

In the early hours of the morning Josella came down to us, looking very tired:

'It's a girl. They're both all right,' she said, and led Dennis up.

She returned a few moments later, and took the drink I had ready for her.

'It was quite simple, thank heaven,' she said. 'Poor Mary was horribly afraid it might be blind, too, but of course it's not. Now she's crying quite dreadfully because she can't see it.'

We drank.

'It's queer,' I said, 'the way things go on, I mean. Like a seed—it looks all shrivelled and finished, you'd think it was dead, but it isn't. And now a new life starting, coming into all this . . .'

Josella put her face in her hands.

'Oh, God! Bill. Does it have to go on being like this? On—and on—and on——?'

And she, too, collapsed in tears.

Three weeks later I went over to Tynsham to see Coker and make arrangements for our move. I took an ordinary car in order to do the double journey in a day. When I got back Josella met me in the hall. She gave one look at my face.

'What's the matter?' she said.

'Just that we shan't be going there after all,' I told her. 'Tynsham is finished.'

She stared back at me.

'What happened?'

'I'm not sure. It looks as if the plague got there.'

I described the state of affairs briefly. It had not needed much investigation. The gates were open when I arrived, and the sight of triffids loose in the park half-warned me what to expect. The smell when I got out of the car confirmed it. I made myself go into the house. By the look of it it had been deserted two weeks or more before. I put my head into two of the rooms. They were enough for me. I called, and my voice ran right away through the hollowness of the house. I went no further.

There had been a notice of some kind pinned to the front door, but only one blank corner remained. I spent a long time searching for the rest of the sheet that must have blown away. I did not find it. The yard at the back was empty of lorries and cars, and most of the stores had gone with them, but where to I could not tell. There was nothing to be done but get into my car again, and come back.

'And so—what?' asked Josella, when I had finished.

'And so, my dear, we stay here. We learn how to support ourselves. And we go on supporting ourselves—unless help comes. There may be an organization somewhere . . .'

Josella shook her head.

'I think we'd better forget all about help. Millions and

millions of people have been waiting and hoping for help that hasn't come.'

'There'll be something,' I said. 'There must be thousands of little groups like this dotted all over Europe—all over the world. Some of them will get together. They'll begin to rebuild.'

'In how long?' said Josella. 'Generations? Perhaps not until after our time. No—the world's gone, and we're left. . . . We must make our own lives. We'll have to plan them as though help will never come . . .' She paused. There was an odd, blank look on her face that I had never seen before. It puckered.

'Darling . . .' I said.

'Oh, Bill, Bill, I wasn't meant for this kind of life. If you weren't here I'd . . .'

'Hush, my sweet,' I said, gently. 'Hush.' I stroked her hair.

A few moments later she recovered herself.

'I'm sorry, Bill. Self-pity . . . revolting. Never again.'

She patted her eyes with her handkerchief, and sniffed a little.

'So I'm to be a farmer's wife. Anyway, I like being married to you, Bill—even if it isn't a very proper, authentic kind of marriage.'

Suddenly she gave the smiling chuckle that I had not heard for some time.

'What is it?'

'I was only thinking how much I used to dread my wedding.'

'That was very maidenly and proper of you—if a little unexpected,' I told her.

'Well, it wasn't exactly that. It was my publishers, and the newspapers, and the film people. What fun they would have had with it. There'd have been a new edition of my silly book—probably a new release of the film—and pictures in all the papers. I don't think you'd have liked that much.'

'I can think of another thing I'd not have liked much,' I told her. 'Do you remember—that night in the moonlight you made a condition?'

She looked at me.

'Well, maybe some things haven't fallen out so badly,' she said.

15. World Narrowing

FROM then on I kept a journal. It is a mixture of diary, stock list, and commonplace-book. In it there are notes of the places to which my expeditions took me, particulars of the supplies collected, estimates of quantities available, observations on the states of the premises, with memos on which should be cleared first to avoid deterioration. Foodstuffs, fuel, and seed were constant objects of search, but by no means the only ones. There are entries detailing loads of clothing, tools, household linen, harness, kitchenware, loads of stakes, and wire, wire, and more wire, also books.

I can see there that within a week of my return from Tynsham I had started on the work of erecting a wire fence to keep the triffids out. Already we had barriers to hold them away from the garden and the immediate neighbourhood of the house. Now I began a more ambitious plan of making some hundred acres or so free from them. It involved a stout wire fence which took advantage of the natural features and standing barriers, and inside it a lighter fence to prevent either the stock or ourselves from coming inadvertently within sting range of the main fence. It was a heavy, tedious job which took me a number of months to complete.

At the same time I was endeavouring to learn the a-b-c of farming. It is not the kind of thing that is easily learnt from books. For one thing, it had never occurred to any writer on the subject that any potential farmer could be starting from absolute zero. I found, therefore, that all works began, as it were, in the middle, taking for granted both a basis and a vocabulary that I did not have. My specialized biological knowledge was all but useless to me in the face of practical problems. Much of the theory called for materials and substances which were either unavailable to me, or unrecognizable by me if I could find them. I began to see quite soon that by the time I had dismissed the things that would shortly be unprocurable such as chemical fertilizers, imported feeding-stuffs, and all but the simpler kinds of machinery there was going to be much expenditure of sweat for problematical returns.

Nor is book-instilled knowledge of horse-management, dairy-work, or slaughterhouse procedure by any means an adequate groundwork for these arts. There are so many points where one cannot break off to consult the relative chapter. Moreover, the realities persistently present baffling dissimilarities from the simplicities of print.

Luckily there was plenty of time to make mistakes and to learn from them. The knowledge that several years could pass before we should be thrown anywhere near on our own resources saved us from desperation over our disappointments. There was the reassuring thought, too, that by living on preserved stores we were really being quite provident in preventing them from being wasted.

For safety's sake I let a whole year pass before I went to London again. It was the most profitable area for my forays, but it was the most depressing. The place still contrived to give the impression that a touch of a magic wand would bring it to life again, though many of the vehicles in the

streets were beginning to turn rusty. A year later the change
was more noticeable. Large patches of plaster detached from
housefronts had begun to litter the pavements. Dislodged
tiles and chimney-pots could be found in the streets. Grass
and weeds had a good hold in the gutters and were choking
the drains. Leaves had blocked downspoutings so that more
grass, and even small bushes, grew in cracks and in the silt
in the roof gutterings. Almost every building was beginning
to wear a green wig beneath which its roofs would damply
rot. Through many a window one had glimpses of fallen
ceilings, curves of peeling paper, and walls glistening with
damp. The gardens of the Parks and Squares were wilder-
nesses creeping out across the bordering streets. Growing
things seemed, indeed, to press out everywhere, rooting in
the crevices between the paving stones, springing from cracks
in concrete, finding lodgements even in the seats of the
abandoned cars. On all sides they were encroaching to
repossess themselves of the arid spaces that man had created.
And curiously, as the living things took charge increasingly,
the effect of the place became less oppressive. As it
passed beyond the scope of any magic wand, most of
the ghosts were going with it, withdrawing slowly into
history.

Once—not that year, nor the next, but later on—I stood
in Piccadilly Circus again, looking round at the desolation,
and trying to recreate in my mind's eye the crowds that once
swarmed there. I could no longer do it. Even in my memory
they lacked reality. There was no tincture of them now.
They had become as much a backcloth of history as the
audiences in the Roman Colosseum or the army of the
Assyrians, and somehow, just as far removed. The nostalgia
that crept over me sometimes in the quiet hours was able
to move me to more regret than the crumbling scene itself.
When I was by myself in the country I could recall the

I

pleasantness of the former life: among the scabrous, slowly perishing buildings I seemed able to recall only the muddle, the frustration, the unaimed drive, the all-pervading clangour of empty vessels, and I became uncertain how much we had lost. . . .

My first tentative trip there I took alone, returning with cases of triffid-bolts, paper, engine parts, the Braille books and writing machine that Dennis so much desired, the luxuries of drinks, sweets, records, and yet more books for the rest of us. A week later Josella came with me on a more practical search for clothing, not only, or even chiefly for the adults of the party, so much as for Mary's baby and the one she herself was now expecting. It upset her, and it remained the only visit she made.

I continued to go there from time to time in search of some scarce necessity, and used to seize the opportunity of a few little luxuries at the same time. Never once did I see any moving thing there save a few sparrows and an occasional triffid. Cats, and dogs, growing wilder at each generation, could be found in the country, but not there. Sometimes, however, I would find evidence that others besides myself were still in the habit of quarrying supplies there, but I never saw them.

It was at the end of the fourth year that I made my last trip, and found that there were now risks which I was not justified in taking. The first intimation of that was a thunderous crash behind me somewhere in the inner suburbs. I stopped the truck and looked back to see the dust rising from a heap of rubble which lay across the road. Evidently my rumbling passage had given the last shake to a tottering housefront. I brought no more buildings down that day, but I spent it in apprehension of a descending torrent of bricks and mortar. Thereafter I confined my attention to smaller towns, and usually went about them on foot.

Brighton, which should have been our largest convenient source of supplies, I let alone. By the time I had thought it fit for a visit, others were in charge there. Who or how many they were I did not know. I simply found a rough wall of stones piled across the road, and painted with the instruction:

KEEP OUT!

The advice was backed up by the crack of a rifle and a spurt of dust just in front of me. There was no one in sight to argue with—besides, it wasn't an arguing kind of gambit.

I turned the lorry round, and drove away thoughtfully. I wondered if a time would come when the man Stephen's preparations for defence might turn out to be not so misplaced after all. Just to be on the safe side I laid in several machine guns and mortars from the source which had already provided us with the flame-throwers we used against the triffids.

In the November of that second year Josella's first baby was born. We called him David. My pleasure in him was at times alloyed with misgivings over the state of things we had created him to face. But that worried Josella much less than it did me. She adored him. He seemed to be a compensation to her for much that she had lost, and, paradoxically, she started to worry less over the condition of the bridges ahead than she had before. Anyway, he had a lustiness which argued well for his future capacity to take care of himself, so I repressed my misgivings and increased the work I was putting into that land which would one day have to support all of us.

It must have been not so very long after that that Josella turned my attention more closely to the triffids. I had for years been so used to taking precautions against them in my work that their becoming a regular part of the landscape was far less noticeable to me than it was to the others. I had been accustomed, too, to wearing meshed masks and gloves when I dealt with them, so that there was little novelty for me in donning these things whenever I drove out. I had, in fact, got into the habit of paying little more attention to them than one would to mosquitoes in a known malarial area. Josella mentioned it as we lay in bed one night when almost the only sound was the intermittent, distant rattling of their hard little sticks against their stems.

'They're doing a lot more of that lately,' she said.

I did not grasp at first what she was talking about. It was a sound that had been a usual background to the places where I had lived and worked for so long, that unless I deliberately listened for it I could not say whether it was going on or not. I listened now.

'It doesn't sound any different to me,' I said.

'It's not *different*. It's just that there's a lot more of it—because there are a lot more of them than there used to be.'

'I hadn't noticed,' I said, indifferently.

Once I had the fence fixed up, my interest had lain in the ground within it, and I had not bothered what went on beyond it. My impression on my expeditions was that the incidence of triffids in most parts was much the same as before. I recalled that their numbers locally had caught my attention when I had first arrived, and that I had supposed that there must have been several large triffid nurseries in the district.

'There certainly are. You take a look at them to-morrow,' she said.

I remembered in the morning, and looked out of the window as I was dressing. I saw that Josella was right.

One could count over a hundred of them behind the quite small stretch of fence visible from the window. I mentioned it at breakfast. Susan looked surprised.

'But they've been getting more all the time,' she said. 'Haven't you noticed?'

'I've got plenty of other things to bother about,' I said, a little irritated by her tone. 'They don't matter outside the fence, anyway. As long as we take care to pull up all the seeds that root in here, they can do what they like outside.'

'All the same,' Josella remarked, with a trace of uneasiness, 'is there any particular reason why they should come to just this part in such numbers? I'm sure they do—and I'd like to know just why it is.'

Susan's face took on its irritating expression of surprise again.

'Why *he* brings them,' she said.

'Don't point,' Josella told her, automatically. 'What do you mean? I'm sure Bill doesn't bring them.'

'But he does. He makes all the noises, and they just come.'

'Look here,' I said. 'What are you talking about? Am I supposed to be whistling them here in my sleep, or something?'

Susan looked huffy.

'All right. If you don't believe me, I'll show you after breakfast,' she announced, and withdrew into an offended silence.

When we had finished she slipped from the table, returning with my twelve-bore and field-glasses. We went out on to the lawn. She scoured the view until she found a triffid on the move well beyond our fences, and then handed the glasses to me. I watched the thing lurching slowly across a field. It was more than a mile away from us, and heading east.

'Now keep on watching it,' she said.

She fired the gun into the air.

A few seconds later the triffid perceptibly altered course towards the south.

'See?' she inquired, rubbing her shoulder.

'Well, it did look—— Are you sure? Try again.' I suggested.

She shook her head.

'It wouldn't be any good. All the triffids that heard it are coming this way now. In about ten minutes they'll stop and listen. If they're near enough then to hear the ones by the fence clattering, they'll come on. Or if they're too far away for that, but we make another noise, then they'll come. But if they can't hear anything at all, they'll wait a bit, and then just go on wherever they were going before.'

I admit that I was somewhat taken aback by this revelation.

'Well—er,' I said. 'You must have been watching them very closely, Susan?'

'I always watch them. I hate them,' she said, as if that were explanation enough.

Dennis had joined us as we stood there.

'I'm with you, Susan,' he said. 'I don't like it. I've not liked it for some time. Those damn things have the drop on us.'

'Oh, come——' I began.

'I tell you there's more to them than we think. How did they *know*? They started to break loose the moment there was no one to stop them. They were around this house the very next day. Can you account for that?'

'That's not new for them,' I said. 'In jungle country they used to hang around near the tracks. Quite often they would surround a small village and invade it if they weren't beaten off. They were a dangerous kind of pest in quite a lot of places.'

'But not here—that's my point. They couldn't do that here until conditions made it possible. They didn't even try. But when they could, they did it *at once*—almost as if they *knew* they could.'

'Come now, be reasonable, Dennis. Just think what you're implying,' I told him.

'I'm quite aware of what I'm implying—some of it, at any rate. I'm making no definite theory, but I do say this: they took advantage of our disadvantages with remarkable speed. I also say that there is something perceptibly like method going on among them right now. You've been so wrapped up in your jobs that you've not noticed how they've been massing up, and waiting out there beyond the fence, but Susan has—I've heard her talking about it. And just what do you think they're waiting *for?*'

I did not try to answer that just then. I said:

'You think I'd better lay off using the twelve-bore which attracts them, and use a triffid gun instead?'

'It's not just the gun, it's all noises,' said Susan. 'The tractor's the worst because it is a loud noise, and it keeps on, so that they can easily find where it comes from. But they can hear the lighting-plant engine quite a long way, too. I've seen them turn this way when it starts up.'

'I wish,' I told her, irritably, 'you'd not keep on saying "they hear," as if they were animals. They're not. They don't "hear." They're just plants.'

'All the same, they *do* hear, somehow,' Susan retorted, stubbornly.

'Well—anyway, we'll do something about them,' I promised.

We did. The first trap was a crude kind of windmill which produced a hearty hammering noise. We fixed it up about half a mile away. It worked. It drew them away from our fence, and from elsewhere. When there were several hundreds of them clustered about it, Susan and I drove over there and turned the flame-throwers on them. It worked fairly well a second time, too—but after that only a very few of them paid any attention to it. Our next move was to build a kind of stout bay inwards from the fence, and then remove part of the main fence itself, replacing it by a gate. We had chosen a point within earshot of the lighting engine, and we left the gate open. After a couple of days we dropped the gate, and destroyed the couple of hundred or so that had come into the pen. That, too, was fairly successful to begin with, but not if we tried it twice in the same place, and even in other places the numbers we netted dropped steadily.

A tour of the boundaries every few days with a flame-thrower could have kept the numbers down effectively, but it would have taken a lot of time and soon have run us out of fuel. A flame-thrower's consumption is high, and the stocks held for it in the arms depots were not large. Once we finished it, our valuable flame-throwers would become little better than junk, for I knew neither the formula for an efficient fuel nor the method of producing it.

On the two or three occasions we tried mortar-bombs on concentrations of triffids the results were disappointing. Triffids share with trees the ability to take a lot of damage without lethal harm.

As time went on the numbers collected along the fence continued to increase in spite of our traps and occasional holocausts. They didn't try anything or do anything there. They simply settled down, wriggled their roots into the soil, and remained. At a distance they looked as inactive as any other hedge, and but for the pattering that some few of them were sure to be making, they might have been no more remarkable. But if one doubted their alertness it was only necessary to take a car down the lane. To do so was to run a gauntlet of such viciously slashing stings that it was necessary to stop the car at the main road and wipe the windscreen clear of poison.

Now and then one of us would have a new idea for their discouragement such as spraying the ground beyond the fence with a strong arsenical solution, but the retreats we caused were only temporary.

We'd been trying out a variety of such dodges for a year or more before the day when Susan came running into our room early one morning to tell us that the *things* had broken in, and were all round the house. She had got up early to do the milking, as usual. The sky outside her bedroom window was grey, but when she went downstairs she found everything there in complete darkness. She realized that should not be so, and turned on the light. The moment she saw leathery green leaves pressed against the windows, she guessed what had happened.

I crossed the bedroom on tiptoe, and pulled the window shut sharply. Even as it closed a sting whipped up from below and smacked against the glass. We looked down on a thicket of triffids standing ten or twelve deep against the wall of the house. The flame-throwers were in one of the outhouses. I took no risks when I went to fetch them. In thick clothing and gloves, with a leather helmet and goggles beneath the mesh mask I hacked a way through the throng of triffids with the largest carving knife I could find. The stings whipped and slapped at the wire mesh so frequently that they wet it, and the poison began to come through in a fine spray. It misted the goggles, and the first thing I did in the outhouse was to wash it off my face. I dared not use

more than a brief, low-aimed jet from one of the throwers
to clear my way back for fear of setting the door and window
frames alight, but it moved and agitated them enough for
me to get back unmolested.

Josella and Susan stood by with fire-extinguishers while
I, still looking like a cross between a deep-sea diver and a
man from Mars, leant from the upper windows on each side
of the house in turn and played the thrower over the besieg-
ing mob of the brutes. It did not take very long to incinerate
a number of them and get the rest on the move. Susan, now
dressed for the job, took the second thrower and started on
the, to her, highly congenial task of hunting them down
while I set off across the fields to find the source of the
trouble. That was not difficult. From the first rise I was able
to see the spot where triffids were still lurching into our
enclosure in a stream of tossing stems and waving leaves.
They fanned out a little on the nearer side, but all of them
were bound in the direction of the house. It was simple to
head them off. A jet in front stopped them; one to either side
started them back on the way they had come. An occasional
spurt over them and dripping among them hurried them up,
and turned back later-comers. Twenty yards or so away a
part of the fence was lying flat, with the posts snapped off.
I rigged it up temporarily there and then, and played the
thrower back and forth, giving the things enough of a
scorching to prevent more trouble for a few hours at
least.

Josella, Susan, and I spent most of the day repairing the
breach. Two more days passed before Susan and I could be
sure that we had searched every corner of the enclosure and
accounted for the very last of the intruders. We followed
that up with an inspection of the whole length of the fence
and a reinforcement of all doubtful sections. Four months
later they broke in again. . . .

This time a number of broken triffids lay in the gap. Our impression was that they had been crushed in the pressure that had been built up against the fence before it gave way, and that, falling with it, they had been trampled by the rest.

It was clear that we should have to take new defensive measures. No part of our fence was any stronger than that which had given way. Electrification seemed the most likely means of keeping them at a distance. To power it I found an army generator mounted on a trailer, and towed it home. Susan and I set to work on the wiring. Before we had completed it the brutes were through again in another place.

I believe that system would have been completely effective if we could have kept it in action all the time—or even most of the time. But against that there was the fuel consumption. Petrol was one of the most valuable of our stores. Food of some kind we could always hope to grow, but when petrol and diesel oil were no longer available, much more than our mere convenience would be gone with them. There would be no more expeditions, and consequently no more re-plenishments of supplies. The primitive life would start in earnest. So, from motives of conservation, the barrier wire was only charged for some minutes two or three times a day. It caused the triffids to recoil a few yards, and thereby stopped them building up pressure against the fence. As an additional guard we ran an alarm wire on the inner fence to enable us to deal with any breaks before they became serious.

The weakness lay in the triffids apparent ability to learn, in at least a limited way, from experience. We found, for instance, that they grew accustomed to our practice of charging the wire for a while night and morning. We began to notice that they were usually clear of the wire at our customary time for starting the engine, and they began to close in again soon after it had stopped. Whether they actually associated the charged condition of the wire with the sound of the engine was impossible to say then, but later we had little doubt that they did.

It was easy enough to make our running times erratic, but Susan, for whom they were continually a source of inimical study, soon began to maintain that the period for which the shock kept them clear was growing steadily shorter. Nevertheless the electrified wire and occasional attacks upon them in the sections where they were densest kept us free of incursions for over a year, and of those that occurred later we had warning enough to stop them being more than a minor nuisance.

Within the safety of our compound we continued to learn about agriculture, and life settled gradually into a routine.

On a day in the summer of our sixth year Josella and I went down to the coast together, travelling there in the half-tracked vehicle that I customarily used now that the roads were growing so bad. It was a holiday for her. Months had passed since she had been outside the fence. The cares of the place and the babies had kept her far too tied to make more than a few necessary trips, but now we had reached the stage where we felt that Susan could safely be left in charge sometimes, and we had a feeling of release as we climbed up and ran over the tops of the hills. On the lower southern slopes we stopped the car for a while, and sat there.

It was a perfect June day with only a few light clouds flecking a pure blue sky. The sun shone down on the beaches and the sea beyond just as brightly as it had in the days when those same beaches had been crowded with bathers, and the sea dotted with little boats. We looked down on it in silence for some minutes. Josella said:

'Don't you *still* feel sometimes that if you were to close your eyes for a bit you might open them again to find it all as it was, Bill?—I do.'

'Not often now,' I told her. 'But I've had to see so much more of it than you have. All the same, sometimes . . .'

'And look at the gulls—just as they used to be.'

'There are many more birds this year,' I agreed. 'I'm glad of that.'

Viewed impressionistically from a distance the little town was still the same jumble of small red-roofed houses and bungalows populated mostly by a comfortably retired middle-class—but it was an impression that could not last more than a few minutes. Though the tiles still showed, the walls were barely visible. The tidy gardens had vanished under an unchecked growth of green, patched in colour here and there by the descendants of carefully-cultivated flowers. Even the roads looked like strips of green carpet from this distance. When we reached them we should find that the effect of soft verdure was illusory; they would be matted with coarse, tough weeds.

'Only so few years ago,' Josella said reflectively, 'people were wailing about the way those bungalows were destroying the countryside. Now look at them.'

'The countryside is having its revenge, all right,' I said. 'Nature seemed about finished then—"who would have thought the old man had so much blood in him"?'

'It rather frightens me. It's as if everything were breaking out. Rejoicing that we're finished, and that it's free to go its own way. I wonder . . .? Have we been just fooling ourselves since it happened? Do you think we really are finished with, Bill?'

I'd had plenty more time when I was out on my foragings to wonder about that than she had.

'If you weren't you, darling, I might make an answer out

of the right heroic mould—the kind of wishful thinking that so often passes for faith and resolution.'

'But as I *am* me?'

'I'll give you the honest answer—not quite. And while there's life, there's hope.'

We looked on the scene before us for some seconds in silence.

'I think,' I amplified, 'only think, mind you. That we have a narrow chance—so narrow that it is going to take a long long time to get back. If it weren't for the triffids, I'd say there was a very good chance indeed—though still taking a longish time. But the triffids are a real factor. They are something that no rising civilization has had to fight before. Are they going to take the world off us, or are we going to be able to stop them?

'The real problem is to find some simple way of dealing with them. We aren't so badly off—we can hold them away. But our grandchildren—what are they going to do about them? Are they going to have to spend all their lives in human reservations only kept free of triffids by unending toil?

'I'm quite sure there is a simple way. The trouble is that simple ways come out of such complicated research. And we haven't the resources.'

'Surely we have all the resources there ever were, just for the taking,' Josella put in.

'Material, yes. But mental, no. What we need is a team, a team of experts really out to deal with the triffids for good and all. Something could be done, I'm sure. Something along the lines of a selective killer, perhaps. If we could produce the right hormones to create a state of imbalance in triffids, but not in other things . . . It must be possible—if you have enough brain power turned on to the job. . . .'

'If you think that, why don't you try?' she asked.

'Too many reasons. First, I'm not up to it—a very mediocre biochemist, and there's only one of me. There'd have to be a lab. and equipment. More than that, there'd have to be time, and there are too many things which I have to do as it is. But even if I had the ability, then there would have to be the means of producing synthetic hormones in huge quantities. It would be a job for a regular factory. But before that there must be the research team.'

'People could be trained.'

'Yes—when enough of them can be spared from the mere business of keeping alive. I've collected a mass of bio-chemical books in the hope that perhaps some time there will be people who can make use of them—I shall teach David all I can, and he must hand it on. But unless there is leisure for work on it some time, I can see nothing ahead but the reservations.'

Josella frowned down on a group of four triffids ambling across a field below us.

'They used to say that man's really serious rivals were the insects. It seems to me that the triffids have something in common with some kinds of insects. Oh, I know that biologically they're plants. What I mean is they don't bother about their individuals, and the individuals don't bother about themselves. Separately they have something which looks slightly like intelligence; collectively it looks a great deal more like it. They sort of work together for a purpose the way ants or bees do—yet you could say that not one of them is aware of any purpose or scheme although he's part of it. It's all very queer—probably impossible for us to understand, anyway. They're so *different*. It seems to me to go against all our ideas of inheritable characteristics. Is there something in a bee or a triffid which is a gene of social organization, or does an ant have a gene of architecture? And if they have these things why haven't we in all this time developed a gene for language, or cooking? Anyway, whatever it is, the triffids do seem to have something like it. It may be that no single individual knows why it keeps on hanging around our fence, but the whole lot together knows that its purpose is to get us—and that sooner or later it will.'

'There are still things that can happen to stop that,' I said. 'I didn't mean to make you feel quite despondent about it all.'

'I don't—except sometimes when I'm tired. Usually I'm much too busy to worry over what may happen years ahead. No, as a rule I don't go much beyond getting a little sad— the sort of gentle melancholy that the eighteenth century thought so estimable. I go sentimental when you play records—there is something rather frightening about a great orchestra which has passed away still playing on to a little group of people hemmed in and gradually growing more primitive. It takes me back, and I begin to feel sad with thinking of all the things we can never do again—however things go now. Don't you sometimes feel like that?'

'H'm,' I admitted. 'But I find that I accept the present more easily as it goes on. I suppose that if there were wishes that could be granted, I would wish the old world back—but there'd be a condition. You see, in spite of everything, I'm happier inside me than I ever was before. You know that, don't you, Josie?'

She put her hand on mine.

'I feel that, too. No, what saddens me is not so much the things we've lost, as the things that the babies will never have the chance to know.'

'It's going to be a problem to bring them up with hopes and ambitions,' I acknowledged. 'We can't help being orientated backwards. But they mustn't look back all the time. A tradition of a vanished golden age and ancestors who were magicians would be a most damning thing. Whole

races have had that sort of inferiority complex which has
sunk into lassitude on the tradition of a glorious past.
But how are we going to stop that kind of thing from
happening?'

'If I were a child now,' she said, reflectively, 'I think I
should want a reason of some kind. Unless I was given it—
that is, if I were allowed to think that I had been born into
a world which had been quite pointlessly destroyed, I should
find living quite pointless, too. That does make it awfully
difficult, because it seems to be just what *has* happened. ...'

She paused, pondering, then she added:

'Do you think we could—do you think we should be
justified in starting a myth to help them? A story of a world
that was wonderfully clever, but so wicked that it had to be
destroyed—or destroyed itself by accident? Something like
the Flood, again. That wouldn't crush them with inferiority
—it could give the incentive to build, and this time to build
something better.'

'Yes ...' I said, considering it. 'Yes. It's often a good idea
to tell children the truth. Kind of makes things easier for
them later on—only why pretend it's a myth?'

Josella demurred at that.

'How do you mean? The triffids were—well, they were
somebody's fault, or mistake, I admit. But the rest ...?'

'I don't think we can blame anyone too much for the
triffids. The extracts they give were very valuable in the
circumstances. Nobody can ever see what a major discovery
is going to lead to—whether it is a new kind of engine or a
triffid, and we coped with them all right in normal conditions. We benefited quite a lot from them, as long as the
conditions were to their disadvantage.'

'Well, it wasn't our fault the conditions changed. It was—
just one of those things: like earthquakes or hurricanes—
what an insurance company would call an Act of God.

K

Maybe that's just what it was—a judgment. Certainly we never brought that comet.'

'Didn't we, Josella? Are you quite sure of that?'

She turned to look at me.

'What do you mean, Bill? How could we?'

'What I mean, my dear, is—was it a comet at all? You see, there's an old superstitious distrust of comets pretty well grained in. I know we were modern enough not to kneel down in the streets and pray at them—but all the same, it's a phobia with centuries of standing. They've been portents and symbols of heavenly wrath and warnings that the end is at hand, and used in any amount of stories and prophecies. So, when you get an astonishing celestial phenomenon, what more natural than to attribute it straight off to a comet? A denial would take time to get around— and time was just what there was not. And when utter disaster follows, it just confirms it for everyone that it must have been a comet.'

Josella was looking at me very hard.

'Bill, are you trying to tell me that you don't think it was a comet at all?'

'Just exactly that,' I agreed.

'But—I don't understand. It must—— What else *could* it have been?'

I opened a vacuum-packed tin of cigarettes, and lit one for each of us.

'You remember what Michael Beadley said about the tight-rope we'd all been walking on for years?'

'Yes, but——'

'Well, I think that what happened was that we came off it—and that a few of us just managed to survive the crash.'

I drew on my cigarette, looking out at the sea and at the infinite blue sky above it.

'Up there,' I went on, 'up there, there were—and maybe there still are—unknown numbers of satellite weapons circling round and round the Earth. Just a lot of dormant menaces, touring around, waiting for someone, or something, to set them off. What was in them? You don't know; I don't know. Top-secret stuff. All we've heard is guesses— fissile materials, radio-active dusts, bacteria, viruses . . . Now suppose that one type happened to have been constructed especially to emit radiations that our eyes would not stand—something that would burn out, or at least damage, the optic nerve . . .?'

Josella gripped my hand.

'Oh, no, Bill! No, they couldn't. . . . That'd be—diabolical. . . . Oh, I can't believe . . . Oh, *no*, Bill!'

'My sweet, all the things up there were diabolical. . . . Then suppose there were a mistake, or perhaps an accident— maybe such an accident as actually encountering a shower of comet debris, if you like—which starts some of these things popping. . . .

'Somebody starts talking about comets. It might not be politic to deny that—and there turned out to be so little time, anyway.

'Well, naturally these things would have been intended to operate close to the ground where the effect would be spread over a definitely calculable area. But they start going off out there in space, or maybe when they hit the atmosphere— either way they're operating so far up that people all round the world can receive direct radiations from them. . . .

'Just what did happen is anyone's guess now. But one thing I'm quite certain of—that somehow or other we brought this lot down on ourselves. And there was that plague, too: it wasn't typhoid, you know. . . .

'I find that it's just the wrong side of coincidence for me to believe that out of all the thousands of years in which a destructive comet could arrive, it happens to do so just a few years after we have succeeded in establishing satellite weapons—don't you? No, I think that we kept on that tight-rope quite a while, considering the things that might have happened—but sooner or later the foot had to slip.'

'Well, when you put it that way——' murmured Josella. She broke off, and was lost in silence for quite a while. Then she said:

'I suppose in a way that should be more horrible than the idea of nature striking blindly at us. And yet I don't think it is. It makes me feel less hopeless about things because it makes them at least comprehensible. If it *was* like that, then it is at least a thing that can be prevented from happening again—just one more of the mistakes our very great-grandchildren are going to have to avoid. And, oh dear, there were so many, many mistakes! But we can warn them.'

'H'm—well——' I said. 'Anyway, once they've beaten the triffids and pulled themselves out of this mess they'll have plenty of scope for making brand-new mistakes of their very own.'

'Poor little things,' she said, as if she were gazing down rows of increasingly great-grandchildren, 'it's not much that we're offering them, is it?'

'People used to say: "life is what you make it." '

'That, my dear Bill, outside very narrow limits is just a load of—well, I don't want to be rude. But I believe my Uncle Ted used to say that—until somebody dropped a bomb which took both his legs off. It changed his mind. And nothing that I personally did caused me to be living at all now.' She threw away the remains of her cigarette. 'Bill, what *have* we done to be the lucky ones in all this. Every now and then—when I stop feeling overworked and selfish, that is—I think how lucky we really have been, and I want to give thanks to something or other. But then I find I feel that if there were anybody or anything to give thanks to they'd have chosen such a much more deserving case than me. It's all very confusing to a simple girl.'

'And I,' I said, 'feel that if there were anybody or anything at all in the driving-seat quite a lot of the things in history could not have happened. But I don't let it worry me a lot. We've had luck, my sweet. If it changes to-morrow, well, it changes. Whatever it does, it can't take away the time we've had together. That's been more than I ever deserved, and more than most men get in a lifetime.'

We sat there a little longer, looking at the empty sea, and then drove down to the little town.

After a search which produced most of the things on our wants list we went down to picnic on the shore in the sunshine—with a good stretch of shingle behind us over which no triffid could approach unheard.

'We must do more of this while we can,' Josella said. 'Now that Susan's growing up I needn't be nearly so tied.'

'If anybody ever earned the right to let up a bit, you have,' I agreed.

I said it with a feeling that I would like us to go together and say a last farewell to places and things we had known while it was still possible. Every year now the prospect of imprisonment would grow closer. Already to get northward from Shirning it was necessary to make a detour of many miles to pass the country that had reverted to marshland. All the roads were rapidly becoming worse with the erosion by rain and streams, and the roots that broke up the surfaces. The time in which one would still be able to get an oil-tanker back to the house was already becoming measurable. One day one of them would fail to make its way along the lane, and very likely block it for good. A half-track would continue to run over ground that was dry enough, but as time went on it would be increasingly difficult to find a route open enough even for that.

'And we must have one real last fling,' I said. 'You shall dress up again, and we'll go to——'

'Sh-sh!' interrupted Josella, holding up one finger, and turning her ear to the wind.

I held my breath, and strained my ears. There was a feeling rather than a sound of throbbing in the air. It was faint, but gradually swelling.

'It *is*—it's a plane!' Josella said.

We looked to the west, shading our eyes with our hands. The humming was still little more than the buzzing of an insect. The sound increased so slowly that it could come from nothing but a helicopter, any other kind of craft would have passed over us or out of hearing in the time it was taking.

Josella saw it first. A dot, a little out from the coast, and apparently coming our way, parallel with the shore. We stood up, and started to wave. As the dot grew larger, we waved more wildly, and, not very sensibly, shouted at the tops of our voices. The pilot could not have failed to see us there on the open beach had he come on, but that was what he did not do. A few miles short of us he turned abruptly north to pass inland. We went on waving madly, hoping that he might yet catch sight of us. But there was no indecision in the machine's course, no variation of the engine note. Deliberately and imperturbably it droned away towards the hills.

We lowered our arms, and looked at one another.

'If it can come once, it can come again,' said Josella sturdily, but not very convincingly.

But the sight of the machine had changed our day for us. It destroyed quite a lot of the resignation we had carefully built up. We had been saying to ourselves that there must be other groups, but they wouldn't be in any better position than we were, more likely in a worse. But when a helicopter

could come sailing in like a sight and sound from the past,
it raised more than memories: it suggested that someone
somewhere was managing to make out better than we were.
—Was there a tinge of jealousy there?—And it also made
us aware that lucky as we had been, we were still gregarious
creatures by nature.

The restless feeling that the machine left behind destroyed
our mood and the lines along which our thoughts had been
running. In unspoken agreement we began to pack up our
belongings, and, each occupied with our thoughts, we made
our way back to the half-track, and started for home.

16. Contact

WE had covered perhaps half the distance back to
Shirning when Josella noticed the smoke. At first
sight it might have been a cloud, but as we neared
the top of the hill we could see the grey column beneath the
more diffused upper layer. She pointed to it, and looked at
me without a word. The only fires we had seen in years had
been a few spontaneous outbreaks in later summer. We both
knew at once that the plume ahead was rising from the
neighbourhood of Shirning.

I forced the half-track along at a greater speed than it had
ever done on the deteriorated roads. We were thrown about
inside it, and yet still seemed to be crawling. Josella sat
silent all the time, her lips pressed together and her eyes
fixed on the smoke. I knew that she was searching for some
indication that the source was nearer or further away, anywhere but at Shirning itself. But the closer we came, the less
room there was for doubt. We tore up the final lane quite
oblivious of the stings whipping at the vehicle as it passed.
Then, at the turn, we were able to see that it was not the
house itself, but the wood-pile that was ablaze.

At the sound of the horn Susan came running out to pull
on the rope which opened the gate from a safe distance. She

shouted something which was drowned in the rattle of our driving in. Her free hand was pointing, not to the fire, but towards the front of the house. As we ran further into the yard we could see the reason. Skilfully landed in the middle of our lawn stood the helicopter.

By the time we were out of the half-track a man in a leather jacket and breeches had come out of the house. He was tall, fair, and sunburned. At the first glance I had a feeling I had seen him somewhere before. He waved and grinned cheerfully as we hurried across.

'Mr. Bill Masen, I presume. My name is Simpson—Ivan Simpson.'

'I remember,' said Josella. 'You brought in a helicopter that night at the University Buildings.'

'That's right. Clever of you to remember. But just to show you you're not the only one with a memory: you are Josella Playton, author of——'

'You're quite wrong,' she interrupted him, firmly. 'I'm Josella Masen, author of "David Masen".'

'Ah, yes. I've just been looking at the original edition, and a very creditable bit of craftsmanship too, if I may say so.'

'Hold on a bit,' I said. 'That fire——?'

'It's safe enough. Blowing away from the house. Though I'm afraid most of your stock of wood has gone up.'

'What happened?'

'That was Susan. She didn't mean me to miss the place. When she heard my engine she grabbed a flame-thrower, and bounded out to start a signal as quickly as she could. The wood-pile was handiest—no one could have missed what she did to that.'

We went inside, and joined the others.

'By the way,' Simpson said to me, 'Michael told me I was to be sure to start off with his apologies.'

'To me?' I said, wondering.

'You were the only one who saw any danger in the triffids, and he didn't believe you.'

'But—do you mean to say you knew I was here?'

'We found out very roughly your probable location a few days ago—from a fellow we all have cause to remember: one Coker.'

'So Coker came through, too,' I said. 'After the shambles I saw at Tynsham I'd an idea the plague had got him.'

Later on, when we had had a meal and produced our best brandy, we got the story out of him.

When Michael Beadley and his party had gone on, leaving Tynsham to the mercies and principles of Miss Durrant, they had not made for Beaminster, nor anywhere near it. They had gone north-east, into Oxfordshire. Miss Durrant's misdirection to us must have been deliberate, for Beaminster had never been mentioned.

They had found there an estate which seemed at first to offer the group all it required, and no doubt they could have entrenched themselves there as we had entrenched ourselves at Shirning, but as the menace of the triffids increased, the disadvantages of the place became more obvious. In a year, both Michael and the Colonel were highly dissatisfied with the longer-term prospects there. A great deal of work had already been put into the place, but by the end of the second summer there was general agreement that it would be better to cut their losses. To build a community they had to think in terms of years—a considerable number of years. They also had to bear in mind that the longer they delayed, the more difficult any move would be. What they needed was a place where they would have room to expand and develop; an area with natural defences which, once it had been cleared of triffids, could economically be kept clear of them. Where they now were a high proportion of their labour was occupied with maintaining fences. And as their numbers increased, the length of fence line would have to be increased. Clearly, the best self-maintaining defence line would be water. To that end they had held a discussion on the relative merits of various islands. It had been chiefly climate that had decided them in favour of the Isle of Wight, despite some misgivings over the area that would have to be cleared. Accordingly, in the following March they had packed up again, and moved on.

'When we got there,' Ivan said, 'the triffids seemed even thicker than where we'd left. No sooner had we begun to settle ourselves into a big country house near Godshill than they started collecting along the walls in thousands. We let 'em come for a couple of weeks or so, then we went for 'em with the flame-throwers.

'After we'd wiped that lot out, we let them accumulate again, and then we blitzed 'em once more—and so on. We could afford to do it properly there, because once we were clear of them, we'd not need to use the throwers any more. There could only be a limited number in the island, and the more of them that came round us to be wiped out, the better we liked it.

'We had to do it a dozen times before there was any appreciable effect. All round the walls we had a belt of charred stumps before they began to get shy. There were a devil of a lot more of them than we had expected.'

'There used to be at least half a dozen nurseries breeding high quality plants in the island—not to mention the private and park ones,' I said.

'That doesn't surprise me. There might have been a hundred nurseries by the look of it. Before all this began I'd have said there were only a few thousand of the things in the whole country, if anyone had asked me, but there must have been hundreds of thousands.'

'There were,' I said. 'They'll grow practically anywhere, and they were pretty profitable. There didn't seem to be so many when they were penned up in farms and nurseries. All the same, judging from the amount round here, there must be whole tracts of country practically free of them now.'

'That's so,' he agreed. 'But go and live there and they'll start collecting in a few days. You can see that from the air. I'd have known there was someone here without Susan's fire. They make a dark border round any inhabited place.

'Still, we managed to thin down the crowd round our walls after a bit. Maybe they got to find it unhealthy, or maybe they didn't care a lot for walking about on the charred remains of their relatives—and, of course, there were fewer of them. So then we started going out to hunt them instead of just letting them come to us. It was our main job for months. Between us we covered every inch of the island—or thought we did. By the time we were through, we reckoned we'd put paid to every one in the place, big and small. Even so, some managed to appear the next year, and the year after that. Now we have an intensive search every spring on account of seeds blowing over from the mainland, and settle with them right away.

'While that was going on, we were getting organized. There were some fifty or sixty of us to begin with. I took flips in the helicopter, and when I saw signs of a group anywhere, I'd go down and issue a general invitation to come along. Some did—but a surprising number simply weren't interested: they'd escaped from being governed, and in spite of all their troubles they didn't want any more of it. There are some lots in South Wales that have made sorts of tribal communities, and resent the idea of any organization except the minimum they've set up for themselves. You'll find similar lots near the other coalfields, too. Usually the leaders are the men who happened to be on the shift below ground so that they never saw the green stars—though God knows how they ever got up the shafts again.

'Some of them so definitely don't want to be interfered with that they shoot at the aircraft—there's one lot of that sort at Brighton——'

'I know,' I said, 'they warned me off, too.'

'Recently there are more like that. There's one at Maidstone, another at Guildford, and other places. They're the real reason why we hadn't spotted you hidden away here before. The district didn't seem too healthy when one got close to it. I don't know what they think they're doing— probably got some good food dumps and are scared of anyone else wanting some of it. Anyway, there's no sense in taking risks, so I just let 'em stew.

'Still, quite a lot did come along. In a year we'd gone up to three hundred or so—not all sighted, of course.

'It wasn't until about a month ago that I came across Coker and his lot—and one of the first things he asked, by the way, was whether you'd shown up. They had a bad time, particularly at first.

'A few days after he got back to Tynsham, a couple of women came along from London, and brought the plague with them. Coker quarantined them at the first symptoms, but it was too late. He decided on a quick move. Miss Durrant wouldn't budge. She elected to stay and look after the sick, and follow later if she could. She never did.

'They took the infection with them. There were three more hurried moves before they succeeded in shaking free of it. By then they had gone as far west as Devonshire, and they were all right for a bit there. But then they began to find the same difficulties as we had—and you have. Coker stuck it out there for nearly three years, and then reasoned along much the same lines as we did. Only he didn't think of an island. Instead, he decided on a river boundary and a fence to cut off the toe of Cornwall. When they got there they spent the first months building their barrier, then they went for the triffids inside, much as we did on the island. They had much more difficult country to work with, though, and they never did succeed in clearing them out completely. The fence was fairly successful to begin with, but they never could trust it as we could the sea, and too much of their manpower had to be wasted on patrols.

'Coker thinks they might have made out all right once the children had grown old enough to work, but it would have been tough going all the time. When I did find them, they hadn't much hesitation about coming along. They set about loading up their fishing boats right away, and they were all on the island in a couple of weeks. When Coker found you weren't with us, he suggested you might still be somewhere in these parts.'

'You can tell him that wipes out any hard feelings about him,' said Josella.

'He's going to be a very useful man,' Ivan said. 'And from what he tells us, you could be, too,' he added, looking at me. 'You're a biochemist, aren't you?'

'A biologist,' I said, 'with a little biochemistry.'

'Well, you can hold on to your fine distinctions. The point is, Michael has tried to get some research going into a method of knocking off triffids scientifically. That *has* to be found if we are going to get anywhere at all. But the trouble so far is that the only people we have to work on it are a few who have forgotten most of the biology they learned at school. What do you think—like to turn professor? It'd be a worth-while job.'

'I can't think of one that would be more worth while,' I told him.

'Does this mean you're inviting us all to your island haven?' Dennis asked.

'Well, to come on mutual approval, at least,' Ivan replied. 'Bill and Josella will probably remember the broad principles laid down that night at the University. They still stand. We aren't out to reconstruct—we want to build something new and better. Some people don't take to that. If they don't, they're no use to us. We just aren't interested in having an opposition party that's trying to perpetuate a lot of the old bad features. We'd rather that people who want that went elsewhere.'

'Elsewhere sounds a pretty poor offer, in the circumstances,' remarked Dennis.

'Oh, I don't mean we throw them back to the triffids. But there were a number of them, and there had to be some place for them to go, so a party went across to the Channel Isles, and started cleaning up there on the same lines as we'd cleaned up the Isle of Wight. About a hundred of them moved over. They're doing all right there, too.'

'So now we have this mutual approval system. Newcomers spend six months with us, then there's a Council hearing. If they don't like our ways, they say so; and if we don't think they'll fit, we say so. If they fit, they stay; if not, we see that they get to the Channel Isles—or back to the mainland, if they're odd enough to prefer that.'

'Sounds to have a touch of the dictatorial—how's this Council of yours formed?' Dennis wanted to know.

Ivan shook his head.

'It'd take too long to go into constitutional questions now. The best way to learn about us is to come and find out. If you like us, you'll stay—but even if you don't, I think you'll find the Channel Isles a better spot than this is likely to be a few years from now.'

In the evening, after Ivan had taken off, and vanished away to the south-west, I went and sat on my favourite bench in a corner of the garden.

I looked across the valley, remembering the well-drained and tended meadows that had been there. Now it was far on the way back to the wild. The neglected fields were dotted with thickets, beds of reeds, and stagnant pools. The bigger trees were slowly drowning in the sodden soil.

I thought of Coker and his talk of the leader, the teacher, and the doctor—and of all the work that would be needed to support us on our few acres. Of how it would affect each of us if we were to be imprisoned here. Of the three blind ones, still feeling useless and frustrated as they grew older. Of Susan who should have the chance of a husband and babies. Of David, and Mary's little girl, and any other children there might be who would have to become labourers as soon as they were strong enough. Of Josella and myself having to work still harder as we became older because there would be more to feed and more work that must be done by hand . . .

Then there were the triffids patiently waiting. I could see hundreds of them in a dark green hedge beyond the fence. There must be research—some natural enemy, some poison, a debalancer of some kind, something must be found to deal with them; there must be relief from other work for that— and soon. Time was on the triffids' side. They had only to go on waiting while we used up our resources. First the fuel, then no more wire to mend the fences. And they or their descendants would still be waiting there when the wire rusted through. . . .

And yet Shirning had become our home. I sighed.

There was a light step on the grass. Josella came and sat down beside me. I put an arm round her shoulders.

'What do *they* think about it?' I asked her.

'They're badly upset, poor things. It must be hard for them to understand how the triffids wait like that when they can't see them. And then, they can find their way about here, you see. It must be dreadful to have to contemplate going to an entirely strange place when you're blind. They only know what we tell them. I don't think they properly understand how impossible it will become here. If it were not for the children, I believe they'd say "No," flatly. It's their place, you see, all they have left. They feel that very much.' She paused, then she added: '*They* think that—but, of course, it's not really their place at all; it's ours, isn't it? We've worked hard for it.' She put her hand on mine. 'You've made it and kept it for us, Bill. What do you think? Shall we stay a year or two longer?'

'No,' I said. 'I worked because everything seemed to depend on me. Now it seems—rather futile.'

'Oh, darling, don't! A knight-errant isn't futile. You've fought for all of us, and kept the dragons away.'

'It's mostly the children,' I said.

'Yes—the children,' she agreed.

'And all the time, you know, I've been haunted by Coker —the first generation labourers; the next, savages . . . I think we had better admit defeat before it comes, and go now.'

She pressed my hand.

'Not defeat, Bill dear, just a—what's the phrase?—a strategic withdrawal. We withdraw to work and plan for the day when we can come back. One day we will. You'll show us how to wipe out every one of these foul triffids, and get our land back from them for us.'

'You've a lot of faith, darling.'

'And why not?'

'Well, at least I'll be fighting them. But first, we go— when?'

'Do you think we could have the summer out here? It

could be a sort of holiday for all of us—with no preparations to make for the winter. We deserve a holiday, too.'

'I should think we could do that,' I agreed.

We sat, watching the valley dissolve in the dusk, Josella said:

'It's queer, Bill. Now I can go, I don't really want to. Sometimes it's seemed like prison—but now it seems like treachery to leave it. You see, I—I've been happier here than ever in my life before, in spite of everything.'

'As for me, my sweet, I wasn't even alive before. But we'll have better times yet—I promise you.'

'It's silly, but I shall cry when we do go. I shall cry buckets. You mustn't mind,' she said.

But, as things fell out, we were all of us much too busy to cry. . . .

17. Strategic Withdrawal

THERE was, as Josella had implied, no need for hurry. While we saw the summer out at Shirning I could prospect a new home for us on the island, and make several journeys there to transport the most useful part of the stores and gear that we had collected. But, meanwhile, the wood-pile had been destroyed. We needed no more fuel than would keep the kitchen going for a few weeks, so the next morning Susan and I set off to fetch coal.

The half-track wasn't suitable for that job, so we took a four-wheel drive lorry. Although the nearest rail coal depot was only ten miles away, the roundabout route due to the blockage of some roads, and the bad condition of others meant that it took us nearly the whole day. There were no major mishaps, but it was drawing on to evening when we returned.

As we turned the last corner of the lane, with the triffids slashing at the truck as indefatigably as ever from the banks, we stared in astonishment. Beyond our gate, parked in our yard, stood a monstrous-looking vehicle. The sight so dumbfounded us that we sat gaping at it for some moments before Susan put on her helmet and gloves and climbed down to open the gate.

After I had driven in we went over together to look at the vehicle. The chassis, we saw, was supported on metal tracks which suggested a military origin. The general effect was somewhere between a cabin-cruiser, and an amateur-built caravan. Susan and I looked at it, and then looked at one another, with raised eyebrows. We went indoors to find out more about it.

In the living-room we found, in addition to the household, four men clad in grey-green ski-suits. Two of them wore pistols holstered to the right hip: the other two had parked their sub-machine guns on the floor beside their chairs.

As we came in, Josella turned a completely expressionless face towards us.

'Here is my husband. Bill, this is Mr. Torrence. He tells us he is an official of some kind. He has proposals to make to us.' I had never heard her voice colder.

For a second I failed to respond. The man she indicated did not recognize me, but I recalled him all right. Features that have faced you along sights get sort of set in your mind. Besides, there was that distinctive red hair. I remembered well the way that efficient young man had turned back my party in Hampstead. I nodded to him. Looking at me, he said:

'I understand you are in charge here, Mr. Masen?'

'The place belongs to Mr. Brent here,' I replied.

'I mean that you are the organizer of this group?'

'In the circumstances, yes,' I said.

'Good.' He had a now-we-are-going-to-get-somewhere air. 'I am Commander, South-East Region,' he added.

He spoke as if that should convey something important to me. It did not. I said so.

'It means,' he amplified, 'that I am the Chief Executive Officer of the Emergency Council for the South-Eastern Region of Britain. As such, it happens to be one of my duties to supervise the distribution and allocation of personnel.'

'Indeed,' I said. 'I have never heard of this—er—Council.'

'Possibly. We were equally ignorant of the existence of your group here until we saw your fire yesterday.'

I waited for him to go on.

'When such a group is discovered,' he said, 'it is my job to investigate it and assess it and make the necessary adjustments. So you may take it that I am here officially.'

'On behalf of an official Council—or does it happen to be a self-elected Council?' Dennis inquired.

'There has to be law and order,' the man said, stiffly. Then, with a change of tone, he went on:

'This is a well-found place you have here, Mr. Masen.'

'Mr. Brent has,' I corrected.

'We will leave Mr. Brent out. He is only here because you made it possible for him to stay here.'

I looked across at Dennis. His face was set.

'Nevertheless, it is his property,' I said.

'It *was*, I understand. But the state of society which gave sanction to his ownership no longer exists. Titles to property have therefore ceased to be valid. Furthermore, Mr. Brent is not sighted, so that he cannot in any case be considered competent to hold authority.'

'Indeed,' I said again.

I had had a distaste for this young man and his decisive ways at our first meeting. Further acquaintance was doing nothing to mellow it. He went on:

'This is a matter of survival. Sentiment cannot be allowed to interfere with the necessary practical measures. Now, Mrs. Masen has told me that you number eight altogether. Five adults, this girl, and two small children. All of you are sighted except these three.' He indicated Dennis, Mary, and Joyce.

'That is so,' I admitted.

'H'm. That's quite disproportionate, you know. There'll have to be some changes here, I'm afraid. We have to be realistic in times like this.'

Josella's eye caught mine. I saw a warning in it. But in any case, I had no intention of breaking out just then. I had seen the red-headed man's direct methods in action, and I wanted to know more of what I was up against. Apparently he realized that I would.

'I'd better put you in the picture,' he said. 'Briefly it is this. Regional Headquarters is at Brighton. London soon became too bad for us. But in Brighton we were able to clear and quarantine a part of the town, and we ran it. Brighton's a big place. When the sickness had passed and we could get about more, there were plenty of stores to begin with. More recently we have been running in convoys from other places. But that's folding up now. The roads are getting too bad for lorries, and they are having to go too far. It had to come, of course. We'd reckoned that we could last out there several years longer—still, there it is. It's possible we undertook to look after too many from the start. Anyway, now we are having to disperse. The only way to keep going will be to live off the land. To do that we've got to break up into smaller units. The standard unit has been fixed at one sighted person to ten blind, plus any children.

'You have a good place here, fully capable of supporting two units. We shall allocate to you seventeen blind persons. making twenty with the three already here—again, of course, plus any children they may have.'

I stared at him in amazement.

'You're seriously suggesting that twenty people and their children can live off this land,' I said. 'Why, it's utterly impossible. We're been wondering whether we shall be able to support ourselves on it.'

He shook his head, confidently.

'It is perfectly possible. And what I am offering you is the command of the double unit we shall instal here. Frankly, if you do not care to take it, we shall put in someone else who will. We can't afford waste in these times.'

'But just look at the place,' I repeated. 'It simply can't do it.'

'I assure you that it *can*, Mr. Masen. Of course, you'll have to lower your standards a bit—we all shall for the next few years, but when the children grow up a bit you'll begin to have labour to expand with. For six or seven years it's going to mean personal hard work for you, I admit—that can't be helped. From then on, however, you'll gradually be able to relax until you are simply supervising. Surely that's going to make a good return for just a few years of the tougher going?

'Placed as you are now, what sort of future would you have? Nothing but hard work until you die in your tracks—and your children faced with working in the same way, just to keep going, not more than that. Where are the future leaders and administrators to come from in that kind of set-up? Your way, you'd be worn out and still in harness in another twenty years—and all your children would be yokels. Our way, you'll be the head of a clan that's working for you, *and* you'll have an inheritance to hand on to your sons.'

Comprehension began to come to me. I said, wonderingly:

'Am I to understand that you are offering me a kind of—feudal seigneury?'

'Ah,' he said. 'I see you do begin to understand. It is, of course, the obvious and quite natural social and economic form for that state of things we are having to face now.'

There was no doubt whatever that the man was putting

this forward as a perfectly serious plan. I evaded a comment on it by repeating myself:

'But the place just can't support that many.'

'For a few years undoubtedly you'll have to feed them mostly on mashed triffids—there won't be any shortage of that raw material by the look of it.'

'Cattle food!' I said.

'But sustaining—rich in the important vitamins, I'm told. And beggars—particularly blind beggars, can't be choosers.'

'You're seriously suggesting that I should take on all these people, and keep them on cattle fodder?'

'Listen, Mr. Masen. If it were not for us, none of these blind people would be alive at all now—nor would their children. It's up to them to do what we tell them, take what we give them, and be thankful for whatever they get. If they like to refuse what we offer—well, that's their own funeral.'

I decided it would be unwise to say what I felt about his philosophy at the moment. I turned to another angle:

'I don't see—— Tell me, just where do you and your Council stand in all this?'

'Supreme authority and legislative power is vested in the Council. It will rule. It will also control the armed forces.'

'Armed forces!' I repeated, blankly.

'Certainly. The forces will be raised as and when necessary by levies on what you called the seigneuries. In return, you will have the right to call on the Council in cases of attack from outside or unrest within.'

I was beginning to feel a bit winded.

'An army! Surely a small mobile squad of police——?'

'I see you haven't grasped the wider aspect of the situation, Mr. Masen. This affliction we have had was not confined to these islands, you know. It was world wide. Everywhere there is the same sort of chaos—that must be so, or we should have heard differently by now—and in every country there are probably a few survivors. Now, it stands to reason, doesn't it, that the first country to get on its feet again and put itself in order is also going to be the country to have the chance of bringing order elsewhere? Do you suggest that we should leave it to some other country to do this, and let it become the new dominant power in Europe—and possibly further afield? Obviously not. Clearly it is our national duty to get ourselves back on our feet as soon as possible and assume the dominant status so that we can prevent dangerous opposition from organizing against us. Therefore, the sooner we can raise a force adequate to discourage any likely aggressors, the better.'

For some moments silence lay on the room. Then Dennis laughed, unnaturally:

'Great God almighty! We've lived through all this—and now the man proposes to start a *war!*'

Torrence said, shortly:

'I don't seem to have made myself clear. The word "war" is an unjustifiable exaggeration. It will be simply a matter of pacifying and administrating tribes that have reverted to primitive lawlessness.'

'Unless, of course, the same benevolent idea happens to have occurred to them,' Dennis suggested.

I became aware that both Josella and Susan were looking at me very hard. Josella pointed at Susan, and I perceived the reason.

'Let me get this straight,' I said. 'You expect the three of us who can see to be entirely responsible here for twenty blind adults and an unspecified number of children. It seems to me——'

'Blind people aren't quite incapable. They can do a lot, including caring for their own children in general, and helping to prepare their own food. Properly arranged, a great deal can be reduced to supervision and direction. But

THE DAY OF THE TRIFFIDS

it will be two of you, Mr. Masen—yourself and your wife, not three.'

I looked at Susan sitting up very straight in her blue boiler-suit, with a red ribbon in her hair. There was an anxious appeal in her eyes as she looked from me to Josella.

'Three,' I said.

'I'm sorry, Mr. Masen. The allocation is ten per unit. The girl can come to headquarters. We can find useful work for her there until she is old enough to take charge of a unit herself.'

'My wife and I regard Susan as our own daughter,' I told him shortly.

'I repeat, I am sorry. But those are the regulations.'

I regarded him for some moments. He looked steadily back at me. At last:

'We should, of course, require guarantees and undertakings regarding her if this had to happen,' I said.

I was aware of several quickly drawn breaths. Torrence's manner relaxed slightly.

'Naturally we shall give you all practicable assurances,' he said.

I nodded. 'I must have time to think it all over. It's quite new to me, and rather startling. Some points come to my mind at once. Equipment here is wearing out. It is difficult to find more that has not deteriorated. I can see that before long I am going to need good strong working horses.'

'Horses are difficult. There's very little stock at present. You'll probably have to use man-power teams for a time.'

'Then,' I said, 'there's accommodation. The outbuildings are too small for our needs now—and I can't put up even prefabricated quarters singlehanded.'

'There we shall be able to help you, I think.'

We went on discussing details for twenty minutes or more. By the end of it I had him showing something like affability, then I got rid of him by sending him off on a tour of the place, with Susan as his sulky guide.

'Bill, what on earth——?' Josella began, as the door closed behind him and his companions.

I told her what I knew of Torrence and his method of dealing with trouble by shooting it early.

'That doesn't surprise me at all,' remarked Dennis. 'But, you know, what is surprising me now is that I'm suddenly feeling quite kindly towards the triffids. Without their intervention I suppose there would have been a whole lot more of this kind of thing by now. If they are the one factor that can stop serfdom coming back, then good luck to 'em.'

'The whole thing's clearly preposterous,' I said. 'It doesn't have a chance. How could Josella and I look after a crowd like that *and* keep the triffids out? But——' I added, 'we're scarcely in a position to give a flat "No" to a proposition put up by four armed men.'

'Then you're not——?'

'Darling,' I said, 'do you really see me in the position of a seigneur, driving my serfs and villeins before me with a whip?—even if the triffids haven't overrun me first?'

'But you said——'

'Listen,' I said. 'It's getting dark. Too late for them to leave now. They'll have to stay the night. I imagine that to-morrow the idea will be to take Susan away with them— she'd make quite a good hostage for our behaviour, you see. And they might leave one or two of the others to keep an eye on us. Well, I don't think we're taking that, are we?'

'No, but——'

'Well, I hope I've convinced him now that I'm coming round to his idea. To-night we'll have the sort of supper that might be taken to imply accord. Make it a good one. Everybody's to eat plenty. Give the kids plenty, too. Lay on our best drinks. See that Torrence and his chaps have plenty, but the rest of us go very easy. Towards the end of the meal I shall disappear for a bit. You keep the party going to cover up. Play rowdy records at them, or something. And everybody help to whoop it up. Another thing—nobody must mention Michael Beadley and his lot. Torrence must know about the Isle of Wight set-up, but he doesn't think we do. Now what I'll be wanting is a sack of sugar.'

'Sugar?' said Josella, blankly.

'No? Well, a big can of honey, then. I should think that would do as well.'

Everyone played up very creditably at supper. The party not only thawed, it actually began to warm up. Josella brought out some of her own potent mead to supplement the more orthodox drinks, and it went down well. The visitors were in a state of happily comfortable relaxation when I made my unobtrusive exit.

I caught up a bundle of blankets and clothes and a parcel of food that I had laid ready, and hurried with them across the yard to the shed where we kept the half-track. With a hose from the tanker which held our main petrol supply I filled the half-track's tanks to overflowing. Then I turned my attention to Torrence's strange vehicle. With the help of a hand-dynamo torch I managed to locate the filler-cap, and poured a quart or more of honey into the tank. The rest of the large can of honey I disposed of into the tanker itself.

I could hear the party singing, and seemingly, still going well. After I had added some anti-triffid gear and miscellaneous afterthoughts to the stuff already in the half-track, I went back and joined it until it finally broke up in an atmosphere which even a close observer might have mistaken for almost maudlin goodwill.

We gave them two hours to get well asleep.

The moon had risen, and the yard was bathed in white light. I had forgotten to oil the shed doors, and gave them a curse for every creak. The rest came in procession towards me. The Brents and Joyce were familiar enough with the place not to need a guiding hand. Behind them followed Josella and Susan, carrying the children. David's sleepy voice rose once, and was stopped quickly by Josella's hand over his mouth. She got into the front, still holding him. I saw the others into the back, and closed it. Then I climbed into the driving seat, kissed Josella, and took a deep breath.

Across the yard the triffids were clustering closer to the gate as they always did when they had been undisturbed for some hours.

By the grace of heaven the half-track's engine started at once. I slammed into low gear, swerved to avoid Torrence's vehicle, and drove straight at the gate. The heavy fender took it with a crash. We plunged forward in a festoon of wire-netting and broken timbers, knocking down a dozen triffids while the rest slashed furiously at us as we passed. Then we were on our way.

Where a turn in the climbing track let us look down on Shirning, we paused, and cut the engine. Lights were on behind some of the windows, and as we watched, those on the vehicle blazed out, floodlighting the house. A starter began to grind. I had a twinge of uneasiness as the engine fired, though I knew we had several times the speed of that lumbering contraption. The machine began to jerk round on its tracks to face the gate. Before it completed the turn, the engine sputtered and stopped. The starter began to whirr again. It went on whirring, irritably, and without result.

The triffids had discovered that the gate was down. By a blend of moonlight and reflected headlights we could see their tall, slender forms already swaying in ungainly

procession into the yard while others came lurching down
the banks of the lane to follow them. . . .

I looked at Josella. She was not crying buckets: not
crying at all. She looked from me down to David asleep in
her arms.

'I've all I really need,' she said, 'and some day you're
going to bring us back to the rest, Bill.'

'Wifely confidence is a very nice trait, darling, but——
No, damn it, no buts—I *am* going to bring you back,' I said.

I got out to clear the debris from the front of the half-
track, and wipe the poison from the windscreen so that I
should be able to see to drive on and away across the tops
of the hills towards the south-west.

And there my personal story joins up with the rest. You
will find it in Elspeth Cary's excellent history of the colony.

Our hopes all centre here now. It seems unlikely that
anything will come of Torrence's neo-feudal plan, though a
number of his seigneuries do still exist, with their inhabitants
leading, so we hear, a life of squalid wretchedness behind
their stockades. But there are not so many of them as there
were. Every now and then Ivan reports that another has
been overrun, and that the triffids which surrounded it have
dispersed to join other sieges.

So we must regard the task ahead as ours alone. We think
now that we can see the way, but there is still a lot of work
and research to be done before the day when we, or our
children, or their children, will cross the narrow straits on
the great crusade to drive the triffids back and back with
ceaseless destruction until we have wiped the last one of
them from the face of the land that they have usurped.